OAKLAND NOIR

EDITED BY
JERRY THOMPSON & EDDIE MULLER

Published by Akashic Books
©2017 Akashic Books

Series concept by Tim McLoughlin and Johnny Temple
Oakland map by Sohrab Habibion

ISBN: 978-1-61775-530-9
Library of Congress Control Number: 2016953897
All rights reserved

First printing

Akashic Books
Brooklyn, New York
Twitter: @AkashicBooks
Facebook: AkashicBooks
E-mail: info@akashicbooks.com
Website: www.akashicbooks.com

ALSO IN THE AKASHIC NOIR SERIES

BALTIMORE NOIR, edited by LAURA LIPPMAN
BARCELONA NOIR (SPAIN), edited by ADRIANA V. LÓPEZ & CARMEN OSPINA
BEIRUT NOIR (LEBANON), edited by IMAN HUMAYDAN
BELFAST NOIR (NORTHERN IRELAND), edited by ADRIAN McKINTY & STUART NEVILLE
BOSTON NOIR, edited by DENNIS LEHANE
BOSTON NOIR 2: THE CLASSICS, edited by DENNIS LEHANE, JAIME CLARKE & MARY COTTON
BRONX NOIR, edited by S.J. ROZAN
BROOKLYN NOIR, edited by TIM McLOUGHLIN
BROOKLYN NOIR 2: THE CLASSICS, edited by TIM McLOUGHLIN
BROOKLYN NOIR 3: NOTHING BUT THE TRUTH, edited by TIM McLOUGHLIN & THOMAS ADCOCK
BRUSSELS NOIR (BELGIUM), edited by MICHEL DUFRANNE
BUFFALO NOIR, edited by ED PARK & BRIGID HUGHES
CAPE COD NOIR, edited by DAVID L. ULIN
CHICAGO NOIR, edited by NEAL POLLACK
CHICAGO NOIR: THE CLASSICS, edited by JOE MENO
COPENHAGEN NOIR (DENMARK), edited by BO TAO MICHAËLIS
DALLAS NOIR, edited by DAVID HALE SMITH
D.C. NOIR, edited by GEORGE PELECANOS
D.C. NOIR 2: THE CLASSICS, edited by GEORGE PELECANOS
DELHI NOIR (INDIA), edited by HIRSH SAWHNEY
DETROIT NOIR, edited by E.J. OLSEN & JOHN C. HOCKING
DUBLIN NOIR (IRELAND), edited by KEN BRUEN
HAITI NOIR, edited by EDWIDGE DANTICAT
HAITI NOIR 2: THE CLASSICS, edited by EDWIDGE DANTICAT
HAVANA NOIR (CUBA), edited by ACHY OBEJAS
HELSINKI NOIR (FINLAND), edited by JAMES THOMPSON
INDIAN COUNTRY NOIR, edited by SARAH CORTEZ & LIZ MARTÍNEZ
ISTANBUL NOIR (TURKEY), edited by MUSTAFA ZIYALAN & AMY SPANGLER
KANSAS CITY NOIR, edited by STEVE PAUL
KINGSTON NOIR (JAMAICA), edited by COLIN CHANNER
LAS VEGAS NOIR, edited by JARRET KEENE & TODD JAMES PIERCE
LONDON NOIR (ENGLAND), edited by CATHI UNSWORTH
LONE STAR NOIR, edited by BOBBY BYRD & JOHNNY BYRD
LONG ISLAND NOIR, edited by KAYLIE JONES
LOS ANGELES NOIR, edited by DENISE HAMILTON
LOS ANGELES NOIR 2: THE CLASSICS, edited by DENISE HAMILTON
MANHATTAN NOIR, edited by LAWRENCE BLOCK
MANHATTAN NOIR 2: THE CLASSICS, edited by LAWRENCE BLOCK
MANILA NOIR (PHILIPPINES), edited by JESSICA HAGEDORN
MARSEILLE NOIR (FRANCE), edited by CÉDRIC FABRE
MEMPHIS NOIR, edited by LAUREEN CANTWELL & LEONARD GILL
MEXICO CITY NOIR (MEXICO), edited by PACO I. TAIBO II
MIAMI NOIR, edited by LES STANDIFORD
MISSISSIPPI NOIR, edited by TOM FRANKLIN
MOSCOW NOIR (RUSSIA), edited by NATALIA SMIRNOVA & JULIA GOUMEN
MUMBAI NOIR (INDIA), edited by ALTAF TYREWALA
NEW JERSEY NOIR, edited by JOYCE CAROL OATES
NEW ORLEANS NOIR, edited by JULIE SMITH
NEW ORLEANS NOIR: THE CLASSICS, edited by JULIE SMITH
ORANGE COUNTY NOIR, edited by GARY PHILLIPS

PARIS NOIR (FRANCE), edited by AURÉLIEN MASSON
PHILADELPHIA NOIR, edited by CARLIN ROMANO
PHOENIX NOIR, edited by PATRICK MILLIKIN
PITTSBURGH NOIR, edited by KATHLEEN GEORGE
PORTLAND NOIR, edited by KEVIN SAMPSELL
PRISON NOIR, edited by JOYCE CAROL OATES
PROVIDENCE NOIR, edited by ANN HOOD
QUEENS NOIR, edited by ROBERT KNIGHTLY
RICHMOND NOIR, edited by ANDREW BLOSSOM, BRIAN CASTLEBERRY & TOM DE HAVEN
RIO NOIR (BRAZIL), edited by TONY BELLOTTO
ROME NOIR (ITALY), edited by CHIARA STANGALINO & MAXIM JAKUBOWSKI
SAN DIEGO NOIR, edited by MARYELIZABETH HART
SAN FRANCISCO NOIR, edited by PETER MARAVELIS
SAN FRANCISCO NOIR 2: THE CLASSICS, edited by PETER MARAVELIS
SAN JUAN NOIR (PUERTO RICO), edited by MAYRA SANTOS-FEBRES
SEATTLE NOIR, edited by CURT COLBERT
SINGAPORE NOIR, edited by CHERYL LU-LIEN TAN
STATEN ISLAND NOIR, edited by PATRICIA SMITH
ST. LOUIS NOIR, edited by SCOTT PHILLIPS
STOCKHOLM NOIR (SWEDEN), edited by NATHAN LARSON & CARL-MICHAEL EDENBORG
ST. PETERSBURG NOIR (RUSSIA), edited by NATALIA SMIRNOVA & JULIA GOUMEN
TEHRAN NOIR (IRAN), edited by SALAR ABDOH
TEL AVIV NOIR (ISRAEL), edited by ETGAR KERET & ASSAF GAVRON
TORONTO NOIR (CANADA), edited by JANINE ARMIN & NATHANIEL G. MOORE
TRINIDAD NOIR (TRINIDAD & TOBAGO), edited by LISA ALLEN-AGOSTINI & JEANNE MASON
TWIN CITIES NOIR, edited by JULIE SCHAPER & STEVEN HORWITZ
USA NOIR, edited by JOHNNY TEMPLE
VENICE NOIR (ITALY), edited by MAXIM JAKUBOWSKI
WALL STREET NOIR, edited by PETER SPIEGELMAN
ZAGREB NOIR (CROATIA), edited by IVAN SRŠEN

FORTHCOMING

ACCRA NOIR (GHANA), edited by MERI NANA-AMA DANQUAH
ADDIS ABABA NOIR (ETHIOPIA), edited by MAAZA MENGISTE
AMSTERDAM NOIR (HOLLAND), edited by RENÉ APPEL & JOSH PACHTER
ATLANTA NOIR, edited by TAYARI JONES
BAGHDAD NOIR (IRAQ), edited by SAMUEL SHIMON
BERLIN NOIR (GERMANY), edited by THOMAS WOERTCHE
BOGOTÁ NOIR (COLOMBIA), edited by ANDREA MONTEJO
BUENOS AIRES NOIR (ARGENTINA), edited by ERNESTO MALLO
JERUSALEM NOIR, edited by DROR MISHANI
LAGOS NOIR (NIGERIA), edited by CHRIS ABANI
MARRAKECH NOIR (MOROCCO), edited by YASSIN ADNAN
MONTANA NOIR, edited by JAMES GRADY & KEIR GRAFF
MONTREAL NOIR (CANADA), edited by JOHN McFETRIDGE & JACQUES FILIPPI
NEW HAVEN NOIR, edited by AMY BLOOM
PRAGUE NOIR (CZECH REPUBLIC), edited by PAVEL MANDYS
SANTA CRUZ NOIR, edited by SUSIE BRIGHT
SÃO PAULO NOIR (BRAZIL), edited by TONY BELLOTTO
SYDNEY NOIR (AUSTRALIA), edited by JOHN DALE
TRINIDAD NOIR: THE CLASSICS (TRINIDAD & TOBAGO), edited by EARL LOVELACE & ROBERT ANTONI

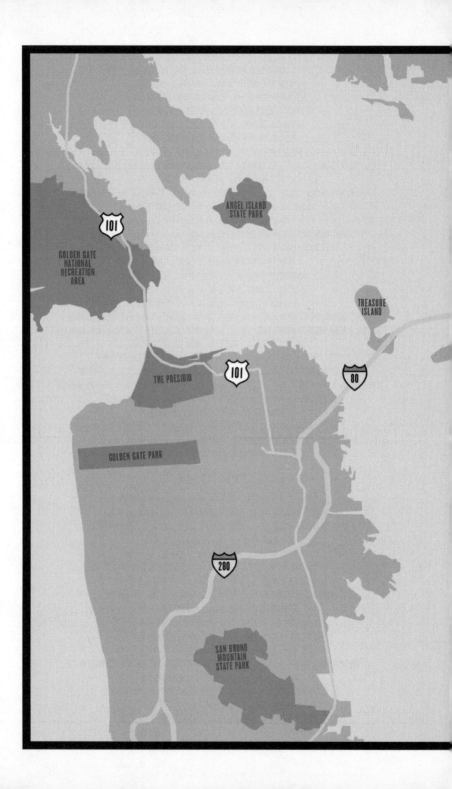

OAKLAND

TILDEN
REGIONAL
PARK

SIESTA VALLEY
RECREATION AREA

80

24

BUSHROD PARK

PIEDMONT AVENUE   MONTCLAIR

PILL HILL   OAKLAND HILLS

McCLYMONDS

DOWNTOWN   HADDON HILL   13   REDWOOD
                                                            REGIONAL
                                                            PARK

SAUSAL CREEK

ALAMEDA   MILLS COLLEGE
ISLAND
                FRUITVALE BRIDGE
ALAMEDA   EASTMONT

                                        TOLER HEIGHTS
                        HEGENBERGER ROAD

BAY FARM
ISLAND   BROOKFIELD VILLAGE

                                                580

                        880

TABLE OF CONTENTS

11   *Introduction*

PART I: NOT A SOFT CITY

19   **NICK PETRULAKIS**   Fruitvale Bridge
The Bridge Tender

33   **KIM ADDONIZIO**   Pill Hill
The Wishing Well

41   **KEENAN NORRIS**   Toler Heights
A Murder of Saviors

60   **KERI MIKI-LANI SCHROEDER**   Piedmont Avenue
Divine Singularity

72   **KATIE GILMARTIN**   Bushrod Park
White Horse

PART II: WHAT THEY CALL A CLUSTERFUCK

87   **DOROTHY LAZARD**   Downtown
A Town Made of Hustle

106   **HARRY LOUIS WILLIAMS II**   Brookfield Village
The Streets Don't Love Nobody

115   **CAROLYN ALEXANDER**   McClymonds
Bulletproof

124   **PHIL CANALIN**   Sausal Creek
The Three Stooges

143   **JUDY JUANITA**   Eastmont
Cabbie

152   **JAMIE DEWOLF**   Oakland Hills
Two to Tango

PART III: A VIEW OF THE LAKE

165   **NAYOMI MUNAWEERA**   Montclair
Survivors of Heartache

179   **MAHMUD RAHMAN**   Mills College
Prophets and Spies

200   **TOM MCELRAVEY**   Haddon Hill
Black and Borax

217   **JOE LOYA**   Hegenberger Road
Waiting for Gordo

251   **EDDIE MULLER**   Alameda
The Handyman

268   **About the Contributors**

INTRODUCTION

EDDIE MULLER: I grew up in San Francisco in the sixties and seventies, so my impression of Oakland—an impression the media fostered—was the badass black brother across the bay. Definitely dangerous. That was my image of Oakland from an early age. The Black Panthers, the Nation of Islam, right down to Jack "The Assassin" Tatum and the outlaw Oakland Raiders. Scary, mean, borderline uncivilized. It took awhile to wise up and grasp the political and economic realities behind the image. Now that I've lived in the East Bay for almost thirty years, I've come to understand and appreciate the hardscrabble, working-class roots of Oakland—and I prefer it to what San Francisco has allowed itself to become.

Jerry, as a transplanted East Coaster, what were your first impressions of the city?

JERRY THOMPSON: Like you, I saw the city as a place soaked in racial and political contradictions. Scary, fabulously underrated, and fabulously criminalized. It's the mothership of delicious and dangerous bad lighting and double gin martinis.

My first impressions are of full busloads of soul music–loving, twelve-year-old superstar ghetto celebs, crackin' on each other while laughing about the day and the years before them. It all blazed fearlessly in front of my nine-year-old East Coast eyes. I was seduced by an ancestral internal drumming that I knew little about but felt deeply—in the folks who looked like me, danced like me, and fought like me on classic soul recordings, dance floors, black movement magazines, and articles shared by Hazel and Larry, my wildly funky parents. It was no accident I was inspired by the collage of blaxploitation posters spread across entire walls in our ghetto-fabulous TV room with its shag carpet. Remember those?

EM: Yeah, I remember . . . though I had other stuff on my walls. So what you're saying is that while everybody else was coming to San Francisco wearing flowers in their hair, you had your sights definitely set on Oakland.

JT: Discovering the wang-dang-doodle jams of the Pointer Sisters shifted my entire focus. Stunning black women were scatting and bebopping all the way into my soul. I think what we've put together in *Oakland Noir* is a volume where this city is a character in every story. He's a slick brother strutting over a bacon-grease bass line and tambourine duet. She's a white chick with a bucket of hot muffins heading to farmer and flea markets, to sell crafts and get hooked up with some fine kat with dreadlocks and a criminal record. And it's in the faces of young fearless muthafuckas pounding keyboards and snapping fingers, lips, Snapchats, and Facebook timelines. It's the core of not only Black Lives Matter but *all* lives matter. We are the children of fantasy and of the funk.

EM: My hometown did not have a Tower of Power. The funk was definitely on the east side of the bay.

JT: Yes, back then inviting some fucker to a party in the East Bay was like asking them to murder your dog. The rusty blue and gold cranes and flickering shipyard lights were like the hems of red leather skirts or second-hand leather bomber jackets, winking into the startled blue and green eyes of Bay Area transplants who have begun to remove the soul of what was created—forgetting that Oakland, with all its myth, was still a city that held a grudge.

EM: Oakland was once considered a predominantly African American city, so I find it interesting that the cultural mix happening here now is much deeper than in the once-liberal bastion of San Francisco. That's been going on for a while, but now the landowners and developers in San Francisco seem to be aggressively marginalizing everyone who's not a high-paid techie. So Oakland is picking up the slack, whether the old guard likes it or not.

There's this restaurant in downtown Oakland called Le Cheval, a Vietnamese place; it's huge and bustling and has survived numerous attempts to displace it. Every time I eat there I feel like the great American experiment has actually worked. A Vietnamese immigrant family runs the place and the patrons are a cross section of the city: middle-class African Americans, starving artists, Catholic nuns, blinged-out gangbangers, off-duty cops, relocated hipsters, Raider cheerleaders celebrating a birthday. *Feed us well and we'll all get along!*

JT: I would only discover Oakland's true voice after realizing one day that I had been living here longer than all the years back east put together. I was not a native but I was not a stranger. Being afraid, and pretending not to be, was like stretching myself out. Learning how to stare life in the face as a black man in a city of black men systematically being erased. I'd find myself in conversations with brother and sisters who loved testifying that they were born and raised in Oakland. Born and raised, a native to all first impressions.

EM: My favorite Oakland moment was when I went with my wife to Maxwell's, a downtown nightclub—now closed, sadly. It may have been the *one* time I went out into the night kinda hipster casual, and the brother at the door turned me away, saying I was "underdressed." Now, I'll work a suit-and-tie morning, noon, and night—but I got 86'd from this place. Went back a week later, got the once-over, and the doorman announced, "This gentleman is clean and sharp and ready for an evening!" I loved that. I'd found a new home away from home. Forget the color, forget the class—just show up turned-out and ready to party.

JT: I feel that my mission is to stand up, to create, to connect, and to carry on in some way—the flip side of ripping down the history of all those brothers and sisters and other minorities who found their way to the end of the train tracks in West Oakland.

EM: I'm really glad there are a couple of midcentury stories in this collection—from Dorothy Lazard and Katie Gilmartin—because as time passes, not many people may remember how Oakland came to be the city it is today—that it was a migration of Southern African Americans who came here during World War II to work in the shipyards. This changed the racial makeup of the city. In my house, the upstairs had been converted into a separate apartment, with its own kitchen and gas, to provide living quarters for WWII shipyard workers. That happened all over the East Bay, and the vast majority of those migrant workers stayed. Who wouldn't?

JT: True. Many did stay—the Pullman porters, civil rights leaders, trailblazers, legendary early black business owners who are still considered by many to be unsung heroes, but by others to be gangsters, pimps, and swindlers. And yet at the same time they are fathers, sons, and brothers raising a living history.

EM: We agreed, right off the bat, that this book would be most interesting to readers if the lineup of writers loosely reflected the demographics of the city. I know a *lot* of crime-fiction writers—the Bay Area is a breeding ground for them these days—but it didn't feel right to have, dare I say, "outsiders" telling stories about Oakland from a distance. Because you've worked in bookstores here for many years, you were aware of local voices I would have overlooked.

JT: This collection reflects the families who moved here, found their voices, created art, built their homes here. It was paramount that we kept close to the pioneers like Ishmael Reed, Amy Tan, Gary Soto, and modern mystery writers like Nichelle Tramble, who set their stories in and around Blues City. I set out to find the writers who were inspired by our history, Oakland's black, Hispanic, LGBT history, its Black Panther history. I did what any eighties East Coast nerdy writer would do: I called on the ancestrals and they guided me. I asked Dorothy Lazard, Judy Juanita, and Keenan Norris for stories, and they answered that call without hesitation, as did new writers like Mahmud Rahman and Keri Miki-Lani Schroeder.

Of course, the collection could not be complete without giving some rebels the mic. "Two to Tango" by Jamie DeWolf and "The Wishing Well" by Kim Addonizio put the ride into high gear. Eddie, I think we share a mutual attraction for what lives in the shadows. Would you say that the shadows are teaching us or guiding us?

EM: That's an interesting way of looking at it. I don't think the shadows do either. I think they're just *there*, always. It's up to us whether we learn anything traipsing through them. These days, writers and readers aren't denying the darker parts of our existence as much as they used to, especially in crime fiction. Some writers just do it for fun, because it's become the fashionable way to get published. You know, "gritty violence" and all that bullshit. The genuine darkness in noir stories comes from two places—the cruelty of the world's innate indifference, and the cruelty that people foster within themselves. If you're not seriously dealing with one, the other, or both, then you're not really writing noir.

JT: I see the stories in this collection as manifestations of thousands of unfinished conversations, gang songs, street hustles— lovers and haters creating art from their pain and regret. Oh, you better believe the Black Panthers are in these stories, as are the next wave of hip-hop noir rappers, like Ise Lyfe, Cookie Money, and Thizz Nation, who are slapping big beats behind their pains and passions. Oakland is a city of black power, brown power, people power . . . Let's roll, people!

Eddie Muller & Jerry Thompson
Oakland, California
January 2017

PART I

NOT A SOFT CITY

THE BRIDGE TENDER

BY NICK PETRULAKIS

Fruitvale Bridge

"A re those sirens? Gotta be. What do you think? Fire? Police?" She tilted her head and tried to catch more of the siren symphony below us. Whether or not the sirens were headed to the bridge depended on which side the call came from. If it came from the Alameda side, those sirens were ours; if the call came from the Oakland side, the sirens wouldn't be headed our way, not yet. Always too much going on in Oakland, never enough in Alameda.

"You were talking about your boy," I said, and that made her look back at me.

Because the sun lay low—and behind—her face was shadowed by her black curls, making it hard to see the eyes that were soft brown, a shade lighter than her skin. But just the mention of her son made her smile. I had to remember that.

"You'd like him," she said. Then the wind got strong and she had to finger some of those curls away from her face. She'd started crying again so she took a deep breath and then released it, slow. "Close your eyes," she said, yelling because of the wind.

I did, shut out the deepening sun, and everything got louder. The wind against my ears, the traffic from the bridge below us. But not the sirens, they'd grown faint—so they hadn't been for us.

"You close your eyes strange," she said.

I cupped a hand behind my ear.

"*Salty people,*" yelling again. "You make your eyes all

squinchy when you close them. Rest of us? We just close our eyes when we close our eyes."

I smiled, but then a gust shot up from over the water, shot up from way down, buffeted hard against me, and I rocked back, scared again, because when you're sixty-five feet in the air— legs dangling from the side of a railroad bridge, and your eyes are closed, and you feel an unexpected blast of wind against your chest—you fucking rock back and clench your hands even harder against the rail, digging grit into your palms, slicing your skin with flaked paint, and you involuntarily breathe in and hold it, and then realize that only two seconds have passed since you smiled.

I wanted to check my fingers, see if I'd cut them, but I'd have to open my eyes and loosen my grip to do that.

Exhale.

"No peeking," she said, still loud. "Now, make a picture of my boy inside your head. First, think about chubby cheeks. But chubby cheeks with attitude, am I right? Now amp up the cute. Definitely amp up the attitude." The wind quieted. "I used to have cheeks like that."

I pictured her reaching up, almost touching her face with her delicate hands, then stopping.

"It was time for the talk," she said. "You know? The Talk. Everyone thought he was too young."

Dead air.

With my eyes shut I was left to wonder what she was doing in the sudden still of the day. Smoothing her dress? Strumming the nylon rope with her left hand?

"They don't know how curious he is. My boy kept asking questions, real crazy ones. 'Specially after he got Hammer."

I missed what she said next because of the wind. It rushed at me again and I opened my eyes. It was *bright*, and she was lovely in the bright light—lovely in her yellow dress, her red sneakers.

Lovely and close. But not close enough.

I squinted from the light and tried not to gawk at her. Or the view—one of the best things about working bridges. The Coliseum in front of us with the hills after; San Francisco behind us with its bay. Its own bridges, its own views.

She stopped talking, seemed to judge the distance between us. Had it changed? Had I moved closer? No, not yet. So she started in on the rope again, tapped it with a fingernail painted as red as her shoes.

"Everybody said getting a kitten was stupid. That *I* was stupid. For getting my boy a cat. And a black cat? Bad luck, am I right? But my boy said that was dumb. Thinking black brought bad."

She smiled again and started crying. Visions of her boy kept her doing that. Cry, smile, cry.

"A female kitten, right? But he called her Hammer. MC would've made it a boy's name, but just Hammer? He didn't see a problem with that."

The wind stilled again and a toddler's shriek cut up through the hush. We peered down at a mom—dressed as Cinderella ready for the ball—pushing a faded green stroller along the bridge below, then I looked at the water churning under that bridge, swirling, the surface of the estuary curling out like breath, the waves an exhalation, angry immediately under us but the whorls calming the farther they spread.

"What's that mom see when she looks up?" she said, and let go of the rope, pointing down, the slanting light catching a flash of shiny red from her nails.

"She's not looking at us," I said as we heard another shriek, "she's got that baby to worry about. And even if she did look up, Cinderella wouldn't notice us, not with those clouds."

If she could let go of her rope, I could let go of the rail, so I did, hitched one thumb over my shoulder at those beautiful clouds, did it fast and then grabbed the rail again. The grit under my palm familiar now, comforting.

"You want me to look at some pretty clouds?" She shook her head. "Not me, I'm past all that."

"Okay," I said, "okay." And I held the rail tight. As long as I clutched the rail I was safe, I wouldn't fall. "Cinderella, she'd see this rail bridge we're sitting on, suspended by those tall, Erector Set towers." I nodded at one, then the other. "That tower in Oakland, that one in Alameda, separated by six hundred feet of water."

"This Erector Set ain't pretty, but she sure works hard." She palmed away more tears. "Story of my life right there."

"This bridge is important—she connects us to California. Don't diminish her."

She wasn't listening. "What does that mom see right now?"

Right after she said *mom*, she touched her belly. A short, soft movement.

"If she looked up, which she didn't, by the way, no one is looking up, no one sees us. But if she did, she'd think she was seeing one bridge when of course it's two. Ours, right here, the rail bridge, looking like an oversize, elongated *H*," I pressed harder on the girder we sat on, "with this huge section of track that just moves as one piece up and down, and when it goes down it connects the rails on the Oakland side to the tracks on the Alameda side."

Another cry from below but I couldn't see Cinderella. Strollering back into Oakland, she was blocked from my view by the north tower.

"Then there's the bridge for cars below us. The Miller-Sweeney—*my* Miller-Sweeney—a workhorse drawbridge. But we all combine them since we're neighbors, and make one span out of two, and call it the Fruitvale Bridge."

"You're not listening to me," she said, and she slapped the girder. "What does she see right now?"

I tried to pitch my voice lower so she had to strain to hear. "Right now she sees what's directly ahead of her, the traffic on Fruitvale, cars headed into Oakland, a few full of trick-or-treaters coming this way to Alameda."

"No, that mom saw us. She saw our legs kicking back and forth. Someone saw us, right? At least one someone saw us, and that someone found a phone and called the police."

"We're not kicking our legs back and forth," I said.

The wind blew and I felt like I was falling, like I'd lost my grip, so I leaned back until the vertigo went away and I was left with the wind and a pretty woman sitting next to me on the bridge—a pretty woman pretending nothing was wrong, nothing out of the ordinary, even as her nails nervously tip-tapped a nylon rope tied to her neck.

Then the wind eased and we could hear a BART train half a mile off accelerating out of Fruitvale Station.

I glanced at the fingers of one hand. Only my thumb had been cut. I put it in my mouth, tasted dust and blood.

"After I finished the Talk," she said, "my boy just looked at me. I started thinking maybe he was too young, maybe they were right and I shouldn't have said anything. But his questions . . . he always has so many questions. Like, *Where did Hammer come from*? And he didn't mean the pound, right?"

The breeze whipped one of her long black curls in front of her eyes. "He didn't want me making up some fool story about storks, he wanted to know. So that's why we had the Talk. But after?" She reached for the curl, wrapped it around her finger. "You know how some kids, when they have a question for you, they do that dog thing and tilt their head?" She tried to tuck the curl behind her ear but the wind got brutal for a second. "Know how I mean, right? When they look at you all confused? My boy never did that. He's never been confused in his life. But he did it right then. Just that once. Went all spaniel on me and tilted his head, thinking about this hurt I just made real. You ever see your mom cry?"

"No."

"Lucky you. First time my boy saw me cry. First and only. I've had plenty of reasons to, but I never did, until then. This wasn't the birds and the bees. He got the truth. The awful, hurtful truth."

I think she said *hurtful*, but we had the wind again, so loud, so high up. Above the buildings, above the trees. Maybe she'd said *helpful*?

"My boy looked over at Hammer, who was asleep on my bra. That kitty had dragged it into a spot of sun. My boy looks from his cat to me and he asks, *It's the same for cats as it is for people?* I just nodded. *Mom*, he says, *I think you better get fixed like Hammer so it doesn't happen to you again.*"

We laughed, both of us, and it was the prettiest sound I'd heard since I'd braced myself against the V support behind me. I took the cover of laughter to try and inch closer, but she'd gone quiet and as soon as my body moved, hers tensed. So I stopped, of course. I had to.

"That idea from my boy?" Again a soft touch to her belly. "The best advice I ever got. But stupid me, right? Did I follow it?"

A car crossed the bridge, honking, and the honk was contagious because two other cars, then three, joined in. The last was an orange Volkswagen, and, in honor of the day, black triangle-eyes and a blocky mouth had been shoe-polished onto the hood, transforming it into a rolling jack-o'-lantern.

She waited like she knew how, and then all those cars were over the bridge and gone. "You didn't answer my first question about the sirens. Police or fire? I guessed fire." Then she forgot that she was past it all now, forgot that beauty couldn't sway her anymore and suddenly she was distracted by the view.

Alameda stretched out long and low on one side of the estuary; shopping center here, houses with their docks along the water starting there, but most everything screened by trees, so many trees lining the streets. On the Oakland side it was warehouses, the glass recycling plant closest with its smokestacks—tall and oversize like on the *Titanic*. Below them, rising from behind the chain-link fence, were icebergs of crushed glass glittering in the setting sun.

But then the warehouses stopped at the freeway—all traffic, no trees—and the buildings of Fruitvale began. Beyond there were houses on the other side of International, continuing on to 580, then up into the hills where the trees finally regained control.

She looked around us. "Is it always so pretty up here?"

"You are," I said.

Her gaze came back, away from the hills, searched for the outboard motor someone had just started—there, a few docks down and away, the motor spewing smoke, the smoke more blue than black. Why wasn't she looking at those clouds? The clouds that were behind everything, those beautiful clouds taking on color. In the late afternoon there was pretty all around—even Oakland looked pretty because we were far enough away that you couldn't really see the city. If you could really see Oakland you'd turn from it like she'd just done. But now, almost dusk?

With the sun picking out some of the windows—glint, flash—from some of the houses from some of the hills?

Glint, flash, glint, as the sun moved lower.

"Very pretty," I repeated. "Please tell me you know that."

Her fingers on the rope, strumming it. Her fingers so long. Not strumming. Tapping. Fast, fast, fast, slow. Why hadn't I noticed that before?

"Do you still play piano?"

She tensed again, looked down at her fingers. *Tap tap tap taaap*.

She laughed. "I thought you were doing some mind reading there, something fancy. But you aren't fancy at all, are you? And you most definitely don't know pretty."

Some hot, wet smell caught us—diesel, dead fish—swirled around and then was gone.

"Can you get that picture back in your head?" She smiled, thinking about her son again.

I nodded, then tapped my forehead like she'd been tapping—the first four notes of Beethoven's 5th. *Tap tap tap taaap*.

"He's going to be so handsome, the cute is a phase, I can tell. He's going to leave that all behind and then . . ."

And then nothing from her.

"What, like Jim Brown?" I asked.

"Nah, he's going to be more movie-star handsome than football handsome."

"Jim Brown was a movie star too."

She would have been good in an old movie, in that dress. The yellow so faint that in this light you could mistake it for white. A breeze caught the hem and it whispered and I was staring again. I did that when she stopped talking—it was easy to stare. The dress, so sheer, and the fact that she wasn't wearing anything else. Underneath was just her in that beautiful dress and red sneakers, each sneaker with a big white star on the side. It should have been a ridiculous look but it wasn't, not on her.

She was a watcher, like me, and she was watching again, noticed my gaze.

"The shoes. I know." And now she did kick her legs back and forth. "It was the same day he got Hammer. He was so happy. My boy's never happy, not ever. But that whole week he was happy. And that day? He couldn't stand it, right? He said, *I got my most favorite wish. Now it's your turn.*"

"He made you buy those shoes?" I said.

"I know, right?"

I noticed that one of them was untied and she dangled it from her foot. This beautiful woman just dangling a red sneaker like she hadn't a care in the world—when obviously she was being crushed by it.

I thought she was going to kick the shoe off but she left it there, dangling high over the water.

"You think I was going to disappoint him? Not that day."

"Can I move a little closer?" I asked.

Behind her, the sun had almost disappeared and her face gained detail in the softer light.

"No. Just stay."

"Okay, okay, I'm staying." There was too much space be-tween us—six feet, probably more. Too much space. "It's just, the sun's almost gone, and with this wind you must be getting cold."

"Is it that obvious?" She looked down—right, then left. "I guess it is." She drew her arms around herself. "What's the worst thing you've ever done?"

I didn't have to think about that. "I steal books."

Two geese—not enough for a formation—flew at us, then the lead angled its wings and the other followed, up and over.

"Well, just one book. But lots of copies of that book. Every time I see it, I steal it. Then I burn it."

"Burning books is wrong," she said.

"Not if you copy a poem from a book, put that poem in a letter to a girl, and tell the girl the poem is yours."

"You tried to show off by writing a letter you didn't write?"

"Pretty much."

"So, your plan is to steal every copy of that book and this girl, she's never gonna know you lied? Is that right?"

"Pretty much," I repeated.

"What do you do, break into people's houses and go hunting for books? That's messed up."

"Not houses," I said. "Sometimes libraries, but mainly it's bookstores. If they're selling it, I just—"

"Steal it. That's the Eighth Commandment you're breaking right there." She looked at the railroad tracks next to us, then back at me. "The trains, they hardly ever come anymore. Why not?"

"Just less need. This year is their last."

"I thought they'd run forever," she said.

"You'll have to trust me on this one."

She continued tapping on the rope. Blue nylon bigger around than the fingers she tapped it with.

"1999 is the end of a lot, then," she said.

"It doesn't have to be."

"Oh? Can you keep the trains running?"

"No," I said.

"Then shut up."

The clouds behind her glowed like embers from the sun's last light.

"How long have you worked here?" she asked. She was just killing time now—that couldn't be good.

"Five years," I said.

"How did you decide this was for you?"

The questions were as ridiculous as her shoes should have been, but she was earnest—like she really thought there might be answers.

"I stay because I like being in the middle. Not Oakland, not Alameda. I like it, being halfway. At first it was just a job. It's not like in kindergarten when all the other kids were saying astronaut, or Wonder Woman, that I said bridge tender."

"That's what you're called?"

New sirens now, not going somewhere else. They were headed here.

"Someone has to be on site in case the bridges need raising, so yes, that's us. Bridge tenders."

"But the trains are ending. So you'll be watching over nothing? Halfway over nothing?"

With the sun having just disappeared, the clouds were magnificent, glowing even brighter orange, brighter red. She moved her head, heard the sirens for sure. Behind her—San Francisco's skyline, backlit with the glory of those clouds. The clouds really on fire now. And the tears on her face, so many tears.

"Your son—"

"Don't," she cut in. "Please. Not him, not now."

"But you're his mom," I said. "A good one."

"You don't know anything. Not one thing. Not about him, not about me."

On the water, a lone rower in a single scull leaned forward, then pulled back on her long oars, her motion powerful, fluid. Lean, pull. Lean, pull.

"How many of you work here?" she said as her fingers tightened on the rope. Where had she learned to tie a knot like that?

"Four. There's at least one of us here around the clock."

"And you have to raise the bridge for boats? Whenever? They have right of way, always?" She was talking so fast.

"Don't do this, not today," pleading now. "Not on such an easy day to remember, a holiday."

"It's not Christmas."

The rower was already on the other side of the bridge. Her boat skimmed fast, its narrow shell slicing open the skin of the water.

"This is gonna cause trouble for you." She started crying again. "Sorry about that."

I wanted to get her away from thinking about the trouble she could cause. "What's your son's name?" I asked.

"No, that's mine." A flurry came out of the orange light and carried away what she said next, so she repeated herself: "What's yours?"

"I'll tell you if you tell me," I said.

"No, you didn't answer my question." She cried harder, shaking from the tears.

"Okay, okay. There's two times a day when the bridge is down and stays down—an hour in the morning, two at night. Otherwise, yes, we're all of us at the mercy of the boats."

Her nose had started running so she blew it, wet and messy, into her fingers, wiped her fingers on her dress. Then she looked between us at the railroad track nestled between girders.

"This one's almost always up. Only comes down for the trains, am I right?" She tugged on the other end of the blue nylon, checking that it held. "How high are we?"

"Not that high. It just feels that way with Oakland there, and Alameda here, and the road and water below."

She shook her head. "Not high enough to just jump. That's why." She tapped the rope.

Oakland, I wanted to tell her, *it's so very pretty right now.*

And San Francisco? With its outline on fire? "Look," I said.

"No." She drew the back of her hand against her slick cheeks before she tugged on the rope again. Then her fingers slid up the rope's other end to the figure eight she'd tightened against her neck.

"Your son," I tried to say, but I was crying now too, and I couldn't see the fire in San Francisco—it was just a smear of red.

"So curious," she said. "He is so curious. And going to be so handsome."

The sirens were loud, the wind couldn't take away the sirens, not now, and they were coupled with flashing lights strobing from between the trees, the red light mimicking the colors of the clouds. The wind was so strong, I was trying to dry my eyes, but there was no way.

"Please, c'mon. Please. I can help you but you have to help me. I get it, okay? It's the hardest thing in the world, the asking. I've never asked for help. Ever. So I understand how hard it is. I get it, I do. You don't want to ask for help. I don't want to ask for help. But this is my life—keeping people safe on my bridge. Let me do my job. Right now. I'm begging, okay? Help me. Please."

"I have to go now." She put her hands down. Her long fingers on the girder, feeling the grit like I felt it but finding no comfort in the roughness, none.

Oh God. I swung my arm out, pivoted as fast as I could, the dirt and chipped paint ripping the skin on my fingers that still held on while my other hand shot toward her, reaching through nothing. But I was too far away, six feet was too far, she hadn't let me get any closer, not even an inch, and it was like she didn't have any last words—*I have to go now*—because they were gone as soon as they were spoken, erased by the wind, and the final thing she did was look up before she pushed herself off the bridge.

Her dress blurred yellow through the air. She fell so fast. Five feet, ten—then the rope snapped taught and her body jerked. The shoe that she'd dangled was flung off, and fell graceful and red through the wind.

I watched it fall, and fall, and hit the water.

THE WISHING WELL

BY KIM ADDONIZIO

Pill Hill

There are no magic walnuts in this story, or wise flounders who speak in rhyme.

Or princes hacking their way through brambles for princesses who shit roses.

None of that here.

All of these people are doomed—they just don't know it yet.

They're all jittering and talking and jonesing in the Kaiser Dependency Recovery Center.

They're keeping their fate at bay, just barely, maybe thinking they're getting a handle on their lives. They hold out a little hope.

I don't belong anywhere near them.

We sit in a circle talking about our week and one guy says, "I know I'm going to start using when I start hating people, judging people on the bus," and the woman next to him says, "What do you do when you start to get critical, then?" and the guy—he's a meth head—leans back in his chair, crosses his arms, and answers, "Just say to yourself, *Who the hell am I?*"

Exactly.

My friend Elena has two subjects of conversation: her family and the lottery. The problem and the solution.

Elena never has money for cigarettes because her monthly check goes to stuff she can't buy with food stamps, to PG&E,

and to the corner liquor store for SuperLottoPlus tickets.

Elena is my next-door neighbor. I'm here at Kaiser to keep her company. She's recovering, and I don't intend to.

I believe that alcohol and drugs are a life choice, not a sickness.

A sickness is when you love someone you shouldn't. There is no recovery.

Elena's granddaughter Darnique lives across town in East Oakland with her shit-for-brains father, Elena's son Anton.

Anton makes movies, which means he illegally downloads and sells them.

Anton also sells drugs, which means people come and go from his place at all hours.

He puts Darnique's glue and colored markers and construction paper on a high shelf so she can't get to them when he's not around.

Among other, worse things.

I feel bad for Darnique because she's another doomed soul who doesn't know it.

Or maybe she does.

During the break, Elena smokes my cigarettes. "Last week Darnique be talkin' about people who kill themselves from stress. Why she askin' about that?" Elena says. "She only ten years old. I tell her, *Uh-uh, girl, you gonna live a long time. Those people that kill themselves, they just got nobody to talk to.*"

There is a gun in this story, so probably you know what that means.

Elena doesn't know shit. I like her.

Ɂ

"So, what's your story?" a guy at the Kingfish asks when I'm about six beers in.

"Just a girl having a drink," I say.

Though "girl" at forty-five is kind of a stretch.

"Feel my ears," he says.

He's clearly looking for something, rather than someone. We both know what it is.

"Like stones," I say, touching them.

"I used to wrestle. It smashes the cartilage."

The Kingfish is close enough to walk home from, which makes up for it not serving hard liquor. Plus, there's fresh popcorn and a shuffleboard table. The guy and I slide a few pucks down the table, and then we walk to my place, and soon we're naked on my living room rug and he shows me some wrestling moves.

My house is a little 1920s bungalow on a quiet street, a few blocks off Telegraph Avenue.

Usually quiet, anyway. Every so often someone runs through the backyard. Once I opened my back door and two cops were there, looking for a gun someone dropped.

Mostly older black folks live here. There's a white lesbian couple that keeps chickens. There's also an old Polish guy in a wheelchair who owns three houses on the block. One he lives in, and the other two look condemned.

"What's your story," the wrestler says again, when we're sitting on the front porch afterward.

Not like he really wants to know.

I tell him anyway.

I tell him my parents died a few years ago in a car crash and left me some money, enough for a down payment on this house and something left over.

I tell him about Nick taking out a whopping loan on our equity line of credit at the bank—I put him on the mortgage as a tenant-in-common—without bothering to mention it. I tell him how I kicked Nick out when I found out, and how much I hate him. I keep saying his name: *Nick, Nick, Nick.*

Fucking Nick.

Right now all the houses on the street are dark and somehow seem smaller, like they shrink a little when the light goes out, and I imagine that everyone else is asleep and not having bad dreams.

"I guess I should go," the wrestler says.

I find the dropped gun the next day, in the potted bamboo on the deck, and I keep it.

∂

Nick and I were together ten years, which means things were both good and bad. When I think about him, I think about us having sex.

And sometimes him standing at the stove cooking.

But mostly the sex.

Everyone you love leaves a hole in you.

A blast crater.

Soon there aren't any more flowers or birds and the rivers dry up.

The wrestler's been gone about ten minutes when a car pulls up next door and cuts its lights. I pull back a little, into the shadowed part of the porch where the streetlamp doesn't reach.

The back door of the car opens.

Someone gets pushed out.

There's a little chiming sound from the wind chimes.

There's a motorcycle backfiring on the freeway two blocks away.

I've never seen a dead person. I've seen birds lying stiff under a tree, or next to a window they slammed into. Once I saw a half-eaten deer in the Oakland Hills. I watched my cat be put to sleep. They looked like nothing—a rock, a fence post, a throw rug.

This looks like shit-for-brains Anton.

He's lying on the curb where they pushed him out.

The car drives off without turning on its lights. It passes the house where the Polish man lives. It passes the house where the old woman sits on her porch all day, her hands folded in her lap. I follow the car until I can't see it anymore and have to imagine where it goes.

I head inside, get a bottle from the built-in shelving, and drink without looking to see what's in it.

Gin.

I met Anton a few times in Elena's kitchen. She was making macaroni and government cheese, ground beef round and Hamburger Helper, chicken thighs. He was just this side of sullen, talking to me but not making eye contact.

I try to imagine where Anton has gone. If he might see my parents and pass on a message.

He let Darnique go to school without breakfast most days. Once he slammed her head against a washing machine.

So fuck drug-dealing movie-making shit-for-brains Anton.

The message I would give my parents is this: *Please come back.*

And this: *I know you were both drunk off your asses when you crashed the car.*

I add some Snapple Lemonade to the gin.

I call Nick.

❧

My mother used to read me stories. They ended happily, but before that there was usually sadness or difficulty. I never understood why they ended just when the good part was starting.

Elena tried to kill herself at least once that I know of. She had a baby back in Tennessee. The baby was born crack-addicted, and died.

I learned this from Darnique.

I tried to kill myself at least twice. There might have been a third time, or I might have just been drunk and taken more pills than I realized.

This was always after Nick had sex with someone else.

I love Nick with all my heart and soul, and he's a complete asshole.

He comes right over when I call.

"I'm scared, Nick," I say. "What if they come back? What if they know I saw their car? What about Elena? She's going to come outside with her coffee in the morning, come over here to bum a cigarette, and see her dead son lying there. Should I call the cops?"

"I'm sorry about the money," Nick says.

"You're such a dick," I say. Then he kisses me and we go to bed.

Afterward I lie awake. Nick is snoring a little. I can hear cars on the street.

I imagine that my heart looks like the moon, the surface all fucked up from space rocks.

The moon has no atmosphere.

Red lights swirl around the bedroom.

Elena mourns Anton with a houseful of people and a lot of potato salad and ribs.

I bring her a grocery bag from the Alameda Food Bank. Tangerines. Chocolate fudge Jell-O. Cans of tuna and vegetables.

At her church they play tambourines and talk about Jesus's love.

There is no God.

Nick and I bought a grill.

Which means he's moved back in.

"Next time I'll bring you a barbequed turkey," I tell Elena.

"I ain't had no barbequed turkey ever," Elena says. "Ain't you got to defrost it first?"

"We're getting a fresh one."

"Fresh? Where you get that at?"

"Andronico's, in Berkeley."

Which means in a galaxy far, far away.

Darnique comes to live with Elena. They get out the glue and glitter and colored markers. Elena cornrows Darnique's hair. She makes her Eggo Cinnamon Toast waffles for breakfast.

Everything works out fine, except in the end it doesn't.

Elena will get diabetes. Darnique will be pregnant by fourteen.

I'm nobody's fucking fairy godmother.

≈

This is the part where the gun goes off. I was drunk, and mad at Nick again after he'd been back a couple of months.

It turns out he had another girlfriend.

Everyone leaves me sooner or later.

I kind of waved the gun around and screamed at him. Then I aimed it at my head, but I changed my mind and turned it toward him instead.

Years before, when Elena tried to kill herself, the recoil of the gun jerked her hand away from her temple. The bullet only grazed her neck, leaving a little scar.

So I knew to hold the gun steady.

There is no recovery.

When I was little, my parents used to take me to bars with them.

Shit works out for other people sometimes, but not for me.

And not for the other women in here.

In here we're all doomed, and we know it.

My parents' favorite bar when we lived in San Francisco was the Wishing Well.

It's gone now.

I sat on a stool and drank Shirley Temples.

In my glass, three bright-as-neon cherries were impaled on a plastic sword.

I pulled it from the melting ice.

They were cold, and delicious.

A MURDER OF SAVIORS

BY KEENAN NORRIS

Toler Heights

I remember hearing about the incident in the news, and considering it with all the sentimentality of a seven a.m. BART train crowd, battered black briefcases and visionless stares. I'm a real romantic, you can tell. Perfect for reporting on Oakland's death spirals—not so much for San Francisco, but this story doesn't have shit to do with San Francisco.

The kid was found in the commercial truck bay of the plaza that divides East Oakland from the suburbs just beyond. A gravel ramp runs up from the bay to the upper level of the plaza, where there is a police station. Someone had tracked the victim's blood up the black ramp, right past the police. Granted, it was a rough section of town, but even by tough-town standards, this seemed impetuous. Not only were the police stationed there, there were also a children's dance studio, a decent-quality supermarket, and a Wells Fargo bank in the plaza. A murder committed so close to so much innocence and authority was rash, even if it happened in the early morning, before business hours.

Nobody knew what to make of it, least of all the local media and police. The press gave the boy's name—Shaun Sobrante—his age—sixteen—and his surprisingly strong grade-point average—3.3. The local gumshoes, going light on the investigative aspect of their work, redundantly noted the manner of his murder and the fact that there was no known culprit, nor motive, nor any witnesses. This was a prediction and justification of what came next: nothing.

The police offered only the unhelpful fact that Shaun was apparently unaffiliated with street gangs and had a marijuana possession charge on his record. The intent-to-distribute case was still pending at the time he was murdered. I recall wishing that I was a police investigator, or a paid reporter on the crime beat, so I could put in some real work on the case. That's assuming there was still such a thing as a "crime beat" when it came to local news. It sure didn't seem like it.

Where Shaun's murder barely registered with the media or the law, it resonated deeply along the blocks surrounding the plaza—his community. Shaun's elaborate graffiti visage went up on the wall of a handball court at the nearby middle school. His funeral brought out several hundred mourners. A basketball tournament was staged at the courts on Seminary Avenue, to mark his passing and the deaths of the many other young people who'd lost their lives to East Oakland violence. Underground rap music blared his name in deafening tribute down the boulevards.

And an Oakland-born businessman with friends in high places came home and founded a school in his honor: Sobrante Preparatory Academy.

The charter schools had swooped in like a black murder of crows over Oakland, resectioning the city's schools and recalibrating its civics. No Child Left Behind money was flowing to a few select men and women handpicked to recode the curriculum. It was only later, after Principal Hill at Sobrante Prep excited my investigative streak, that I learned of this trend, but I might as well set the stage with it now so that what happened, the whole mystery at the heart of things, will come clear to you faster than it did to me.

There was James Chavo of the Native American Middle School; Lexington Fowler at Inspired Tech Academy; Mrs. Majesty Blanche Boudreaux at Leaders Born High School. There were others too, believe me. The time was ripe for saviors: our president was a great born-again Christian and the City of Dope, that Too $hort had told us couldn't be saved by John the Pope, was being born again too. No, it was no longer the drug-plagued eighties, or the bullet-riddled nineties. It was a new century and saviors were everywhere in Oakland. The town was being chartered out.

By the time of the Sobrante murder, the schools were already receiving quite a bit of press for their ties to the Republican Party and their exceptional test scores. Chavo at the Native American school in the Laurel District was said to be a miracle worker—his students' Annual Yearly Progress scores had reached 860 for two years in a row, an elite level rarely accomplished by any but the most privileged private schools. Chavo was also said to be a born-again of particular fervor and Bible-beating prowess. Fowler's Inspired Tech Academy was, like the Native American school, situated in one of East Oakland's diverse, borderline neighborhoods, where the announcement of an AYP above 800 was often followed by word that a police informant had been executed in an alleyway, or that SWAT was busting in someone's door down the street. The kind of neighborhood that could go either way at any moment. Fowler, for his part, had been among Bush 41's Thousand Points of Light back in '90 or '91, and he had not lost favor with the paradise-inclined mind of 43, the son.

Everything about the charters was story-worthy. Yet there was an undercurrent in every article that went uninterrogated. Each piece would mention, in passing, the schools' high teacher turnover and militant reliance on nineteenth-century schoolhouse discipline. Chavo, it was reported, angrily ended a pep rally in mid-hoorah because some boys were sagging their pants in violation of his dress code. Fowler, meanwhile, took it upon himself to patrol the halls of Inspired Tech and volubly chastise girls if they were cuddled up with the lower-performing boys. Mrs. Majesty Blanche Boudreaux, the *Tribune* reported, actually went to the trouble of keeping a public tally of students whose grade-point averages statistically qualified them for acceptance to four-year colleges and universities, implying that the rest were wastrels and losers. Cash Hill bought ad space in the *Tribune* where he proclaimed his school would be "the lynching that Thug Life and all the other culture cancers have coming."

Why weren't these signs of unstable leadership investigated? I can't say. What I do know now, but only suspected back then, is that local newspapers were experiencing the wrath of the Internet, and budgets were being slashed like a machete dropping cane. Investigative reporting was going the way of my own broken dream of being the next Woodward, Pilger, and Wells, all wrapped into one. News anchors and popular editorialists might demand high salaries, but the actual nature of their work was inexpensive. By contrast, the costs for actual investigative work could spiral stratospherically. What if the story went deeper and involved more players than originally expected? What if the saga ran longer than anyone suspected it would? A news agency couldn't just pull out midinvestigation and act like the story had run its course. It was an all-or-nothing deal—and the media increasingly opted for nothing.

I had always imagined myself haunting the halls of the state capitol, doggedly delivering on the intentionally obscured issues of political glad-handing and corruption. Maybe if I made it out of local news, I'd one day work for CNN or CBS, and find myself holed up with Congolese rebels or unembedded in Iraq or Afghanistan. At the very least I'd end up on the Big Pharma beat, stalking CEOs from boardrooms to brunch dates with doctors on the make. But by the time I was out of college, that deeply researched reporting on local politics and events was dead. If it had to do with a war in the Middle East—fuck the Congo, Uganda, or Sri Lanka—there was always money and a few warm bodies to throw at it. But what went on in Sacramento day to day, let alone Oakland, might as well have been happening on another planet.

I was still trying my hand at freelance reporting back then, although a year clear of school I was just as broke and unpublished as I'd been on my graduation day. Oh, the pride of my parents, you can only imagine. I picked up a part-time job at a Mexican supermarket on East 14th near the Allen Temple Baptist Church, and I worked parking lot security for the church on Wednesdays and Sundays. My savings had run dangerously low before the part-time jobs and I had been forced to move into a three-bedroom duplex off 85th Avenue where I was the only tenant. This was way before gentrification so I could afford it. Nobody but a naïve college kid wanted that rattrap, which was right above a homeless encampment that doubled as an open-air drug den. Looming over the many elderly, addled homeless was a billboard advertising pet rescue and adoption: *Save Fido. Rescue Kitty.* Happy, smiley, white Disney cartoon people nuzzled their anthropomorphic pets right on top of rickshaw shopping carts, broken black people, syringes, and vials. The landlady was more than happy to get my six hundred dollars in rent every month. Half the faucets didn't work, the electrical outlets were all ungrounded so powering up my PC was taking my life in my hands, and there was no heating or air-conditioning in the whole place. The building was as dangerous, really, as anything outside its walls. But I wasn't ready to give up on myself as a journalist. I had no desire to admit defeat and fall back on my parents in suburban Sacramento, so I holed up in the hood and held tight. I drank a lot, and read books about washouts on the outskirts of Hollywood throwing their ideas down the toilet along with their liquor vomit.

I wasn't sure if I was embarking on an article about a hero leading a great educational effort in an East Oakland ghetto, running a preparatory academy literally founded upon a murder scene and dedicated to the victim—or if what I was after was something more sinister. But I had to tell the story everyone else was slighting, even if my only means of publication was a blog that no one but its author ever read.

I started schooling myself on the inner workings of Sobrante. Eventually, I wanted to talk to the principal himself, but first I needed to know more about his operation from people around the fringes. I couldn't interview students who were minors without complications arising, so I settled for janitorial staff, clerical workers, and former employees who were already making their presence known on *Glassdoor.com*.

"A Trump-like figure," one post read, "a mannerless Wall Street lout." It was the language of a teacher or HR staffer from the hills, maybe even from Marin, who was trying to compute the existence of a man so connected and yet so uncouth.

"The educational equivalent of a prosperity preacher," another post read.

"Like the Eddie Longs and T.D. Jakes of the world, he's receiving the largesse of the Bush administration—except instead of faith-based initiatives it's No Child Left Behind federal funding," another writer noted.

Others were more opinionated: "What a black cracker!

Not to play the 'race card,' but is there any chance in hell that white kids would get guinea-pigged like this by an education fascist?"

Glassdoor disrobed the town and had a million stories to share about its birthday suit, but it was still just a website. For all the Internet could reveal and make accessible, it couldn't replace the intimately felt reality of genuine reporting. There was no flesh to grasp onto online, no facial cues, hushed tones, or eyes that would rather wander a million miles than meet your own. No viscera. Everything was cloaked in keyboards and anonymity. I had to get on the campus (through the plaza mall, past the Wells Fargo and the dance studio) and talk to real people, on the record.

"The dress code is selective," said one staff member who declined to be identified. "For the record, remember what a charter is and isn't. There are private schools in Oakland's enclaves with bigger endowments than state universities. These schools serve two, three hundred children at most. We are not private, kids actually go to school here. Our endowment is the overtime wages Hill shorts us on. If we didn't receive public monies, we wouldn't exist. But at the same time we're not true public schools because we're not union or school board regulated. There's no unions, no boards—just Hill. Hill regulates us and himself. As far as this school is concerned, he *is* the state. Only the federal government has any say over him, and you know the feds don't come to Oakland unless it's a drug bust. Plus, he's got friends in the White House."

"Friends?"

"That's what I heard."

"Duly noted." I moved us back to firmer ground: "The dress code is selective, how?"

"Selective like this: If your GPA is above a 3.0, your standardized test scores are above proficiency, and you're a girl, you can wear a cropped halter top and high heels. Your blouses can expose back and shoulders. If you're a boy with those same credentials, you still can't sag your pants, because Hill thinks that's coded communication between gang members. But you can wear your hat at any angle you like, you can wear jewelry, and you can curse without facing reprimand. These privileges are not open to the low-performing student."

I remember pausing to take stock of a few of the class photographs that adorned this woman's office walls. The children wore an array of outfits, some with pants sagging ludicrously low, evidently in open rebellion to the rules. Others wore their shorts high-water, like old men, Urkel, and wary boxers. Several of the girls wore "stunner shades," huge block-shaped goggle-like sunglasses that seemed to only come in hot pink, flame orange, or neon blue. These young ladies were also bursting out of their tiny shirts emblazoned with provocative insignias, which drew my attention that much more shamefully to their taut teenage breasts. "These must be the straight-A students," I cracked.

"No," she shrugged, "not even close. This crew isn't exactly headed to Harvard Yard."

"But I thought only the smart kids could dress like they want."

"In theory, that's the rule. But Hill can't patrol the halls every morning and afternoon inspecting each student's clothes. He has a school to run, and day-trading to do," the woman reminded me. "That would be unrealistic, even for a demagogue. The dress code mostly comes into effect the day before standardized tests, and everybody knows it. I think he learned it from Chavo over there at the Indian school. Baggy jeans, exposed boxer briefs, halter tops, and visible bra straps will get you suspended on test day, if you're bad at taking tests."

"Is that legal?" I asked ignorantly. Was the place where I lived *legal* under any compliance code? Was the homeless encampment on the street outside *legal*? Where were their permits? What about the police who curb-crawled the neighborhood nightly, extorting the prostitutes and shoestring pimps? Where was running a protection racket out of a police station endorsed under the law?

"I asked the same question when I first showed up here." She nodded at me somberly. "I don't anymore."

AYP scores came in: Sobrante rated a 650, hardly in the elite category that the Native American Middle School consistently claimed, but it was at least a hundred points higher than the public high schools deep in East Oakland.

According to my inside sources, Principal Hill was unsatisfied. He blamed the mediocre score on race and culture. One source had surreptitiously recorded Hill's rant on her phone: "If these Negroes would consent to an eleven-month school year for their children, we could social engineer our way to a 900 AYP in no time flat. I promise that on my brother's grave. We could create a black Bill Gates. We could make us a Mexican Stephen Hawking, minus his ALS. You know, you can't get that shit if you learn to salsa at three years old. Think about it, you ever known a Mexican falling out of his wheelchair with ALS? Mexicans are a healthy people with a healthy culture, but Negroes are a lost people. They require some inhumanity. They need to be reeducated by any means necessary, and the eleven-month school year is the nicest way of doing it. It could be twelve months. If it were really up to me, I'd do like Mao and send them all back to the land, beat it into them. The Marxists had a good idea—they just applied it to the wrong people.

The rich don't need reeducation. Whites and Asians do not need reeducation, and if they did, they wouldn't bitch about it like blacks do. They would do whatever was necessary not to become a subservient class."

The recording exposed everything that was wrong with Mr. Cash Hill. The guy was sounding more fascistic by the moment. Whatever his business acumen, whatever his connections to born-again Bush, his guidance of children was taking a dark turn. There was no way such a man would have been allowed to lead affluent white children, and no telling what such a man would do to the poor and powerless.

Unfortunately, I knew I couldn't print any of this, or even post it to my blog. It's against California law to record or publish people without their permission. I know FOX News all but destroyed ACORN using it as a tactic, but I'm just a small-time citizen journalist. Hill would be up my ass with lawsuits and countercharges; my underwear would be up for auction if I tempted fate like that. Even now I wonder what will come of it, if he is out there somewhere reading my words, plotting to put me before a judge. All for exposing his mad love.

I located a janitor who had moved on from the high school for reasons he wouldn't discuss. But he admitted on the record that he'd more than once wandered into Principal Hill's motivational sessions while fetching things from the janitorial supply closet. Inside he'd find some banished child wearing a dunce cap that read, *DEPORT THIS LATINO,* or, *CRACK BABY BRAIN,* or, *DANGER: LAZY NEGRO HAPPY SLAVE.* Then there was the tiara, always given vengefully to the boys that bucked against rule and order—*BITCH,* it read in bright white sequins.

"It's not right to teach children that way," the janitor said, "even if they is in high school and they did somethin' wrong."

Add to the alleged wrongs an oft-used method one HR employee explained to me: "You lock the unruly student inside one of the windowless classrooms or a storage closet. All they miscreant asses need is a tablet of some kind and a writing instrument. You turn off the lights and you leave 'em there, go about teaching those who want to learn, then come get he or she who was actin' out from the lock-up at three p.m. when school is out. Now that's a policy that ain't on paper, but one that is practiced here without apology. Shit, if Principal Hill ran East Oakland like he runs this school, these streets wouldn't be lookin' the way they look, I can tell you that much."

I was not looking forward to Hill entering local politics, though perhaps that was where all this was headed. With him at its helm, East Oakland would either transform into a sprawling, chocolate-city suburb, or it would be overtaken with roving bands of disgruntled ex-employees and students who'd been kicked out of the school system.

If Principal Hill would have been a lightning rod as a mayor, Principal Chavo at the Native American school would have been the thunder, plus a few downed power lines. In a turn of events that made local news, Chavo pulled his own card by cursing out a contingent of Berkeley School of Education students who were touring his campus. Apparently they disagreed with the principal patrolling the halls on standardized test day and suspending kids on the spot for the merest of infractions. One kid (who might not have been the sharpest of students) just looked at him wrong and was gone. In another instance, Chavo swooped straight into a classroom, asked everyone if the test was too hard, and then kicked out all those who raised their hands. Several dozen students ended up on the curb, waiting to be picked up by parents, guardians, or whoever scooped them up. Some of the graduate students were concerned by the haphazard pickup situation, others by the initial disposal. Chavo didn't give a damn and had them put out of doors as well.

The Berkeley students went to the papers and local TV. After that, the scrutiny on Oakland's charter school movement increased. Mrs. Majesty's custom-made job applications, with question after question about prior union involvement, came under suspicion; *Glassdoor* was inundated with anonymous complaints; meanwhile, Principal Fowler's penchant for ridding his school of strapping young men, and his frequent cancellation of football games, pep rallies, and school dances suddenly seemed rather suspect.

And Principal Cash Hill, though he had only been in the booming business of high school education briefly, was not immune. A few mothers, wrung raw by the world and by Hill's commandments, complained to the newspapers about the new push for an extended class schedule to ten or eleven months. Their children were not robots, they inveighed. The Ivy League was not the be-all and end-all of life in East Oakland, they said, just in case Hill was unaware. My blog even received some attention—mostly from the lame local media that plundered it for my "exclusive interviews" with employees from the school. I had yet to publish the really explosive stuff about racist dunce caps and locking kids in storage closets. I was holding off on that until a couple more shoes dropped. Also, the "legitimate" reporters had a bad habit of publishing my content without crediting me. Of course, I could have sued them, but in news everything is about timelines—nobody reads the retractions.

Then the Oakland Police Department reopened their investigation into the murder of Sobrante Prep's namesake. A press conference was held, to which I was not allowed entrance. I waited outside next to a network news van parked between the plaza mall and the McDonald's. The gathering was not large and I could hear the spokesman at a distance, describing how Shaun Sobrante was a college-bound student, a good kid, and what had happened to him was an unmitigated tragedy. But he had made a fateful mistake and had gotten himself kicked out of the public school system. Shaun had been asking around about the new charter schools; in particular, he was roaming the plaza halls trying to get a meeting with Principal Hill. Enrollment at what was then called Forging the Future Preparatory Academy was low. There was opportunity there, maybe even for a kid with a pending court date for drug possession. It was unclear if Principal Hill had ever met with Shaun, or whether the school had a policy then against accepting children with pending criminal charges. Charters could keep a lot of things private back then.

"That's all we know right now," the spokesman said. "That, and the fact that it's a shame that Shaun never got a chance to attend the fine school that bears his name."

I imagined the spokesman exiting stage left, cameras flashing on his retreating profile like a harried president disappearing into the White House's inner sanctums.

I knew it was time to interview Cash Hill. Not the next morning, not that night, but right then. And unlike the local media, I knew how to find him.

I'd never dialed it before, but I'd had Hill's cell phone number on speed dial for some time. It was given to me by the disgruntled janitor, who shall remain nameless. I called him while standing beside the network news van.

"Cash Hill?"

"Who's this?"

"The closest thing you have to a friend in the Oakland media. I know you're aware of the televised press conference that just went down at the police station right outside your school. I know you know there's scrutiny on the charters right now. You need to set the record straight—about Shaun Sobrante, your school, and the proposed eleven-month schedule."

"Eleven months isn't shit!" he shouted. "Nothing comes by expectation alone; anyone who tells you success can be had without resistance is lying on their mama! Of course there's people that hate me, so what? When we have our black Bill Gates, they'll thank me. History will absolve me."

"Fair enough. You want to go on the record with that?"

He repeated himself—on the record. "This over now? I've got work to do."

"You've got a public image to maintain, Mr. Hill. People will begin to question the seemliness of naming your school after a murdered child whom you refused to enroll. Unless you get out front of this story. Tell me about yourself, Mr. Hill. I'm not interested in a hit piece or a shock story. I want the people of Oakland to know you, to know why you are enraged about education in the town, and the radical measures you've taken to change it."

Apparently this struck a chord. Thirty minutes later, I was standing at the doorway of Hill's Oakland Hills home. The big man, adorned in vaquero hat and boots, a Sobrante Academy blazer, and slim-fit jeans, summoned me in. He was an imposing man in person, just as he appeared in his newspaper advertisements and TV interviews. He was hard-jawed, broad-shouldered, tall, muscular, lean, and rough-hewn. He looked more like a boxer than a broker, and more like a broker than a school administrator. I could see him striding around Wall Street, but it was much harder to imagine him sitting down to give careful attention to a kid's homework assignment. I wondered if he had any children of his own and scanned the walls of the front room for pictures, but I just saw photograph after photograph of Hill with a woman I took to be his wife. She was dark and striking, angular and alert in her posture, with typically round, lush African facial features that contrasted with her otherwise straight, narrow frame. She was beautiful and she was everywhere, but there were no children in evidence.

Shrouded and dark, curtained in deep blue and purple, the front room felt oceanic. I had the sense that I was sinking into something.

Hill led me down a winding staircase, typical of homes in the hills, and I felt I was wandering beneath the earth into a small, dark chamber. The room he led me to was crowded with shelves and was so tight we had to angle and sidestep our way around before arriving at an area where there was space to stand and furniture in which to sit. The shelves didn't contain many books, I noticed. The few that were there were balanced against dozens of trophies and plaques. At a glance, the books were professional manuals and black nationalist tomes, while the memorabilia celebrated graduations, certifications, and administrations. There was a framed photograph of Hill shaking hands with Bush 43. Something, maybe a signature, was scrawled across the front.

Hill sat down on a large leather chair and motioned me to an office chair nearby.

"We gotta lynch Thug Life on every oak tree in Oaktown!" he thundered. There would be no small talk, I ascertained. "We're making inroads, with President Bush's emphasis on faith-based living and institutions, and the charters breaking up the bad public schools and the bloodsucking teacher unions. Once we get what Malcolm called *them foxy white liberals* outta office, we'll be on our way to real change. Anyway," he said, suddenly breaking from the rhetorical mode, "Shaun Sobrante was a political expedient."

His words fell cold in my mind. "What does that even mean?" I asked.

"Look, kid, if you haven't noticed, Oakland's the kind of place where people get shot every once in a while."

We were clocking in at a murder almost every other day at the time.

"It's not a soft city. Sobrante was interchangeable with others that are just as dead as he is. But he was in the news, there was populist momentum there. As far as not enrolling the brother—you know what I say about Thug Life: it's not tolerated, its perpetrators are not allowed at my school. I don't know why he got killed any more than I know why the last hundred murders happened, but I will say this: you get iced outside a police station, sounds like the 5-O put that work in themselves and are just tryin' to relocate the blame. But you and I know that that shit would never see a courtroom, so what's the point? Better *our* expedient than *their* victim.

"I'm not into murder mysteries, kid. That's why I got the hell outta them East Oakland flats when I was eighteen, saw the writing on the wall. Crack was hittin', bullets was about to be flyin'. But education and capitalism saved me. I capitalized on my brain and some elite private institutions. You see, public schools and universities don't give a fuck about minorities. They're like the Democrats—they got us by the droves. Private institutions, they actually care, they teach and nurture us. That was when I realized public education was fatally flawed. I went from USC to an Ivy League MBA, and then after that I got my real education on Wall Street. Got to be where the kid from East Oakland was about as grassroots as a skyscraper. One day I woke up, checked my bank account, and I was actually kinda rich compared to everybody but my colleagues.

"I'd been asked by an old friend from East Oakland to come speak at her high school. Janie McPherson, her name was. She's Mrs. Cash Hill now, but back then Janie told me I was the kind of role model the kids needed. I had risen up from the same dust, you might say. Back in the day, I just wanted to get the fuck out. But I was aged and experienced when Janie came calling. I had learned some things, been through some things." He paused. "It took my close—"

Hill, shockingly, let forth a noise so desperate and clipped I wasn't sure what it was—a choke, a gasp for air, a cry for peace. I didn't even react to it until after he had regained his voice. "My own family, my brother. Some thug put a bullet in him out of mistaken identity. For no damn reason, just a gun and a mistake.

"In college, I never went to no black-issues rallies, didn't take no African American studies. I didn't go see no ghetto violence movies like *Boyz n the Hood* when they came out. I had seen the caskets closed for real, why I wanna go see Hollywood tell that story all over again? I wasn't really tryin' to change the world or know it three times as deep. You understand me?"

"I'm sorry," I said, not in sympathy, but because I didn't understand. I was a wannabe reporter, diving after my idea of the truth, as unconcerned with the feelings of others as Hill was with his students' feelings when it came to standardized testing.

"After my brother, it was different. So I done did my speech at the little school, and in the Q&A this light-skinned shorty in the front row with cornrows and amberish eyes asks me, *Do you ever wish you could trade places with your brother?* That's why I'm on fire like this. That's why I came home.

"That the story you were searching for?" Hill questioned. "My side of the story, my blood."

"And as for Shaun Sobrante?" I pressed—not because I thought it right or appropriate to do so, but because I was young and lost in complexity and bloodshed, and I didn't know what else to say. "You're willing to let me publish that he is your *political expedient?*"

Hill took a moment to consider that. I could tell by the way he held himself that he was walking out of his history and back into the present. He shrugged. "Maybe Oakland will understand."

Oakland did understand. But it also didn't.

There was a second press conference, this one downtown, led by not a spokesperson but the chief of police. "We have no suspects and have made no arrests in the Sobrante murder investigation," he said. "It's our determination that the integrity of the crime scene was jeopardized by the amount of time and foot traffic that probably went by between when the crime was committed and when law enforcement arrived on the scene. Forensics are minimal and would likely be inadmissible in court. No witnesses have as of yet come forward, either. It's a tough case . . . Sobrante Prep? Look, it isn't for me to comment on the ethicality of naming a high school after a dead child, who was not allowed to enroll at that very school due to a criminal charge. It should be noted that charges are not indictments, and indictments are not convictions. I think Principal Hill's published comments on the matter speak for themselves: unfounded insinuations about police involvement in the death. *He was our expedient.* The police department deals in people, not expedients."

Oakland PD was steadfastly unwilling to do interviews with me, or any other journalist about the matter. FYI: the strictest no-snitching policy of all is the one amongst law enforcement itself. But retaliatory information leaks, they'll give you those in a heartbeat: Cash Hill's serial harassment of underachieving students and his flirtations with grade fraud quickly came to light. The *Chronicle*, the *Trib*, the *Merc*—everybody ran the story. Federal funding for the school was jeopardized.

East Oakland rallied to the black man's defense, reminding law enforcement that there was no love lost, ever. Despite the dunce caps and other creative cruelties, parents started to send their children to the besieged savior in droves—just to spite the police.

The Sobrante case went cold, and justice was of another world.

Meanwhile, Cash Hill's days were numbered. Heightened demand to attend his school only increased the cost pressures, until it was him or Sobrante itself—one or the other had to go.

I've heard tales about Cash Hill's whereabouts since—that his ghost walks the halls of Sobrante Prep; that he went back to Wall Street; that he was sent to Havana to kick up dust and overthrow the communists; that he fell in with an evangelical venture capitalist and created a for-profit online education business bearing his brother's name. If he had told me his brother's name that afternoon, I could at least go searching and find out if the school—or even the brother—was real, rumors, or lies.

But Hill had never spoken his name when he and I were down in that dark chamber, high in the hills. Around here, cases go cold as corpses, and mysteries stay mysteries.

DIVINE SINGULARITY

BY KERI MIKI-LANI SCHROEDER

Piedmont Avenue

I should have known that bitch was lying. All the "Sorry, Maggie, I'm working late" and "last-minute business trips." What utter bullshit. I followed her last night, waited outside her office in Jack London Square and watched her walk to her car. I parked closer to the train tracks, out of sight, safely hidden by bustling tourists crowding the streets doing God-knows-what in this part of town. It must be the only place in Oakland that gets visited solely on its name alone. Jack-fucking-London. The place appeals to people whose tastes never made it past their high school reading list, if you ask me. Anyway, I watched that snake as she crossed 2nd Street and climbed into her fire-red Wrangler. She was wearing her slightly out-of-fashion teal power suit. I'll admit, I once thought it was quirky and cute, but now it just screams LESBIAN. I mean, she already drives a Jeep, isn't that enough? And how was I ever attracted to a woman who wears that much product in her hair? I used to joke that she looked like Molly Ringwald OD'd on gel. As I watched her sitting in the Jeep, messing with her phone, I received a text: *Sorry Maggie, gonna be late tonight. Finishing up a contract with an old client and then for some new place called Divine Singularity, LOL, so lame <3.*

Sure, Sarah. We'll see.

I started up my car (not a Jeep, thank you very much) and followed her from a distance. It was probably the only time I was thankful for Bay Area traffic, as it's great coverage when stalking your lying-piece-of-shit partner. She drove through Lake Merritt to those ranchero-style homes near Piedmont. *Oh, so you got yourself a fancy bitch now, huh?* I could see through her rear window that Sarah was on the phone with someone. Her gestures were exaggerated, almost comical, like how she gets all flustered when we're arguing. Or how she gets sometimes when we're fucking. I could feel my ears burning as the blood pulsated in my head and my belly dropped.

Sure enough, she turned into a fancy brick home in Piedmont, complete with an obnoxious yellow fence around a blossoming garden, and *no . . .* a wishing well in the yard? How tacky. I drove past the house as Sarah turned into their half-circle driveway. She was so preoccupied on the phone that she didn't pay any attention to me. A part of me wishes I had kept driving, just so I could maintain a snippet of blissful doubt. But instead, I turned around.

The typical cheating signs began a few weeks ago: she'd become more secretive, almost defensive, with her phone calls and texts, spending unexplainably longer hours in the office. But what finally made me follow her were the texts I'd read the night before last. I had never looked through Sarah's phone before. I really don't condone this type of behavior, but she'd been acting so strange lately and was in the shower when it buzzed, so I picked it up. I told myself I was only checking quickly to see if it was important, if it was an emergency that I needed to notify her about.

Three unread texts from a number not yet added as a contact, a number without a name. How convenient.

536-7856: *You cannot do this to me Sarah.* [Sent 6:58 p.m.]

536-7856: *I will convince you to change your mind.* [Sent 6:58 p.m.]

536-7856: *Meet me tomorrow evening. I will make it worth your while.* [Sent 6:59 p.m.]

Which brings me to now—sipping on too-strong rum drinks decorated with tiny umbrellas in the Kona Club after she didn't come home last night. The bar smells a bit like wet towels, but the room is dark, and I need some alone time. *That lying, sniveling piece of shit.*

I flag down the bartender. I'm making it a goal to try every tiki drink in the joint before sundown.

"This one," I point to the menu, "the . . . Macadamia Nut . . . Chi-Chi? The fuck is a *Chi-Chi?*"

The bartender is one big man-bun in an aloha shirt; a beach bum surfer who probably hasn't been to the ocean in twenty years. He nods at me while he wipes down a glass. "Sure," he smiles. "But maybe you should take it easy after this one."

"That's not what I asked you, Endless Summer."

"I love that movie, but that doesn't even make sense. Are you calling me Endless Summer? My name is Big Mike."

"Pleased to meet you. I'm Maggie. Now Chi-Chi! With extra umbrellas!"

He serves me my drink, albeit reluctantly, and I replay once again the events of last night. Seeing Sarah's face in the window and the hulking silhouette of whoever was in the room with her. What a beast. I always knew she liked them more butch, the lying dyke . . . I watched from the window of my car for a few minutes, contemplating whether or not to confront them. Whether or not to knock on the front door and spit in Sarah's stupid face when she and her new lover answered.

I could have said something clever, like in the movies when couples break up. Something like, *Ha! You can have her! Psssh . . . good luck!* Or even better, *Good riddance!* Or maybe I would joke about how she dresses terribly, or is lazy in bed, or always lies about being a gold star . . . I should have told them I hoped they would be happy together and then told Sarah to pick up all her shit from the house. I should have told her I never even loved her . . . Fuck.

But the truth is that seeing them together made me feel like something was breaking inside me. The truth is that I sat in disbelief in my car for several minutes, as I watched them through the window. The truth is that when I saw the other woman embrace Sarah, pushing her up against the wall like that, I had to turn away because I thought I was going to be sick.

Aloha Shirt hands me my Macadamia Nut Chi-Chi, a cheerful little drink to offset my sour mood.

I can't take it any longer. I pull out my phone and text her: *I saw you last night. Why did you do it?* [Sent 7:22 p.m.]

I put the phone down on the bar and close my eyes. The syrupy sweetness of the drinks is starting to give me a headache without a buzz. Okay, maybe a little buzz, but it's the warm, sugary, tipsy precursor-to-a-hangover—not worth the high. I keep thinking of all the fun Sarah and I used to have, all the good times: the late-night cuddles and movies; the uncontrollable laughing at the stupidest shit; or when she would squeeze my hand sometimes suddenly, as if to make sure I was still there and still real; or, oh God, the sex . . .

I snap out of it and look at my phone. A note appears under my sent text: *Message Read 7:24 p.m.* It is now 7:49 p.m. with no response. I rationalize this in several ways: Maybe she can't text because she is hurriedly driving home, eager to apologize in person. Maybe her phone died as she was texting back—she was always forgetting to charge it overnight. *Fuck.* She stayed out overnight.

My throat tightens as I begin to accept that: Sarah read my text and chose not to respond. She has not contacted me in nearly twenty-four hours. On purpose. I gulp down the rest of my sickeningly decadent drink.

I cannot believe she didn't come home, that she didn't call or send a message. I had to remove the battery from my own phone to prevent myself from contacting her first. I don't even remember driving home. I was just suddenly there, chainsmoking cigarettes despite having quit over a year ago, sipping the cognac we kept in the cupboard for special occasions. This was a "special occasion" all right, over four and a half years of a relationship abandoned. I didn't even cry. I just sat there dumbfounded until the night melted away into dawn and I woke up sweating in an empty bed a few hours later.

My phone starts buzzing before I can start to tear up again. One new unread text message.

Sarah: *Where are you?* [Sent 8:36 p.m.]

Where am I? That's all she has to say for herself? She wants to know *where I am?* Where are *you*, bitch?

Me: *I'm at the Kona Club getting wasted. What the fuck do you care?* [Sent 8:42 p.m.]

I sit there stewing for a moment before I realize that the sneaky bitch is asking where I am so she can sneak in the house when I'm not there. I pay my tab and leave in a rush to confront her. I walk briskly down the road toward our home. We (or soon to be just *I*) live in one of those little duplexes off of Piedmont Avenue. To be clear, not *Piedmont*—the ritzy-town-inside-a-town where that whore lives—but just the street in North Oakland. It's a deceiving area: in the daytime it can be almost bourgie, with little shops selling useless—but *organic!*—items lining the street, but nighttime is when it gets interesting. Yoga moms and young radicals teach their children about gentrification by giving them books on the subject, while making sure to shield them from the unsightly homeless living in the alleys.

As I pass Sandro's Healthy Lifestyle Boutique, the overwhelming smell of spicy herbs and essential oils wafting from within makes me turn my head. There's a sign showing hands photoshopped over a lavender om symbol attached to the side of the building: *Soon to be the new home of Divine Singularity Yoga Studios.* Well, I'll be damned. I peer inside. Colorful glass bottles of assorted tinctures and vitamin supplements line the shelves. So this is the place Sarah was working on? I make a mental note and keep walking, eager to get to the house before she does.

Our apartment is a fraction of a building that used to be a single home, with one and a half bedrooms and a "balcony" not large enough for a step stool, let alone the both of us. As an amateur interior designer, I try to make the place feel homey by using light colors and as many collapsible, compact fixtures as we can find to open up the space. Sarah's work is a bit more practical, building DIY websites and writing "personal" blogs for people who can't be bothered to do it themselves. She blogs for several businesses on Piedmont Avenue, including Sandro's, which was always a hoot because we have never followed any hip, healthy lifestyle plan. In fact, we used to joke about the regression of health fads like the Paleo diet. I mean, didn't cavemen have a life expectancy of something like thirty-five years?

Sarah snuck in "health facts" borrowed from ancient cultures, because that's what nouveau-hippies are into these days—as if somehow appropriating the cultural traditions of others will bring them longevity and happiness. Sarah once wrote a blog for a boutique chocolate company whose pitch was that "the ancient Mayans ate cocoa for centuries." I'm sure they did, but they also cut the still-beating hearts from virgin sacrifices and wore animal heads as hats. Sure, chocolate is fabulous, but that really seems beside the point. As nonwhite, nonhippie nonconformists ourselves, we found it both flatter-

ing and confusing to see advertisements selling different eth-
nicities to others—as if we have our shit figured out any more
than anyone else. However, Sarah and I were perfectly willing to sell white folks permission to use our cultural identities,
since it helped us start a little nest egg that might one day get
us a "real" home to call our own.

These rambling thoughts end abruptly as I approach our
apartment. Sarah's Jeep is not in the driveway. Walking in, I
realize no one has been here since I left a few hours earlier. My
dirty glass and empty bottle of celebration cognac sit where I
left them, and Sarah's collection of boots and shoes, always an
unsightly tripping hazard, still clutters the hallway.

I shake my head to clear the sugary alcohol clouds and
reach for my phone. *Shit.* I check my purse and coat, but it isn't
there. I suddenly feel agitated and annoyed that I came back.
Do I really want to be here waiting when she gets home, like I
have nothing better to do than sit around feeling sorry for myself? It's true, of course, but I don't want her to see it. I put my
coat back on and return to the bar to retrieve my phone and
some dignity.

Aloha Shirt Big Mike greets me as I walk back in. "Hey,
Maggie, some lady came by looking for you a few minutes ago."

"Who? What did she say?" I'm a little dumbfounded, a
little angry.

"She asked if Maggie was here, and I said you just left."

Sarah came here? Does that mean she came to explain?
Have I been overreacting? Thoughts flood my already cluttered
mind.

"Did I leave my phone here?"

Big Mike thinks for a moment. "Oh, yeah. I did find a
phone." He opens a drawer by the register. "Here you go."

"Thank you. Can I have one more Chi-Chi, please?"

"Extra umbrellas?"

"No, it's okay. I'm cutting down."

He laughs and starts mixing and shaking. I open my phone to three unread messages.

Sarah: *I thought you were at Kona Club?* [Sent 10:16 p.m.]

Sarah: *Where are you now?* [Sent 10:32 p.m.]

Sarah: *You fucking cunt. I'm coming to get you.* [Sent 10:47 p.m.]

"The fuck?" I say aloud. Even at our worst, Sarah has *never* spoken to me like that. It would have been a deal breaker for either of us.

"Everything okay?" Big Mike asks, sliding over a bulbous glass of fluorescent liquid.

"I don't know." My phone's screen saver pops up, a picture of Sarah and me arm in arm at Stinson Beach, smiling.

"She's cute," he says.

"I know," I sigh. "So is that all she said when she came in? Did she seem . . . okay?"

"Who? Her?"

We share a puzzled look. "This isn't who was asking for me? Are you sure?" I hold the phone closer and point at the picture of us: the wind had been blowing Sarah's red ringlets into my face and we were both laughing as I tried to spit out the strands.

"Nope." He wipes down a glass. "I'd remember her. This one was . . . you know." He shrugs.

"*You know*, what?"

"She was . . ." He stands straight and puffs out his arms and chest. "A big ol' gal."

I stare at him blankly. The woman from last night. The one I'd seen with Sarah. *She* had come to see me? Where was Sarah?

I quickly google *Oakland news*. A few shootings here and

there, a vegan bake sale to end gentrification, a youth center displaced by a tech start-up. I scroll on, numbly. Then I see it: *Unidentified woman found dead in Piedmont Friday morning. Foul play suspected.*

My mouth suddenly tastes like bile and a coldness trickles down my spine.

The phone buzzes in my hands. I drop it on the counter and clasp my hands to my mouth, trying to find my bearings. Another text. My hands shake as I lift the phone and unlock the screen.

Sarah: *There's no use in running.* [Sent 10:59 p.m.]

My head is hot and my mouth is dry. I feel dizzy.

Sarah: *I'll kill you like I did your cunt girlfriend.* [Sent 11:01 p.m.]

"Are you all right?" Big Mike looms over me, his husky figure silhouetted in the overhead lights. Flashes of the previous night come rushing back. Sarah. Was she . . . Were they . . . arguing in the shadows? When she pushed Sarah against the wall, was she—holy shit, Maggie, are you so fucked up you mistook violence for sex?

I have to get the fuck out of here.

A cool wind rushes through me as I hurry out the door. The streets are empty. I start walking, trying to gather my thoughts. Do I call the cops? What do I say? Fuck, I wish I hadn't been drinking. The air is cold on my face, but not refreshing. I open my phone to dial 911 and see there's a new text.

Sarah: *You look good from behind.* [Sent 11:13 p.m.]

I whip around, but there's no one in sight anywhere. I walk faster and frantically start dialing. My phone beeps as it drops the call. I try again, and again. *Shit!* Returning to the bar would be backtracking too far—and if this psychopath really is following me, I might run right into her. I realize I have to run.

The gates of the Mountain View Cemetery are at the top of the road. I need to hide. I need to hide and call for help.

I reach the entrance and glance back quickly. There's almost no light, but I can make out a figure trailing me down the road. I squeeze through the tall iron gates and dash up the paved road, past mausoleums and oversized ornate tombstones.

This place is like a park during the day, with families picnicking on the immaculately trimmed lawns, and guided tours pointing out the more famous interred. Now it's dark and suffocating. I duck behind the brick archway of a memorial and cup the phone to cover any light from the screen. The battery icon is flashing red. I dial 911 and raise the phone to my ear, trembling.

A low voice answers, "Hello?"

I whisper, high-pitched hiccups escaping between sobs, "I need help. There's someone after me and I think she killed my girlfriend. I'm in the cemetery—"

"Hi, Maggie," the voice replies.

I jerk the phone away as if it were alive.

Sarah's picture is on the screen. 911 is on hold. I frantically press the button to hang up. The battery icon flashes one more time, then the screen goes black. I can't hold back the choking sobs. Suddenly a firm hand grips my shoulder.

Screaming, I leap up and start sprinting blindly, cold tears streaming down my face. I weave between monstrous weeping angels and huge marble headstones gleaming in the moonlight; I run until my lungs burn and I cannot feel my legs. I scramble uphill through narrow stone pathways, past a pyramid adorned with an eagle and an obelisk jutting from the ground. I look over my shoulder: no one is behind me. I reach a crumbling mausoleum with a broken wooden door. Inside, it smells musty and damp. Things are crawling on the ground but I try to stifle the panic. As my eyes adjust I see a stone tomb in the center of the cramped room. I crouch behind it, covering my mouth to steady my breathing, letting my nose run and tears roll silently down my cheeks.

What the fuck is happening? *Sarah, I'm so sorry.* Time slows down. I can't complete any thoughts other than, *I'm sorry, I'm sorry* . . . I'm consumed with fear, guilt, and regret. Will this be the last thing I feel? Is this what happened to Sarah?

Footsteps crunch in the gravel outside. Louder now, heavier. The sliver of light from under the mausoleum's door is broken by a shadow. I hold my breath, and the shadow retreats. I allow myself a glimmer of relief.

Then the brittle door is kicked open, coming off its hinges. I whimper pathetically as the figure ducks inside.

"You bitches just don't know how to let things be."

"What the fuck do you want?! Who the fuck are you?" I kick out my legs, cowering farther into the corner.

"All she had to do was back off," the voice continues, coming closer. "The same with you."

Through the shadows, I can make out her face. "Sandro?" I stammer.

I've seen her dozens of times as I walked past her shop. The bulging, oversupplemented muscles and henna tattoos are unmistakable. Her nose ring glitters and I see dark scratches across her face. *Sarah* . . .

"That fickle bitch," Sandro spits. "Helping that fucking yoga studio take over my space, driving me out with all that *Divine Singularity* bullshit." She says the name in a mocking sing-song voice.

"Wh-what?" I am genuinely shocked. "It's her *job*, Sandro!"

"She was a motherfucking double agent!" Sandro screams. through clenched teeth: "I work. So. Hard. I paid Sarah good money to write the health blog. I order the supplements from China myself. I make my interns keep perfect inventory. Then I find out she's helping some yoga shithead take over my place? Do you have any fucking idea how impossible it is to find decent commercial space in this city?"

"You're crazy! You don't *do* anything! You throw money at other people to do your work for you! You're a fucking lunatic!"

"You people are all the same. You want handouts but have no loyalty, no vision. I gave Sarah an *opportunity*—and she betrayed me." Sandro's eyes are wide with rage. She lunges forward.

I try to fend her off but she slams my head into the stone wall, over and over. I think of what I saw last night, through the window, my last glimpse of Sarah.

Over and over, I think of Sarah.

WHITE HORSE

by Katie Gilmartin

Bushrod Park

Two women walking down the street together doesn't make sense to anyone when one of them is Negro and the other white. Unless the Negro woman is carrying a bag of groceries or pushing a carriage with a towheaded baby inside. But even then, not after dark. And certainly not if both are dressed to the nines, she in her smart hat and neatly pressed gloves. We always felt eyes on us. The way a hook trolling through water looking for a fish catches on some weed or stump and holds fast, those eyes snagged on our dark and light bodies as we passed. Trying to figure out: what was the relationship between these women that led to the two of them walking down a street together after dark? They don't like the answer they come up with. Or they like it too much. Roll it around in their minds, caress it with their tongues, till they resolve that the right thing for them to do, the only thing for them to do, is to join us.

So we always walked alert, careful. Quickly and with determination, making it clear we had a place to be and it wasn't here on this sidewalk explaining how we came to be walking together. We walked side by side, but not too close, and we never held hands. One day, a year or so ago, we'd gone for a walk up in the hills, where redwoods tower so high they were once used for navigation by boats in the bay. It was a sweet afternoon of dappled sunlight, and when she was sure there was no one to see us but those trees, Mabeline slipped her hand in mine. As it settled in, palm against palm, fingers nested, there was no comfort in it; no home there, the way our bodies felt when we slid against each other, the curves familiar and essential. Our hands were strangers to each other. After seven years of loving, I didn't know her hand inside mine.

On the sidewalk we kept walking when men offered to take us home, bristled when we politely declined. Our place was in the Bushrod neighborhood. The men that followed us were eager to make jokes about *bush* and *rod*. There were three or four variations, you can figure them out yourself. We kept walking, as they told us what they believed we did together and then prescribed a remedy for the ailment they presumed we had. We kept walking, hoping to get where we were going before they'd grab an arm—Mabeline's usually, if he was a white man; mine, often, if he was a Negro, trying to tug us toward a shadowed doorway or dark alley.

That particular night we were headed to the White Horse, so our stroll was brief. Sam greeted us at the door with a curt nod, a nod that warned us not to allow our alert caution to relax down around our shoulders as it usually did when we entered the welcoming warmth of the dark bar. The subdued murmur as we moved inside confirmed it. We'd heard there'd been two unfamiliar visitors the past weekend, with collars buttoned a little too tight for our comfort.

The crowd was thinner than usual, though not by much. Storm clouds led some to flee, but the regulars planted ourselves firmly for the night. We had too few places to let go of any one of them easily. Mabeline and I made our way to the bar, nodding at familiar faces, sizing up the ones that weren't. The two men in tight collars weren't among them. Henry, usually a warm bath of friendliness, served our drinks with a thin-lipped smile and we settled at a table with two couples we knew. Mabeline and I sat facing the rear of the bar, where we could watch the passage that led to bathrooms and the back door. Barbara and Lou had eyes on the entrance. Lester and Evan viewed the bar. We were each other's eyes.

The White Horse had never been raided, at least not in anybody's memory. The place either had some kind of charmed existence or the other shoe was due to drop. We'd all been watching that Senator McCarthy and his Pervert Inquiry unfold across the headlines, reading about the postmaster general's campaign to eliminate filth from the family mailbox. We'd all felt the same ice water flowing through our veins. We wondered when, and how, the crackdown would come for us. Maybe this was it: two men in tight collars.

Mabeline didn't believe in charmed existences, nor did she much worry about other shoes. She was a practical woman. "I'll bet the Johnsons haven't been giving the cops their usual fat envelope."

"You think that's all this is about?" Barb asked.

"That's always what anything is about."

"Well, my drink is still overpriced and watered down," Lester reported, "so the money's flowing in like usual."

"Maybe the police just need to show off."

"No elections on the horizon," Lou countered.

"Maybe the Johnsons hired two friends to wear their best suits and scare us away."

"Could have been some shoe salesmen from out of town," Evan suggested.

"Could have been Santy Claus's travel agent, but I don't think so." Mabeline looked at me sharply. "You're not forgetting our agreement?"

I shook my head. "I'm not forgetting our agreement." *Keep*

your head. Whatever happens, keep your head. I shook my head, and meant it.

Mabeline had known me to be released from jail the morning after a raid and get tossed right back in, fighting with the desk clerk over whether or not she was still inside. She'd known me to be released early and spend the rest of the night under a lamppost not thirty yards from the police station, watching for her to emerge, till I was picked up for vagrancy and thrown back in when she herself was already safely home. That wasn't the worst of it, either. Some man would disrespect her, and instead of ignoring it I'd slug him. Soon enough we'd both be limping home, bruised and battered. *Making a bad situation worse,* that's what she called it. I'm an expert at that. I wanted to be her knight in shining armor. She knew I wanted to ride that horse for her. She'd made me swear that after any raid, once I got released I'd go home, sit down at the kitchen table, and wait for her there.

"Trouble's cousin just arrived," she announced. Otis was a young queen who hadn't yet learned to handle his liquor—or his hands. Last Saturday he'd had his knuckles rapped twice by the bartender, who kept a yardstick behind the bar for that very purpose. Bartenders at the White Horse smacked anybody with the first glimmer of a leer in their eye, before they got so far as putting a hand on a knee, a head on a shoulder, an arm around a waist. All the bars that catered to our kind did much the same thing, though others managed it without the humiliation of a ruler. Since a court ruling had made it legal for our kind to congregate, the cops had to find a new justification for raids. Often as not they created that justification. Luring in youthful ardor was a favored way to do so. Otis was chatting eagerly with a friend, putting quarters in the jukebox, waving his hands around—a bird of paradise in a funeral arrangement. Lester went to speak with him, quietly. The bird's finery drooped, but only slightly. The ones who are a little crazy to begin with get crazier under pressure. I know something about that. I'd grown up in a small town, fighting my way out of most situations. Fighting my way into the others. Not keeping my head.

Mabeline and I had met in the dark, labyrinthine passageways of a ship we were building at Mare Island Naval Base during the war, when the world discovered that women, even Negro women, could do all kinds of work we'd been unable to do five minutes before. Suddenly, riveting was just like sewing, and soldering was just like icing a cake, tasks we were all assumed to be adept at. And suddenly we had decent-paying jobs. We'd ride the same streetcar to and from work, and I noticed her—lips slicked a dark red, eyes with lashes long enough to catch mist when the fog settled deep, and a compact, curvy figure that made me wonder how flesh could be so sculpted and so firm. I also wondered whether she felt my eyes on her, and whether they felt good to her, or bad. She gave no sign that I could read.

At first glance you might think Mabeline was just a cream puff, but you'd be wrong and sure to discover your mistake. I was topside at the end of my shift when I noticed a glove missing, so I headed back down into the maze of steel passageways. Retracing my steps, I heard a muffled cry. Sound bounced and echoed in that hard place, distorted and disorienting, so it took me awhile to find them, and along the way I heard his taunting voice say wetly to her, "The blacker the berry, the sweeter the fruit."

When I reached it the room was gone, its definition lost in darkness—I saw only the white-hot glow of her blowtorch and the crotch it was dangerously close to. Her words were a low, controlled murmur: "The next time you decide to help yourself to a measure of my body, or to show me the great glory God gave you, I'll be going to see your wife." She bit the word off like an epithet. "I'll be telling her about that mole just to the left of your thing. And just in case, when she asks you how a darky girl like me might come to know about it, just in case you plan to tell her I've been throwing myself at you, I'll also let her know that I'm the one who sent you home with the crotch of your work pants singed to ember."

As the tip of that torch crept closer to the center seam of those dungarees, I heard a yelp and a whimper, neither coming from Mabeline. I couldn't tear my eyes away as the torch hovered there, as the fabric darkened and the slightest whisper of a plume of smoke formed. The whimper turned to a yowl. The torch crept to the right, then to the left, creating a blackened patch of fabric that I knew could burst into flame any moment. Then the torch leapt to the side, where it found a headlamp on the ground next to a work pail with its contents spilled across the floor.

She bumped into me at the doorway and hissed, "You in line? I may have to start charging." Then she checked her movement, seeing my eyes—seeing them focus on the darkness where the man she'd left behind stood. "Leave it," she spat. I gave her room, then followed her out. Later, I hung nearby to make sure she got on the streetcar okay. Of course she got on the streetcar okay. I followed because I wanted to be the one ensuring she got on the streetcar okay.

A week later she asked if I wanted to join her for a drink after work. She didn't need to drop any hairpins and wait to see if I picked them up. During the war it was easier to blend in, with so many women wearing pants to work, most keeping their hair shorter for safety, and saving scarce lipstick for weekends. But I was still obvious to anyone who knew the signs. We didn't discuss that encounter in the hull. We talked about work, about the war. We talked about the difficulty of getting meat and sugar, eyes dancing with smiles around the latter. I walked her home, and she allowed me to kiss her in the hollow of her doorway. When we surfaced she gripped my gaze in the dim light. "I don't need any knight in shining armor to save me. Second, I gave him reason not to retaliate—you had none. Third, you'd have put both of us at risk: think what kind of rumors he could have spread." Then she turned and disappeared in her door.

On my back porch I stared up at the night sky, turning over her words, savoring the kiss, pondering the proximity between them. A spiderweb stretched from the eaves to the corner post, its impossibly fine lines etched against the sky's blue-black glow. As my eyes adjusted to the darkness I saw a lower half emerge, catching the faintest light from a neighbor's window, shimmering against silhouetted trees. Suddenly the fat body of the largest spider I'd ever seen dropped precipitously from the roofline and dangled there, legs arranging and rearranging in some inscrutable purpose. It swayed slightly with the air currents but remained casual, luxurious, arranging and rearranging, on its back no less, as though it were bathing rather than suspended a hundred times its body length above the ground from a thread so fine I couldn't see it. I marveled at the confidence it had in that thread, to trust space that way, to dangle there. I wondered if anything would ever sustain me so sturdily, would endow me with that kind of trust in life, so that I might dangle, calmly arranging and rearranging. Mabeline became that thread for me.

'Course, we lost our jobs as soon as the men returned from war. I was back at the cannery, Mabeline back in a kitchen. But come evening, she was on the back porch with me.

"You ever been with a Negro girl before?"

"No. You ever been with a white girl before?"

"No. But it's not the same thing."

"Isn't it?"

"White people believe all kinds of crazy things about Negro girls."

"Do Negroes believe all kinds of crazy things about white girls?"

"Well, I know you ain't Miss Ann."

"I ain't Miss Anybody." I paused. "Who's Miss Ann?"

Mabeline hesitated, then said, "She was a friend of my aunt's. But they had a falling out."

"What was it about?"

"About Miss Ann not understanding."

"Not understanding what?"

"Anything."

"Well, I want to understand everything about you."

"That could take awhile," she said, in a voice so slow that if she'd been on a bicycle she'd have tipped over.

When the war ended we went to the California Hotel to celebrate—Mabeline loves music. We generally encountered fewer hassles at tony places. Not because the people were any nicer, but because the wives would pull their husbands back, saying, *That's your best suit.* Musicians filled the air with jazz so raucous it made colors stream and waft up the aisles. As we floated out on those currents, some man came up close behind Mabeline and started sniffing loudly. She ignored him, but I was ready to haul off and hit him right there in the lobby. Mabeline grabbed my arm, saying grimly under her breath, "Forget it."

She pulled me outside to hail a cab. I kept my gaze on that man—there he was, his eyes still on Mabeline. I watched him watching her, my gaze moving between them. A cab passed by. Then another. It stopped up ahead, for other passengers. Another cab approached and I rushed forward, throwing my arm up and piling Mabeline inside. I wanted her away from that man. When I turned to her, her eyes were angry. The cabbie never stopped watching us in the rearview, so we waited till we got home to speak. Mabeline said there were too many things to talk about.

It took me awhile to understand: she wasn't mad about me getting that cab—didn't I see that she couldn't get one herself? Yes, it was good that I could do that for her, but didn't I understand that I should be mad too, mad that *she* couldn't get us one? I explained that I wanted to be the one to get cabs for her, I wanted to lay down my cloak for her, I wanted to do all those things, but she insisted that I still didn't understand. "Those things only become a welcome gift," she said, "when I could have done them myself."

So then I saw how much of what I had to give could only be an insult, an offense, to Mabeline. Cannery pay is always more than kitchen pay. Those steaks I bought for her—they were a gift she should have been able to buy herself.

Around nine thirty a shadow crossed Evan's face. I followed his eyes: two men in tight collars had just been served at the bar. Glances ricocheted around the room. The bartender stood sentry, his gaze piercing the smoke the way a lighthouse beam cuts the fog. Conversations were suspended in the air for a moment, hardly something you'd notice in another bar. In the lull Mabeline murmured, "We've got company." Then voices resumed and bodies began to move. Two women rose from the bar, leaving their drinks behind, ambling to the front door mighty fast. Several men slipped quietly out the back. I glanced at Mabeline; her eyes were narrow slits.

"They look too young for cops," Lester said.

"They recruit 'em young, hung, and handsome for just this purpose."

"The applicant pool must have been small," Mabeline noted drily.

"Quite a flamboyant tie on the one. Is that puce?"

"The better to eat you with, my dear."

"It's actually quite tasteful. *Can't* be department issue."

The two men got their drinks and came toward our table. Our breaths bottomed out as their shiny shoes squeaked past. They unbuttoned their jackets and settled in at the table behind us. Hands wrapped around their glasses, they leaned back in the universal bar code of invitation. Mabeline and I had front-row seats when Otis weaved his way from the corner, waved merrily as he circled a tableful of friends, and slid sloppily into a seat at the strangers' table. "Haven't seen you here before!" he warbled gaily.

The two men smiled, eyes and all. Mabeline swore under her breath.

"You from around here?" Otis queried.

Both nodded, and said they were from San Francisco.

"Oooh, the big bad city!" Otis crooned.

"I'm Fred," one guy said, extending his hand. "And this is Buck." I considered the old saw about cops always having single-syllable names as Otis complimented Fred on his tie. Otis gestured to it, leaning exuberantly across the table, his hand landing inches from the glass and the hands of Officer Puce. After a moment Otis slid one seat closer, his hand diddling around on the table near Officer Puce's beer.

"Jesus," Mabeline whispered, snapping open her purse and extracting her reading glasses. She slid them on, then quickly smeared away lipstick with the back of her hand, leaving a red streak across her cheek, a macabre mockery of a smile. Then everything happened at once. Otis gave Officer Puce's hand a fond rub, the cop reached in his back pocket for handcuffs,

Mabeline hitched up the front of her dress, pulling it high over her cleavage as bright lights came blasting in the front door. Just before they blinded us Mabeline held my eyes with hers to steady me.

The wagons pulled up to the front of the building, but not to the back. The newly initiated thought this was lucky, and a few made a run for it. Those of us who'd been around awhile knew things were headed south. Wagons at both doors meant they'd load us up, haul us off, and book us. No wagon out back meant other things could happen in that dark alley. Things that made getting hauled off to jail seem like your best option.

The barrage of officers herded us against a wall, shined lights in our eyes, called us *faggot, bulldagger,* and *queer,* called some of us *nigger* and *coon.* They especially liked mixing words from the first category together with words from the second, in various combinations. A cop with a bent nose and a Southern drawl came down the line with a smile, checking faces. He lingered on Mabeline. I could smell his sweat as he hovered, breathing on her. My body was taut as the mooring line of a warship. I remembered Mabeline's eyes and held my breath. I waited for him to pass. As he turned, his eyes already on the next woman down the line, he reached out his hand and cupped Mabeline's breast in a smooth, curving motion. Gave it a squeeze just as he let go. I forgot Mabeline's eyes and swung for his jaw. He reared back. Blue bodies rushed over, blue arms grabbed me and pulled me toward the back door. He followed, dragging Mabeline.

I tried to keep quiet, tried not to let my body make a sound as it hit the wall, the trash cans, the ground, the ground again. I didn't want Mabeline to have to hear all that while the bent-nosed cop pushed her against the wall and felt her up. I kept it quiet until he pushed her down on her knees and said, in his Southern drawl: "The blacker the berry, the sweeter the fruit."

When I heard him say those words, and knew Mabeline was there, and knew it was my fault, I lost it and I roared. Two more blue bodies came and I wanted him to come over too—I roared and raged and clawed and tried to make the cop with the bent nose come over. But he didn't.

My face was pitted with gravel, my legs somewhere far away. All of me ached, no part any more than the others. I assessed the sounds. Almost dawn. No one around. Mabeline gone.

Eventually I gathered enough focus to move. My neck, my arms, then my legs. I headed slowly toward the police station, but halfway I changed course, limping home, toward the kitchen table. When I arrived, the apartment was silent. I gathered the percolator, the coffee, the water, placed it all on the stove, and settled myself at the table. I waited.

At some point I had to check the gash near my eye that wouldn't stop weeping. In the bathroom only one toothbrush was in the little glass. I opened the cabinet. Half of it, empty.

What I never told Mabeline: those were the words that strode, uninvited, into my head the first time I laid eyes on her, the first time I saw her beauty there on the streetcar. I didn't want those words. I didn't want what those words made of her, what those words made of me, and what they made me make of her. Those words were tracks under a train I didn't want to ride, but the ticket stub was already in my pocket.

So I tried to protect her from those words, out in the snarl of the streets, the maze of the ship, the cage of a raid, the madness of my mind. I wanted to ride that horse. For Mabeline.

Opened in or before 1933, Oakland's White Horse Inn is the oldest continuously operating Queer bar in the United States.

PART II
What They Call a Clusterfuck

A TOWN MADE OF HUSTLE

BY DOROTHY LAZARD

Downtown

Poppy Martens trotted out of Selden's Gym close to midnight, his wallet heavy with the cash he'd just won on a prizefight all his friends had advised him to lay off. But Poppy was partial to southpaws. Their stubborn survival in a right-handed world always surprised people. No doubt the favorite in tonight's bout was surprised when a left hook sent him sailing backward, nearly out of the ring. Poppy smiled, remembering the fellas around him falling silent, their cigarettes hanging loose from dry lips. All Poppy could do was laugh at the sight, slapping the shoulders of the guy seated in front of him.

Now he strode up 7th Street, toward downtown, snapping out of his reverie as he passed the French laundry, the shuttered storefronts, and the darkened factories. Just a couple of years earlier these foundries and fabricators would have been buzzing with activity, lights on twenty-four hours a day. There'd be people all over the streets. Guys coming home dead tired from the shipyards, clothes sooty with metal dust and smoke. Apartments functioned like hotel lobbies back then, people occupying them in shifts, sleeping in closets, beds, even tubs. Oakland teemed like an engine. Everybody was working, making something or other for the war. *All that is done now,* Poppy thought as he lifted his jacket collar against the cold.

He smiled again, thinking of all those saps who'd come rushing out here for jobs they thought would never end, to support a war they thought would change their sorry lot in life once and for all. But end they did. And as soon as they did, what happened? What always happens: colored folks were the first to be let go. And where are they now? Back bowing and scraping for a living. Pumping gas, sweeping floors, and slinging hash to the vets who were handed their good-paying jobs. Back to the end of the line, just like before.

The lucky ones got jobs on the Pullman cars, in offices, or at the auto plants in East Oakland. Too smart now to go back home to the fields. And who could blame them? Where could they go, what could they do but stay here and make a way?

These days Poppy made a meager living watching all this change happen, writing down what he saw and what it meant to the Negro. His paper didn't pay him much, but he didn't need much. He was alone now. Wife and kids back east and—he hoped—still safe. Away from the trouble he seemed to always deliver to them, like fresh milk. He scraped together a living at an outfit that could barely eke out a weekly edition, but he liked the job. Cobbled things together with temporary gigs of all sorts. It gave him freedom to roam during the day, talk to people, find out how the city worked and the endless number of ways it didn't. He liked to test his ability to get into their heads and hearts and, sometimes, a little closer. The wad of money he'd just won could certainly help with that.

He headed up to police headquarters in City Hall to sit with the drowsy night desk officer and listen to the police radio.

"Poppy Martens!" the officer called out, his hand held high in greeting as Poppy entered the booking area.

Poppy nodded a greeting, but was all focus. He sat wide-legged in a chair across from the desk and flipped open his notepad, ready to retrieve any leads coming over the speaker. "Anything up tonight?" he asked.

"Nothing yet, but soon enough. It's Saturday night. Still early."

Right then a pair of patrol cops dragged in three men who looked too young to be as drunk as they were. When a cop shoved one kid up to the counter, the guy staggered a bit then hurled his guts across the desk. The night cop jumped back just enough to avoid the bilious spray.

Poppy suppressed a laugh.

"Poppy!" Sergeant Webster stood across the room, hands braced against the doorjambs. "Come in here, I wanna talk with you."

Webster, a burly white man with a perpetually red face, wrestled the jacket off his broad back and draped it over his swivel chair. Poppy approached the man's desk tentatively. The detective expected him to tell a story; that was their deal. Webster fed Poppy leads for his news stories, and in exchange Poppy dropped the names of a few of West Oakland's less savory characters. Poppy felt no guilt about this arrangement. Oakland was a town made of hustle and that's how it would always be. The few bills Webster skimmed off his money clip and gave to Poppy were tucked away, a security blanket in uncertain times.

"Have a seat," Webster said. "What's the latest on Raincoat Jones?"

Charles "Raincoat" Jones was a mover and shaker in West Oakland, working both sides of the law. He ran a gym, nightclubs, gaming houses, and a pawnshop. Folks in the neighborhood loved him. Poppy loved him. You could always count on Raincoat to keep a widow's lights on, or to buy uniforms for some kid's baseball team, or forward you a loan to start up a little business. And because of that, Poppy never leaked a thing about him to Webster. Oakland needed people like Raincoat.

"Haven't seen him," Poppy lied, "not for a while. Heard he was out of town. Reno, someone told me."

"You mean you haven't seen him at Selden's? Not for any fights? I know there's been a lot activity down there lately."

"Raincoat doesn't go to Selden's. You know, he has his own—"

Webster raised his hand. "Yeah, I know, I know. I just wanted to check it out."

Poppy wondered why Webster was suddenly after Raincoat. Maybe the dick wasn't getting what he felt was his due from the protection money Raincoat paid the OPD.

It was nearly two in the morning when Poppy reached his apartment on Jefferson. He found his old friend David "Tak" Takiyama on the sofa. Poppy could smell the bourbon on Tak's breath before he crossed the room. The war had not been kind to Tak and his people. For all their flag-waving patriotism, pledging allegiance, and Boy Scout merit badges, they were still considered the enemy. Two years after the war Tak still couldn't catch on with any paper. No detective agency would hire him either. He and his camera, which had been so productive before the war, had both been stilled. Tak's reentry into society was heartbreaking for Poppy—all the sun had gone out of his pal. It was a daily tragedy to witness. Tak was once the best cameraman in Oakland, but none of that mattered back in '42 when he and his parents and sisters were rounded up like convicts and shipped to Topaz, Utah, to spend the war years in shame and isolation, away from everything and everybody they had known.

Tak had been the first man to offer Poppy a hand in friendship when he landed in Oakland right before Pearl Harbor. And Poppy didn't forget it. He welcomed Tak into his little place, happy his friend had been strong enough to survive such humiliation, but the experience had killed something fine in him.

He didn't read anymore. He wasn't up for club-hopping down 7th Street. No more lusting after the white salesgirls at Owl Drugs on San Pablo. Betrayal had washed him clean of vices, all except one—hatred.

"You're in the same spot I left you in this afternoon," Poppy said as he entered the apartment.

Tak didn't reply.

"You wear a hole in that couch, you're paying for it. I'll rat you out to the landlord."

Tak shifted his body, but said nothing.

Poppy took off his coat and threw it into the bedroom where it landed heavy on the chair. He smiled, remembering the money from the fight. He turned and stepped back toward the couch.

"Man, you shoulda come with me tonight! That light-heavy Selden was bragging about was all bluster. Turns out he had a glass jaw! Went down in the sixth round, hard as a redwood. *Bam!* Bloody nose, big swollen jaw, one eye closed shut!"

Poppy grew excited as he recalled the details, bobbing and weaving to bring the story to life. The fights used to be one of Tak's favorite pastimes, prewar. He had a taken an enviable collection of fight photos to prove his devotion to "the sweet science," which Poppy had saved for him, but Tak showed no interest in doing anything with them now.

Poppy went to the kitchenette and scrambled an egg, made some toast, and drank cold coffee that he or Tak—he couldn't remember who—had made the previous morning.

Poppy wanted to be loyal, but he couldn't bear too much more of Tak's inertia. *You gotta move, man!* Poppy was always telling him. *You still got air in your lungs, use it!* Today he thought he'd try a new approach.

"Hey, Tak, let me use your camera." He said it casually, as if he routinely asked for his pal's most precious possession.

Tak turned, propped himself up on his elbows. "Have you gone insane?"

Poppy shook his head. "Nah."

"If you're asking to use *my* camera, you have. Are you drunk?"

"No," Poppy said, amused at this accusation coming from a drunk man.

"No is right! You touch my camera, I'll break your wrists."

Poppy, a whole head taller than Tak, waved his hands in mock-fright. "Oh no, not my wrists!"

"Yeah. Your wrists. See how many stories you write then. See how many, mister!"

Poppy wanted to laugh but decided not to be cruel. "I'm serious. I need your camera, man. I won't damage it. I swear."

"You don't know nothing about cameras," Tak said.

"What I need to know you can teach me."

"I could, but not using *my* camera. No way, no how."

Poppy finished his food and placed the plate in the sink. He stretched his long body, raising his hands high above his head, and yawned loudly. "All right, my friend, I'll use somebody else's camera. No problem."

Poppy pulled his shirttails out of his pants and headed toward the bedroom. He scratched his head and his balls, said good night, then went into his room, closing the door behind him. He was pulling a shirt over his head when he heard Tak through the door.

"Take pictures of what exactly?"

From there it was easy. Poppy opened the door. "I got a tip from a guy who works the elevator at the Athens Athletic Club."

"Yeah? About what?"

"So, this guy says that there's some shady characters coming into the club through the back service entrance, who've been wheelin' and dealin' with the guys running the place."

"Dealing what exactly?"

"He doesn't know, but it seemed to be something important."

Tak waved his arm and headed back to the couch. "That could be anything."

"True enough. But most people don't go to the Athens Club with muscle. In this case, some thick-necked Irish goon. With something heavy in his pocket." Poppy raised his eyebrows for emphasis and detected a flash of interest on Tak's face.

"So, who's this guy you know?"

"Just some guy." Poppy headed toward the bed, suddenly fatigued from a long day that had already ended. The lure had been set in the water. Tak would be up and dressed early. "See you tomorrow."

The lobby of the Athens Athletic Club may have been serene, but the back rooms buzzed with activity. Negro waiters and busboys bustling through swinging doors, dishwashers orchestrating the flow of dirty dishes into the huge sinks, maids wheeling overloaded linen carts. Negroes ran the back end of this club, although they could never lounge in its plush lobby chairs. Every folded linen napkin bore a Negro's fingerprints.

Poppy and Tak entered through the service entrance, past a gang of smoking waiters blocking the door.

"Say, where's Willie?" Poppy asked a maid.

He was directed deeper into the bowels of the grand building. Poppy and Tak waited for the elevator to touch down in the basement, and Willie stepped out.

They exchanged greetings and Willie sized up Tak. "What's with the camera? You can't bring that in here."

"Sure he can," Poppy said, gently moving Willie back into the elevator and pressing a button at random. "Haven't you ever heard of freedom of the press?"

The elevator started to move.

"Man! What you do?" Willie blocked the panel of buttons with his body.

A call rang in from the sixth floor, so Willie hurried the two men out at the lobby floor, then ascended up to six. They paced anxiously, waiting for Willie to return. Marveling at the detailed painting in the coffered ceiling, Poppy wandered down a hallway.

"Get back here, man!" Tak seethed through his teeth. "C'mon, let's take the stairs."

Poppy was distracted by all the grand architecture, the enveloping chairs and couches, the insouciant privilege that made places like this club so foreign to people like him. No one was on the hustle here. No one was doubled, tripled, quadrupled up in their living quarters. This place was all summertime, where the living is easy.

When Poppy turned to rejoin Tak, he found his friend nose-to-nose with a much larger white man. Poppy paused, peeking into the lobby, assessing the situation. Certainly there'd be guards. They wouldn't look like guards; they'd be in suits, tight across their chests. Poppy knew Tak couldn't take this guy. He shook off the apprehension and hustled back to his friend. Tak had just enough hate in him not to back down from a fight, even one he couldn't win.

"Hey, hey, what is this?" Poppy said as he approached, his left hand already balled into a fist. The man had clutched the shoulder of Tak's coat and was shoving him backward, toward the corner of the vestibule. By the time Poppy reached them, the man had landed two sharp jabs in Tak's gut. Tak clubbed the man's ears with his fists. Poppy grabbed the man's starched shirt collar and pulled him off Tak.

"You back the hell off!" Poppy shook the stranger like a chastised dog, then pushed him away.

The white man stumbled, gasping, and twisted around. He righted himself quickly, ready to swing, but pulled the punch when he saw Poppy had about three inches on him. Tak lunged, but Poppy held him back with his other hand.

The attacker regained his balance. "Don't you touch me," he snorted, straightening his jacket and tie. "Who the hell do you think you're talking to, you black bastard!" The man pulled his shirtsleeves down, ran fingers through his blond hair. "Neither of you should be here. And what do you think you're doing with a camera in here? If you don't leave at once, I'm calling the chief of police."

That's right, white man, Poppy thought, *take it to the extreme. Just a patrolman won't do.*

"C'mon, let's go," Poppy said. But when Tak just stood there, primed to lunge again, Poppy guided him away from the white man and toward the elevator. The stranger was on their heels.

The elevator chimed just as Poppy and Tak reached it. Willie stepped out, putting on a deadpan expression when he spotted them. He stood erect.

"Willie, did you let these men in here?"

"No sir. I just came on shift, sir."

Poppy sneered at Willie as he and Tak boarded the elevator.

"Well, get them out of here! Right now!"

Willie nodded. "Yes sir. Right away, sir." He looked at his riders with scorn.

As the elevator doors closed, Poppy regarded the man he had tussled with. A finely dressed business type with pomaded hair he smoothed down with a hand. Indignant, the man met Poppy's gaze. Something clicked for Poppy. He noticed the sickle-shaped scar that ran from the man's lower lip to his chin. Incongruous on such a refined, aquiline face. Beads of sweat sprouted on Poppy's upper lip. It came to him like thunder. He exited the elevator quickly on the ground floor, his heart pounding.

"Who is that guy?" Poppy asked Willie once they were outside.

"You gotta be kiddin'," Willie said. "He's an assistant DA. In the paper *all* the time."

"What's his name?"

"Daniel Coopersmith. A real comer, they say."

Poppy frowned. "Boy, you wouldn't know a comer if one fell on you."

Daniel Coopersmith had certainly cleaned up his act. When Poppy last saw him, years earlier, the guy was leaving a Buffalo warehouse, wiping off a bloody hunting knife with his pocket square. Coopersmith had been the silent, elegant lieutenant to the area's top bootlegger. Poppy's employer of the past few years had gone into the warehouse that night but had not emerged. Young and desperate, Poppy had stood obediently in the shadows, waiting to bring the car around to his boss once a signal was given. But there was no signal. After a few minutes Poppy headed back to where the cars were parked in the rail yard. He stood between his boss's car and one belonging to the guy his boss had come to meet. The whole thing should have taken no more than ten minutes. He had checked his watch. Something was bad wrong. He'd started to breath deeply, then he began to pant, his heart galloping in his chest. Running liquor across the border had become downright dangerous. It had taken only a few seconds to make up his mind. He climbed into the other car and found the satchel of cash on the front seat that was supposed to go to his boss. He regarded the stacks of neatly packed bills, longing for it like you would an unattainable woman. As he drove away he didn't think about freedom so much as justice. A life for a life.

But somehow Coopersmith cheated what was coming to him. Poppy knew someone would be hunting for him soon enough, so he fled Buffalo with his family that night. How many years ago was it? A whole war's worth and then some. Coopersmith might be legit these days, but Poppy knew he still had to steer clear of him. He knew exactly how lethal the man could be.

The advantage of being a Negro was that, most times, no one paid any attention to you. You were just a black hand that white folks dropped change into or passed luggage to. You were not an individual, a particular set of physical features and behaviors. Poppy counted on this. He couldn't afford to have this man recognize him and threaten the comfortable life he had built in Oakland. Running counter to everything he stood for, he now willed himself to be invisible, hoping Coopersmith wouldn't recognize him and set the dogs loose. Or worse yet, come after him himself.

Poppy fell asleep that night thinking of all the public meetings and social events he had attended over the years, places where Coopersmith must have been. The danger he thought he had escaped was there all along, he just hadn't known it.

The following morning Poppy woke up in a cold sweat, having dreamed of days spent endlessly driving to feed the bottomless thirst of upstate New Yorkers. He had wanted them to stay drunk, to drown in the amber liquids he transported. *Keep drinking! Suits me fine!* It had been an adventure, one he hadn't given up easily. He could finally clothe and house his young family properly. Like a man should be able to.

An undercurrent of fear coursed through him for two days. He called in sick, something he had never done, and laid low. But three days after the encounter at the Athens Club, itching to get back out into the world, Poppy felt like himself again. After a hot shower and a few cups of fresh coffee, he headed out, striding up Jefferson, then up 9th Street to Fitzgerald's Diner on Washington. This was the place where deals were made and promises were broken. This was where the political types mingled with police, delivery men, and office girls. Gossip here was as free-flowing as the coffee.

He wanted to find out how Coopersmith had gone legit, who his political cronies were, if they were alumni from that same unsavory school of business he had left behind in New York.

He sat at the counter listening to chatter from the red leatherette booths and the nearby tables. He had built his reputation on picking up key bits of information, often without even interviewing people directly. Everybody in California talked too much. This, he hoped, would never change. In the long mirror mounted on the wall that separated the dining room from the kitchen, he could see the people behind him. He was dipping his toast into a sunny-side-up egg when he saw four suits enter. These fellas looked slicker than the usual crowd, more buttoned-down than the regulars. Folks you'd see coming out of the Athens Athletic Club. Here they were slumming.

"Say, you finished with this?" Poppy said, nodding at a copy of the *Post-Enquirer* the guy next to him had dragged through spilled coffee.

The man looked down at the wet paper. "Damn! Sure, take it."

"Thanks, man."

Poppy snapped the paper open, reading about last night's fights and the lingering union fallout from the previous year's general strike. He searched for anything coming out of the DA's office, anything about Coopersmith. One of Coopersmith's colleagues, a young cat with lots of promise, had been summarily fired. He had been charged with taking bribes from a developer who had swooped into Oakland after the war to buy up and convert properties belonging to the evacuated Japanese. Now some Japanese families were fighting to get their properties back, charging the federal government with theft and displacement, and this ADA was stalling the proceedings.

Tak would love to get his hands on this guy, Poppy thought. He took a long gulp of coffee, glancing from the paper up into the mirror again. The hairs on the back of his neck bristled— Coopersmith had joined the group of slick men. Poppy took a deep breath, thought about leaving, then exhaled slowly. He surveyed the room. He was the only Negro in the place, so he figured his departure might cause notice. He studied the group. Coopersmith was the top dog; the others leaned in when he spoke and nodded like acolytes to a great master.

Poppy wondered how many bloody knives Coopersmith had cleaned off since that night in Buffalo.

When a group of rowdy workmen came in to grab coffee and day-old donuts, Poppy scurried out behind their hubbub. He headed toward police headquarters, his mind racing as he approached the 14th Street entrance. He pulled the soggy paper from his back pocket and reread the article about the misbehaving ADA. He took out his notepad and scribbled some questions down, not sure of whom to ask them.

White folks *do not* like to be questioned. Poppy couldn't think of a time when he didn't know this fact, but questioning people was his job. Who'd be safe? He headed to the public library on 14th and Grove and asked the librarian for the newspapers from the past few weeks. He combed the *Tribune* and the *Post-Enquirer* for stories about Coopersmith or his beleaguered colleague. The district attorney had been railing hard against corruption in the city and county governments, so this case had legs. Surely Coopersmith's name would come up soon.

Over the next few weeks Poppy dropped a few lines about the case in the Negro newspapers on both sides of the bay. He got Negroes wondering how much deal-making had impacted their judicial outcomes. Stories began to swirl. Coopersmith and his leadership were called into question, which put the district attorney's office on notice.

In no time, patrol cops started to stop Poppy for the most minor infractions: jaywalking, tossing a gum wrapper on the street, loitering while he was waiting for a light to turn green. When he related these incidents to his buddies at the barber shop on 7th Street, they were not compassionate.

"You may be a reporter but you still a colored man," the head barber told him. "Don't let that byline think you above it. You ain't." All the fellas in the chairs nodded their agreement.

When a pair of cops stopped him walking out of the Roxie Theatre on 17th Street, they were unusually rough. One smacked him in the face when he asked why they were stopping him. The other called him Raincoat Jones and said he was wanted for questioning. And though Poppy tried to assure them that he wasn't Raincoat, they prevented him from reaching into his pocket to pull out his driver's license or his reporter's ID. Detective Webster pulled up as the policemen had Poppy's face pressed against the hot hood of their squad car, his arm bent high behind his back. He grimaced in pain, clenched his teeth.

"Let him go," Webster instructed coolly. The cops released him but they didn't retreat far enough for Poppy's comfort. Webster shook a cigarette out of a pack, lit it, then studied the burning tip. He was calm.

"What's up, Webster?" Poppy asked, straightening his clothes. "Why does everybody all of a sudden have a hard-on for Poppy Martens?"

"They just like you, I guess."

"These guys called me Raincoat when you all know who he is. What am I getting shaken down for?"

"You piss people off, Poppy. Always have."

"What did I do?"

"Putting your nose in someone's business, messing in things you don't understand."

"What don't I understand, Webster?" Poppy felt his anger rise.

"Lots. You can't understand how things in a city work. People have to maintain relationships in order to get things done, to keep the city functioning, growing. You get my meaning?"

Poppy shook his head. He got *someone's* meaning, but it wasn't Webster's. He knew Webster well enough to know that these were lines he had heard someone else say.

"You can't go around getting people riled up about something that impedes progress."

Poppy squinted, intrigued by the transformation in Webster's diction. "Can I go? Are you arresting me for . . . something?" he said with his arms outstretched.

"You just mind yourself. Stop being a busybody. And know that the paper that hired you can easily fire you."

"On what grounds, exactly?"

"On poking your big nose where it don't belong!" Webster dragged on his cigarette. He blew smoke in Poppy's face.

"Does any of this harassment have to do with Coopersmith?"

Webster's eyes widened. "What about Coopersmith?"

"He's the one who fired the young turk in his office. Whatever that kid was doing, Coopersmith must've known about it. Had to have sanctioned it. Right?"

Poppy knew he was treading on thin ice. One nod to the rabid cops behind him and Webster could have him pummeled into the sidewalk. But it was a chance worth taking. He realized Coopersmith was now the big boss, with his own henchmen who had their own bloody knives. No need to get his hands dirty unless Poppy came too close. Like he had at the Athens Athletic Club.

The next time Poppy went to the Athens he walked right through the front door, his reporter's ID pinned to the lapel of his coat. A man from the front desk stood up, startled, and asked him if he had a delivery to make.

Poppy looked at his own suit then at the man, but decided to ignore the question. "Is Mr. Coopersmith here?"

"The whereabouts of our clients are private. This is a private club."

"Yeah, I know it's private. I'm not here hunting a membership. Just Coopersmith."

"If I see him, who should I say is looking for him?"

Poppy had to think on this. Coopersmith must know his name if he was behind these run-ins with the police. He drummed his fingers on the desk and scanned the lobby of potted palms and tranquil white faces. Then he left the building.

He walked home with images of that night so many years ago coursing through his mind. He felt now that he had been hiding all along. If not from Coopersmith, then from all the rotten shit that he had to endure just to have a life, to thrive in that life. Coopersmith had gone about his business, had re-invented himself, safely, successfully. Poppy wondered why he couldn't. For the first time in a long while he felt himself unlucky.

Poppy came home to a darkened apartment. He flipped on the light switch, tossed his keys in an ashtray, and turned to find Tak sitting on the couch. His arms were raised above his face, shielding his eyes. Poppy walked closer and saw that Tak had a split lip and a black eye.

"Man, who did this to you?"

"I fell down the back stairs. I told you those stairs were go-ing to kill me one day. Well, today they almost did."

Poppy studied Tak's face. His nose wasn't broken, but his lip would take some time to heal. "You are the worst liar in the known world. Who did this?"

"A couple of guys. I don't know them."

"Where'd it happen? Here?"

Tak closed his eyes and shook his head. "No, man. I was on 18th Street, coming from the bus terminal."

As Tak iced his eye, Poppy looked around the small apart-ment that so many people had found safe harbor in during his time there. He didn't want to run. He hailed from a family of runners, fleeing captors, family, and responsibility. Oakland felt like home—warm and nurturing, the way a home should feel. This raggedy apartment was the first stable house he'd had since leaving his family. As he studied his friend's battered face and eased him out of his bloodied shirt, Poppy Martens decided he wasn't going to run anymore. *This shit stops now.*

With Tak watching in silence, Poppy disemboweled the apartment. From the seams of curtains, from the bottoms of cupboards, from the rotting floorboards behind the toilet, from an envelope pinned to the back of the couch, Poppy Martens pulled all the money he had in the world. Money that had come all the way from Buffalo.

"What the hell is that?" It was the most excited Tak had sounded in years.

Poppy counted the loot, considered moving it, considered giving it to Tak so he could be safe and away from whatever hell was coming, considered asking one of the hop-heads he knew in Cypress Court to dispatch Coopersmith and have this cat-and-mouse routine done once and for all.

He went to his typewriter instead and scrolled in sheet after sheet of white paper, hammering furiously on the keys. Then, on an envelope he wrote, *Open in Case of Emergency or Tragedy,* and slipped the folded pages inside. He waved it at Tak who stood nearby, watching. Poppy placed the envelope on the table. He wrote out a letter in longhand and put it and some cash in another envelope addressed to his wife. This he placed in the breast pocket of his overcoat. He forked over enough bills to Tak to keep him in high cotton for quite awhile. He smiled, feeling as though he was making tithes at St. Francis de Sales.

"Where the hell did you get all this cash?" Tak wanted to know. "What have you been up to?"

"It's from a long time ago. Before California. My rainy day money," Poppy said.

"Is it raining now?"

"Once I drop these letters off, it'll be pouring. You best be ready, my friend."

From the tiny closet Poppy took a leather satchel he'd always been too self-conscious to carry. Though he bought it second hand, it screamed prosperity. In it he put a letter, wrapped five hundred dollars in the funny papers as if it were catfish, and carefully tied the bundle of bills together with twine. He snapped the case shut and handed it to Tak.

"I want you to take this to the courthouse when you're feeling better. Ask for the district attorney." Poppy saw the doubtful look on Tak's face. "Of course, they won't let you see him, but tell whoever's guarding his door that the satchel is for him and him alone. Make a fuss if you have to. But make sure *you* put it in his hands."

"Why me? Why can't you do it?"

"Poetic justice."

Tak didn't have to navigate a gauntlet of underlings at the courthouse. That very evening Poppy and Tak found the district attorney's car parked outside the courthouse and placed the satchel on the passenger seat. In it was an unsigned letter, implicating Coopersmith in the Japanese property scandal that had cost his colleague his career.

It was no bloody knife, Poppy realized, but it would serve.

THE STREETS DON'T LOVE NOBODY
BY HARRY LOUIS WILLIAMS II
Brookfield Village

A fat roach trekked silently across his bloody brown hand. It flicked its antennae as it waddled across fingernails caked thick and black with dirt. Outside, the piercing howl of sirens racing down 98th Avenue collided with the heavy pounding of hip-hop beats from the fifteen-inch speakers in a passing car.

A moan came from the dark couch rank with old beer stains. Super Blast was startled to find that it had emanated out from deep within his own parched throat. Anticipating the call, his homeboy Lyle stepped over to the couch where Super Blast lay sprawled. Lyle bent over and rested the open end of a plastic water bottle on his bottom lip. Then he untied the fat laces on the brand-new Jordans before slipping them off Super Blast's feet.

A damp crimson blotch spread out across the chest of Super Blast's once-white Raiders T-shirt. Lyle had tried to stop the bleeding, to no avail. The .44 slug had hit Super Blast in the center of his chest, sending bone fragments scrambling toward his heart and lungs. It had hit so hard and with such fury that it had actually set his shirt on fire. It scalded his belly and shredded his breastbone.

"Am I . . . going to die?" Super Blast asked.

Lyle chuckled, "Fool, you too rich to die. You got 'em, dude. Don't you remember?"

Yes, he did remember. Super Blast had slipped through an open bedroom window in one of the Black Christmas Mob's trap houses. He had cracked open the safe in the bedroom with an ax. There were two kilos of raw cocaine packed in clear plastic packages, along with three fat stacks of folded money tied with red rubber bands. Super Blast chucked the kis and the dough into a duffel bag. He was home free until he heard someone holler, "Hey, did you hear that? Somebody's in the bedroom!"

Super Blast zipped up the duffel and tossed it through the open window. His mistake was instinctive: turning to see who was coming through the door. And they came in blasting. The first slug hit him before he could jump on the chair to leap over the window ledge. He heard seven shots in all before he fell down into the tall grass outside. For a moment he lay there in the dark, twisting like a snake, waiting for death to come. Somehow, he summoned the will to stand. This feat achieved, he grabbed the duffel bag and ran for his car.

The front door of the trap house opened. Super Blast ducked between parked cars, running with his head down. Bullets whizzed overhead. A Corvette's rear window exploded, showering glass all over him. It wasn't until he'd made it two blocks that the adrenaline rush subsided. He dashed to the Jetta that he'd stashed at the corner of East 106th and San Leandro Boulevard. He started the engine, veered into traffic, and raced in the direction of Sobrante Park in East Oakland. He couldn't go home—War Thug had seen his face, so they'd be looking for him. He took a right on 105th Avenue at Edes, sped past Scotty's Liquor, zoomed across the railroad tracks, and took a left into the stony heart of Brookfield Village.

Super Blast was headed for Lyle's crib. Lyle was the one person he felt he could trust. Once people learned he had those kis, they'd be trying to take everything away from him. But not Lyle. Lyle was his crime protégé; Super Blast had introduced Lyle to the game.

He parked the car around the corner and limped up to the tiny brown wood-frame house at the center of the cul-de-sac. It took Lyle forever to get the door. He was laughing into his cell phone when it swung open. The pain in Super Blast's chest was nearly unbearable; white flashes of light blinked in his skull. His shirt was soaked in blood and the duffel bag dangled from his fingertips. Lyle's eyes settled on the bag and rested there.

"What's up, my dude?" Lyle asked.

"What it look like, playa? Let me in."

Super Blast stumbled through the doorway right into Lyle's awaiting arms. Lyle draped his right arm across his shoulders, then half-carried, half-dragged him into the living room area. He let Super Blast down slowly onto the couch. Finally, he noticed the bleeding chest.

"Damn, man! How is you still alive? What happened?"

Super Black gargled and spit out a mouthful of blood. "War Thug got me."

"War Thug? That Black Christmas Mob capo?

Super Blast nodded. For the moment it was all he could manage.

"Why he do this to you, bruh?"

"Look in the bag." Super Blast thrust it in Lyle's direction, never letting go of the handle.

Lyle unzipped it, peered inside, and grabbed his own chest. "Holy! . . . Man, that's two kis in there. How much money is that?"

Super Blast's smile broke into a laugh but he cut it short. Hurt too much. "C'mon, dude. You know how I get down in these streets."

Lyle's face darkened. "Yeah, and I know how *they* get down too. Drama probably got a whole platoon out in those streets right now looking for this . . . and you."

"Drama don't scare me. He ain't nuthin' but a sucker." Super Blast put up his middle finger. "I got this for Drama."

"I hear you talking, Super Blast. But it's only a minute 'fore they come through here looking for you."

"I know that."

"So then you know you can't stay here. 'Cause they'll kill us both."

"Now that's where you wrong, Lyle."

"'Scuse me?"

"Lyle, go pick up my mama. Tell her to come here and get me."

Lyle scratched his scalp. "Why don't we just call her?"

"Mama ain't got no phone. You gots to go get her." Super Blast pulled a car key from his pocket and thrust it in Lyle's direction.

"Blast, that's crazy. They gon' be looking for that car. I pull out in traffic and those fools will start knocking at the light."

Super Blast sucked his teeth, then raised his voice. "Fool, Mama ain't got no phone. If you too 'fraid to drive my car, that only leave you one choice."

Lyle held up his hand. "No, don't even think about it."

"Yes, youngster. You gon' have to walk it to Mama's house."

Lyle's phone rang.

A nervous tick caused Super Blast's jaw to pulsate. "Who trying to hit you? Cut it off."

"This is *my* cell. I ain't cutting it off."

"I said cut it off. You forget who I am, fool?"

For a second, a bolt of hatred made Lyle's eyes glow in the dark. No, he hadn't forgotten. It was Super Blast who had turned him out, took him on his first drive-by, made him a lookout on his burglary team. There were a dozen or more licks, but Lyle always seemed to come out on the short end of the split. Once, they were driving down International Boulevard near East 83rd when blue lights started flashing behind them. Super Blast said, "I got a .22 in the glove box. If they turn this car upside down, it's your gun. I'm on parole." That was the first time Lyle ever had to do jail time. Now he had a record.

"Where your sister at, man?" Super Blast suddenly said.

"She ain't home."

"Call her."

"I ain't doing that."

"You really feeling yourself tonight, huh, lil' homie?"

Suddenly, Super Blast grabbed his chest and fell back on the couch. To Lyle he appeared asleep, eternally so.

Seconds later, Super Blast's eyes opened. He felt a shadow and smelled Listerine breath. "Fool, why you leaning over me?"

"What you mean?" Lyle said.

"Second ago you was on the other side of the room—now you all over me like a damn vulture."

"You trippin', OG."

Super Blast reached beneath the couch and felt for the duffel bag. Still there. "Now, what was we talking about," Super Blast asked. He propped himself up on his elbows.

"My sister Tanya, 'member?"

Despite his pain, a lewd grin crawled across Super Blast's face. "Yeah, so what's up with old Tanya?"

"You know Tanya got the herpes, right?"

"How would I know that?"

"'Cause she got it from you."

Super Blast smirked and diverted his eyes momentarily, almost displaying a tinge of embarrassment. Then he was right back to his old self. "The herpes ain't nuthin'."

"Ain't nuthin'? My sister started breaking out all over her private parts with these blisters. The doctor say that disease don't never go away. Never."

Super Blast turned slowly on his side to face Lyle. "Tanya want to be my ride-or-die chick. She want to share my glory, she got to share my pain. We all got a price to pay in this world."

"She asked you to wear a condom, man. Why din't you?"

"Didn't want to take away the feeling."

"Blast, why you feel like you can just do people any kind of way you want? You use people, that ain't right."

"Ain't you caught on yet, my dude? The streets don't love nobody. You can't understand that, you'll never understand a man like me. I bred you from a pup, but I must've done something wrong 'cause you weak. You soft, my dude. You ain't nuthin' but a follower. Sure, I used your sister, and I ain't ready to stop there. Is your mama home? 'Cause she can get it too."

"Mama's at church."

Lyle's cell phone rang again.

"Fool, I told you to turn that thing off!"

"Just a second." Lyle looked at the number and then lifted the phone to his mouth. "Can't talk now, I got company." He ended the call.

"Who was that?"

"Telemarketer. Now, let me call a cab so I can get over to your mama's crib."

"Fool, you ain't calling no cab so they can see who's up in this house. Hell naw! You walking."

The phone rang once more.

Before Super Blast could say anything, Lyle picked up the cell and hollered into it, "Don't call here no more! I got company!"

"Who was that, Lyle?"

"Same damn call."

"Fool, why you tell a telemarketer you got company?"

"Only way to get rid of 'em. Law says they can't call you back if you say you got company."

"For real? I never heard of no law like that."

"It's new."

Super Blast sucked his teeth. "Damn, I hate telemarketers." He began to shiver, his teeth chattering. He moaned, "I'm so cold," then gripped his pistol close to his chest as though it were a baby's blanket.

"Try and relax," Lyle said. "Let me go get your mama, now."

Super Blast grunted his approval before slipping into unconsciousness.

He heard the back door open. How long had he been out? No way of telling. It was all good, Mama was here now and she would get him to a doctor. Maybe they'd have to make a run for it. They had family in New Orleans. The money would give them a fresh start, they'd get a nice apartment and a new car. He'd break those kilos down and then cook the rest into rocks. He'd make a killing.

"Mama, I'm in here!" Super Blast cried out.

"*Mama?* I ain't your mama, fool!"

It was a man's voice: cold, angry, ruthless. Super Blast recognized it and almost screamed. He aimed his pistol toward the voice.

Nothing. Just two clicks.

The lights went on. And there he was: the hood god, Drama himself, and two of his goons. Lyle stood behind them.

"Lyle, I told you to go get my mama," Super Blast said.

"Is that what you said? Huh. I thought you said go get Drama."

Even Drama laughed. His trademark ponytail jumped on his back as his head bobbed up and down.

Super Blast winced as the pain shot through his spine. "Judas, you set me up."

"I ain't Judas, because in this scenario that would make you Jesus Christ, and you far from that."

"I hate to break up all this good church talk," Drama cut in. "But Super Blast—where my merchandise at?"

"I ain't got nuthin', Drama. Five-O ran up on me and I dropped the bag."

Drama cursed, then crossed the room and stood over Super Blast. "Where my stuff at, fool?"

"I ain't got—"

Drama slapped Super Blast in the forehead with his pistol. Blood gushed out.

"I can do this all night, player. Do not make me ask you again—where my yay and my money?" Drama's right hand reared back.

"Okay, okay! It's under the couch."

"Give it to me."

A tear slipped from Super Blast's eye as he reached for the duffel bag. A puzzled look came over his face. His hand slid back down and started feeling around under the couch once again, frantically. "It's gone."

"Chump, you halfway to death's door and you still want to play me?" Drama turned to the thugs behind him. "Get him up on his feet."

And the truth hit Super Blast like a cement block falling from the sky. "Lyle! You stole that bag! When I passed out, you came and took the duffel. And you took the bullets outta my gun!"

"Get your story straight, Blast! First, you says you dropped a duffel bag when you were on the run. Then you say it's under the couch. Now you saying I got it? Player, it looks like your run is over. A gangsta who can't keep his alibis straight—I don't know what's to be said for you."

"Let's go," Drama ordered. "I see we gonna have to torture your ass to get my money back."

The goons scooped up Super Blast by his armpits; he was too weak to fight.

"Lyle, don't do this to me! Tell this man something."

"I don't know what I can tell, Blast. But I can tell you like you told me: *The streets don't love nobody.*"

Drama wrapped Super Blast's mouth with duct tape, then pulled a ski mask over his head so he couldn't be recognized.

Before they left, Drama said, "You done good, Lyle. Letting me know this fool was still here when I hit you on the cell. Otherwise he and his deadbeat mama might've got out of town. Come see me at the spot tomorrow—I'll hit you off somethin' proper, just like I promised." Drama was known to be a man of his word, and generous to boot.

Super Blast twisted his head back, his eyes begging. As he was led out, he saw his protégé smile and say, "Have a lovely evening, gentlemen."

BULLETPROOF

BY CAROLYN ALEXANDER

McClymonds

> *I thought I loved you!*
> *Just like I thought I was alive.*
> *Like I wasn't the zombie Phantom of the Opera*
> *Like this hurt I feel didn't slit my throat*
> *Like I didn't bleed out on my favorite outfit*
> *Like these words even matter to you.*

Lisa and Leon didn't know each other, but they both felt the same way.

Lisa knew she was alive because she was hurting. Once again she had caused her own pain. Nothing could staunch the greedy and needy monster inside her who begged for more attention, more words of affirmation, more acts of affection, more, more, more. Her boyfriend finally peered down the bottomless pit of her need and he too ran off, to save his own life.

Leon had always felt he had to buy love, starting with his parents. His brother was an athlete, Leon was only an A student—commendable, but there was no glory in it, no trophies. His brother attracted girls. Leon earned them with gifts and begging. He was actually better looking than his older brother, taller and with dimples. But girls took Leon for granted, got bored, and eventually hooked up with some bad boy who screwed them over and left them, who they could never get over. Yet they would never take Leon back.

Lisa walked out the back of McClymonds High School, past her car in the parking lot, and out the gates, wandering aimlessly down 28th Street. When she crossed Myrtle she entered into the ho stroll of working girls. Even on the sunniest days this block was in shadow. One skinny, saggy-tittied prostitute, smoking a cigarette, eyed her. Lisa was too sad to fear for her own safety. The prostitute wore resignation like the mask of death. A car slowed, the driver leaning over the passenger side and scrutinizing Lisa, but when he didn't hear the question, *Are you looking for a date?* he moved on to the other woman on the block, didn't like what he saw, and sped off. The prostitute took the cigarette out of her mouth, peered at Lisa with pure venom, then settled in against the wall of the storage mart.

Sturdy brown legs under a white skirt skipped by, the trudging steps of her mother right behind, smiling absentmindedly. There was joy in West Oakland, even in the dark shadow of the ho stroll. Lisa always felt sorry for herself after love went bad. It was time to rewrite the script. She reminded her students that most papers could be saved, in fact were not complete without a good and thorough edit. But like her students, she didn't have what it took to do it, at least as far as her life was concerned.

She assessed herself. Five foot nine (too tall), caramel skin, size 12/13 (too big). Thick black hair that was prone to getting poufy in this curly weave world, round face, big eyes, negroid nose, and full lips, wearing a black pencil skirt and a fitted white blouse. Not exactly bad-girl attire.

Leon turned his ride at the corner of 28th Street and saw Lisa standing there. She was a different type of prostitute, one for the guys who wanted to take down a businesswoman, a proper girl. Maybe he could pay up front and have exactly what he wanted.

In her sad, suicidal mood, Lisa decided if he slowed she

would get into the car. He looked harmless enough. A voice in her head whispered, *This ain't* Black Pretty Woman, *you know.* She ignored the voice and got in. There was something about his face, something about him that made her feel it was okay. Leon drove off. He didn't speak and neither did she. He turned right onto Market Street. The light caught him on 27th Street. Lisa opened the door just to see if she could, in case she needed to get out in a hurry.

"What's the matter?" Leon asked. He would be relieved if she got out, but he was also relieved that she stayed. Her energy felt good, it was electrifying.

"Nothing."

Leon looked at her. "How does this work?"

"How do you want it to work?" Lisa didn't even know where that came from.

"Uh, I don't know." Leon's cell phone rang and he reluctantly answered it. "Where . . . ? Yeah, I'm just getting off work but I have someone with me . . . Maybe I don't want to bring them along . . . All right! I'll pick you up." He stole a glance at Lisa. "A slight detour, I need to pick someone up."

"Okay," Lisa whispered. She thought, *Is this the setup for a gang rape?*

He sensed her fear and instinctively reached for her hand. But he caught himself; this was no date. What the hell *was* this anyway? Lisa pulled her hand away at his first furtive movement. Maybe he was trying to hold her so she couldn't jump out.

What type of prostitute is she? Leon wondered. She seemed too shy to be a whore, but if she wasn't, why would she get in his car? Why didn't she talk about price up front? Maybe it was an act to fleece him at the end of the evening. *The bitch!*

"I would say a penny for your thoughts but I know that wouldn't be nearly enough."

"Thoughts? Thoughts are free. I was just thinking it's good to be with a gentleman." She was hoping.

"A gentleman?" Leon snorted. "You find many of those cruising 28th Street?" He turned right on 7th Street.

Lisa didn't answer. They both were thinking, *What the fuck have I got myself into?*

Leon pulled into the West Oakland BART station. A tall, thin, nut-brown guy with a pile of nappy hair approached. Lisa jumped out of the car and Leon's heart lurched with the same feeling of *relieved if she does, relieved if she doesn't.* Lisa opened the rear door and got in the back. Nobody would slip a garrote around her neck.

Leon frowned at her. Lisa managed, "We can talk later," before his friend got in, his shock of hair scraping against the ceiling of the car. "Take care of your friend first."

"Thanks, man," the guy said. He turned around with a semi-smirk on his face. "Who is this?"

Lisa disliked him immediately.

Leon stammered, "This is—"

"Lisa Boudreux," she said, extending her hand. The guy turned away without taking her hand.

"This is Ajani," Leon said.

"Well, Leon, I see you are up to surprises." Ajani cupped his hand to light up a joint, then turned to Lisa. "You a smoking girl?" He had that same quizzical smirk on his face.

God, she couldn't stand him. "No," she said, and shook her head gently.

Leon turned and looked at her. She really was a different type of prostitute. He could use some herbal encouragement.

Lisa noticed the early winter sunset as she watched the bright orange-red end of the joint grow brighter when Leon took a toke.

Leon drove past the Shell station on 7th Street and Market. "I gotta get gas but this place is too high." He headed down to the ARCO on Grand. When he jumped out to pump gas, Ajani stepped out to get something from the AM-PM store.

"So, who's this chick?"

"Somebody I picked up."

"C'mon, man. You don't pick up chicks."

"Today I did." Leon turned his back to the car and leaned toward Ajani. "She's a prostitute."

"A prostitute?" Ajani glowered at her. "She ain't no prostitute."

"I slowed down where the working girls are. She was there and hopped right in my car."

Ajani peered at Leon, then over at Lisa.

As soon as the guys got back in the car, Ajani twisted around to face her and asked, "How about a threesome?"

Lisa stared at Ajani unflinchingly and casually said, "A threesome is more. Who's paying?"

"I don't want a threesome," Leon cut in. "This is between Lisa and me."

"Yeah, I bet," Ajani muttered. "Tell you what. I got a spot; it's a place not too many people know about or *can* know about. You heard about the Power Exchange in San Francisco?" *Crickets.* "Of course not. Well, this is like the Power Exchange only more relaxed. No one is required to do anything. The place has a really chill atmosphere. It's called the Upside of Pandora's Box. You guys seem up for an adventure today, so let's go."

Ajani directed Leon back down Market to 18th and made a right and then a left, stopping at a huge house on Linden Street. The ground floor had been turned into a separate apartment. Ajani ran ahead. A hunky black man in a pinstripe suit opened the door and he and Ajani laughed. The brother let Ajani head inside. When Leon tried to walk past, the guy said,

"Twenty dollars a person." Leon paid for Lisa as well.

The smell of sage greeted them as they stepped over salt sprinkled at the threshold. The air was hazy and blue light barely illuminated the place. "A Love Supreme" by John Coltrane was playing, followed by Prince's "Do Me, Baby." As Leon and Lisa made their way up the stairs they passed Ajani sitting with another guy, pulling on a bong. His eyelids were already drooping. Ajani handed the bong to Leon, who hit, and he passed it to Lisa, and she hit it, and the bong began making its rotations. They didn't feel anything . . . *and then they did.* The world changed. All their senses were heightened. They became hyperaware of everything. Their bodies felt lighter. Gravity was no longer in effect.

Couples were dancing sensuously. A man bent a woman over and ran his hands along her breasts and down the length of her body, grabbing her hips and pulling her into him. A girl came in, demure and sad. "Why you feeling blue, Meg?" a man asked. He cleared a long oak table and helped her lie down on it. He began to disrobe her and others joined in. They rubbed her down with oil, from the bottom of her feet to her scalp, massaging her slowly. Some guy bent over and suckled her breast and a girl on the other side did the same. Meg's eyes were closed as she drank in the tactile pleasures. A man sunk his middle finger between her legs. She gasped and then began a low moan. He mounted her while the others continued to caress her, holding her hands out and rubbing her arms. In a short while she arched her back and pointed her bent legs toward the ceiling. Everyone applauded when they saw the shy smile on her face.

Lisa slurred, "That was lovely."

"You think so?" Leon whispered. Ajani had disappeared to parts unknown. Leon leaned forward and gently kissed her.

"You're lovely." He kissed her again, parting her full lips and tasting her.

A wide-hipped woman, looking like Pocahontas with two thick braids, stood up and began dancing alone. She was dancing so slowly and smoothly that in their drugged state, one of her movements seemed to blur into the next as if her body had no lines or boundaries. Lisa leaned in clumsily and kissed Leon and they both fell over. He rolled on top of her luscious thickness and the weight of his body felt delicious. Their pleasure was liquid and insuppressible. He bunched her skirt up around her waist. Neither was conscious enough of their surroundings to care. Leon began tugging forcefully on Lisa's panties.

"Wow! Can I be next?"

It was as if a beautiful love song playing on vinyl had the needle abruptly ripped off. Lisa and Leon opened their eyes to find Ajani, grinning stupidly at them. The hunky guy in the pinstriped suit was shaking his head at Ajani—his behavior was improper etiquette for the Upside of Pandora's Box.

"Man, can't you find yourself a woman?" Leon said. "And find yourself a ride home!"

"Aw, man, is it like that? Over this bitch?"

Leon tilted his head and just looked at Ajani.

"Yeah, man, I can get a ride," Ajani finally muttered.

"Good!" Leon reached for Lisa's hand and they made for the door.

When they stepped outside, the cold air dissipated the sexual intensity they had felt inside.

"You want to get a room?"

Lisa looked down. "Yes, I do. But I have something to tell you."

"You're not really a prostitute."

"You knew?"

"I guessed. I don't really have any experience with this, but what prostitute doesn't talk money from the jump, unless they want to blindside the guy with the price later? You didn't seem hard enough for that. But why in the world would you get into a stranger's car? That's damn dangerous."

"I know, but you had a look and I had a feeling. I was feeling low and so I took a chance."

"Man, that could have been the deadliest chance of your life."

"Well, why did you pick me up?"

"I was feeling down too. I looked at you and I just did it. Paying for sex, however you want it. At the time it seemed like a good idea."

They stared at each other for a moment.

"It's getting late. I better go back to my car." Lisa said.

"Are we going to exchange numbers?" Leon asked.

"No, the night was perfect. It would probably go downhill from here."

"You're probably right."

"But if I ever see you again . . ." they both said at the same time.

"We'll know it was fate," Lisa finished.

He drove her back to 28th Street, the block between Myrtle and Market. A car passed by and Lisa thought she saw Ajani's face. "Are you sure you don't want a ride to your car?" Leon asked. "You already dodged one bullet."

"No, I'll be fine. Let's keep the mystery going."

He kissed her once again and let her out. She was walking back to McClymonds, one short block, when she noticed a lump of something on the sidewalk. When she got closer she saw it was the prostitute in a heap, her eyes half open, a cigarette hanging out the side of her mouth. Lisa didn't know if she was alive or dead. Either way it was too late for the woman to rewrite this chapter of her life, and Lisa wondered if it was too late for her too. She pulled out her phone to call 911. The heavy footsteps behind her came so fast she had no time to feel fear or dread.

THE THREE STOOGES

BY PHIL CANALIN

Sausal Creek

Tonight the three guys felt good. All of them had scored some schwag and were about to blaze big in a minute. But they sat, stalling and shooting the shit for a little bit, knowing that the first hit was always the best hit, and waiting for it could be almost as good.

They were hanging out in the forgotten back end of Austen Square, near East 22nd Street. Not far from them, a mural had been gloriously painted on the old concrete retaining wall along that portion of Sausal Creek. The mural, about thirty feet long, depicted a woman's face with a series of scared and startled expressions, ending, or perhaps beginning, with Pinocchio's cartoon face, also startled, even horrified. Meaning what, exactly? That someone cannot tell a lie? Or that someone's about to tell a lie? It depended on the direction in which the observer viewed the painted mural, maybe. Either way, a lie about what?

The three of them were all but hidden by tall, grassy weeds and wild shrubs, broad-leafed, hollow-limbed, and ignored for years. None of the boys cared one bit about the artwork or its intended meaning. The boys—really, they were men in stature—sat sprawled atop a portion of the low wall of cheap, crumbling concrete. The city had probably saved a few cents on the dollar using inferior product back when they first put the wall up ages ago, maybe saving a few more cents by hiring inferior city workers.

What was supposed to be a wall to stop Sausal Creek from eroding the land was now a crumbling, unkempt eyesore, like the rest of the creek trail most of the way down to the Oakland Estuary. Hell, a lot people lived in Oakland all their lives and didn't even know Sausal Creek existed, let alone that it ran from the northeast hills up near Mountain Boulevard down to the estuary and San Leandro Bay. It didn't help that city forefathers had installed metal culvert pipes to direct much of the creek underground, causing a lot of it to dry up. Even in the winter months many parts of Sausal Creek were thin, filthy beds of jumbled rocks embedded in flat sections of gray, smelly clay. All this was why the three of them could hole up there forever most nights, rarely bothered. Of course, their ragged, dirty clothes and overall grossness kept folks at a distance too.

On one end Maurice was holding up a cheap plastic sandwich baggie, shaking it and gleefully bragging in front of the others. Maurice was eighteen, originally from LA. He'd dropped out of high school after the very first day of freshman year, just never went back. No one cared. His mother and father were already long gone and his sister was a whore. She worked in West LA, making just enough cash to sustain her meth stash and keep a room in a cockroach-infested motel where Maurice crashed. She was so out of it she rarely knew that Maurice was there, sleeping in the bathroom tub, eating stolen food or fast food he bought using money pinched from her. After finally taking off, Maurice never saw or heard from her again. Hell, she may not have realized he was ever there and gone. If she was still alive. Sometimes, in his dreams, Maurice still heard her (fake) and her johns' (scary) moans and groans, bleeding through the bathroom walls from the living room. Maurice used to cover his ears and pretend to sleep through it. He was better off alone.

"Got me two good ol' blunts here, you know. Took them right off that crazy white mo'fo at the 26th Avenue bus stop," Maurice said. "Dude was soft, man, couldn't do a thing, you know what I mean? I just took his backpack, took it right from him. Snatch. He thought I was sleepin'."

Maurice was one of those big, really fat homeless guys. Huge. Gross. He had to weigh at least three and a half bills and he was only five foot five. Maurice rarely had a lot to eat, so keeping all that weight on must have been some biological DNA thing. It didn't help his girth that he spent so much time lying around sleeping, wherever and whenever he could find some quiet place, alone. Hell, it was all he could do, dragging his humongous body around was exhausting. He had on the usual three pairs of sweatpants, old now, the top one black, soiled and ragged, torn at both knees, a dirty gray one showing through. Maurice also wore a giant navy-blue hoodie beneath a 5XL cotton shirt, fading green and orange plaid, ripped at both elbows and a foot too long for his squat body. When Maurice found something that fit over his huge frame, he held onto it, never sure when the next load of Bigandbigger clothing would come. Covering his fashion ensemble was a simply made poncho, a hole cut out for his head, his arms sticking out of the corners on either side. That poncho was big enough to be a kid's tent, made of some dark indoor/outdoor material that was soft and pliable, but waterproof and tough. It looked like something a giant cowboy would have worn to survive long cattle drives through harsh winters atop beautiful Wyoming mountain ranges. It was Maurice's prized possession, cinched at the waist now with a piece of rope, but big and long enough to curl his large body into later, keeping him warm and dry at night, right here atop the ugly, dirty Oakland city streets.

Lawrence Booker, in the middle, spoke: "Lessee what you

got, Maurice . . . *hhssssp* . . . make sure it's real stuff, not dried-up nickel ragweed. *Hhssssp.* Don't want you burning out a lung or anything . . . *hhssssp.*"

Lawrence sat there on his cold perch, both hands pulled up into the sleeves of his green army coat. The coat was stained and had a nasty stench from years of use and limited washings. His messy, gnarled Afro was stuffed into an equally gnarled black knit hat that more than suggested he needed a larger one. Puffs of Lawrence's dry ratty hair stuck out randomly along the edge of the hat; it wasn't easy to tell what was hair and what was unraveling hat yarn. "Come on, Mo, first spark up a little of your stuff . . . *hhssssp.* I'm a little light right now. Get it? A little light? *Hhssssp.* That's what we need."

As he talked, Lawrence had this habit of sucking air into his mouth through a gap made by two missing teeth. Not his two front teeth, but the first two immediately off-center on the top right side. About two years ago, Lawrence "found" a pretty fat wallet in a coat hanging in a coffee shop down on International. Later that night he bonged a boatload of kick-ass hashish while guzzling a quart of cheap tequila—eventually he passed out and keeled over, smashing his face on some steps. Those two teeth had taken the brunt of his fall. When Lawrence awoke, sleeping in a small pool of his own congealed blood, he had his own permanent mouth instrument to keep him amused.

Lawrence had been living on the streets longer than either of the other two. An orphan, he had never known his mother or father, living in a multitude of foster homes in the East Bay as a child, a vagabond in a woebegone government system that neither budgeted enough money to monitor what was really happening out there in Foster Kid World, or cared enough to even give a rat's ass. Maybe government folks figured as long as you were in a home and had a place to eat and sleep, well then, you damn well must be happy. After his millionth beating from the last of a series of foster parents who used his stipend money to buy booze and drugs, Lawrence had simply said, *Screw this*, run off, and permanently escaped. He was eleven years old then, and no one was going to know what Lawrence had had to do sometimes to survive all this time. He'd take that crap to his grave. No one. *Hhssssp.*

The last guy on the other end, that was Champ, who chimed in, "Yeah, Mo, you know that dirty old dude coulda been rollin' anything, man, you know like he had no cash to get nothing rich either, right, know what I'm sayin'?"

Maurice chuckled low. "Yeah, I hear you, Champ. Come on, man, I already had a couple early tokes. Stuff's for reals, I'm tellin' ya. Fo'. Reals." He smiled and winked at the others, teasing them with his fluttering joint bag. "Wutchoo idiots get? More to share? Cuz you know, two fatties ain't much to pass around, you know, mostly good for me, maybe a free toke or so for you, maybe not."

"Dang, Mo, you jumped the gun on us, man," Champ replied. "You know, shoulda waited on us, man."

His real name was Champion DeLeon Cromarté. He told everyone he was named Champion by his proud father, who was once the Este Región Guantes de Oro Peso Welter Campeón. In English: the East Region Welterweight Golden Gloves Champion—in the Dominican Republic. His father moved to the States in '91, fell in with some bad gamblers, and didn't make it in boxing. Finally, fifty pounds over his fighting weight and sporting an obnoxious cauliflower ear, Señor Cromarté got hired as a thug for some nobody drug pusher. As was usually the case in that line of work, Señor Cromarté was paid in drugs, booze, and a place to crash, and even then some woman loved him enough to marry him and bear his only child.

Champ told everyone, "Yeah, man, you know, my father held me up in the county clinic, right, and shouted at the top of his lungs, *He's gonna be a champion, a champion like me!* That was just a week before he and my mother both OD'd on some shit smack, you know. So you can call me Champ—more like Chump—but don't call me Champion, cuz it ain't so, know what I mean?"

Child Protective Services took custody of baby Champ and eventually found some long-disconnected uncle and aunt and, bless them, they at least consented, raising Champ as best they could. But they were barely making it themselves and never really knew his father, who was only some very, very distant third cousin or something, and they knew Champ's mother not at all. So forgive them if they didn't lavish much attention or support on the kid. *Hijo de punto*, he wasn't their kid anyway. Champ understood that, even at age nine when he ran away for the first of many times, and definitely at fourteen when he ran all the way away once and for all.

Champ sat there, outfitted like the others that evening, in layers of smelly, dirty clothes, anything to keep warm at night: two or three hoodies, the requisite knit hat, khaki pants over sweats; indiscriminate colors, since colors don't matter when the clothes you're wearing are torn, filthy, reeking rags. Champ did sport a greasy red, white, and blue do-rag tied around his head, crammed under his knit hat—not for the good old US of A, but proudly for the colors of the Dominican Republic national flag. Champ looked tired, like the others, dark bags beneath sunken brown eyes. He had unruly facial hair growing in uneven patterns on his mocha-colored face, dirty and mucky from being on the street without a shower or shave for over ten days now. Champ was thin, medium height, but his frazzled appearance made him look twenty years older than he was. His frazzled life made him feel forty years older.

Earlier that day Champ had made a couple of bucks and some change sweeping out King's Gym alongside the disgusted glances of the sweaty regulars working out. Mr. Gordon, or just Gordon as he was called, was the head janitor and had worked for the Kings for many years, had even known Champion's *padre* years before. Gordon felt badly for Champ, so occasionally the old janitor would let the kid sweep or pick up garbage and towels in the gym for a few dollars and loose change, anything to help him out. But the handouts came less and less frequently, especially as Gordon saw that Champ was more and more often just hanging out with the other alley bums, not even trying to help himself. And Champ smelled flawed somehow, like all the bums did, slipping further and further into that gory morass of wasted human lives. Gordon saw it too often and it pained him to no end. He knew for certain that if Champ's father were still alive, he would never have let this happen, no way. He would have knocked some sense into his only son, literally.

"Self-pride is another long-lost art, like the art of boxing," Gordon often tried to explain when he thought he had Champ's attention. "You gotta learn to take care of yourself. You can train and train and work out all you want, but once you're in that ring it's only you."

Gordon even tried to get Champ to go back to school—a program at Laney College for dropouts and homeless kids he had read about in the *Tribune*. Gordon went so far as to contact the school's director, someone named Tom Gelman. Coach Gelman told him all Champ had to do was call and Gelman promised he'd take care of the rest. Seemed like a good guy. But when Gordon invited Champ into his messy, cramped supply office to explain about the school and have Champ make the call, he saw immediately in the kid's eyes that he didn't give a crap. Gordon realized he had just been wasting his own time, and why should he do that? Hell, he was no Mother Teresa, he had a job to take care of. Too lazy to get off the streets? Welcome to the streets, kid! But every once in a while, Gordon still felt badly and he'd help Champ out, for old times and for Champ's *padre*, Señor Cromarté, the last real champion of anything from around there.

"Dudes," Champ was now telling his street buddies, "you won't believe what happened today, you know. Ol' Gordon gave me two-fifty for sweeping up his ratty ol' boxing gym. What an idiot, you know what I mean? So I bought me some sweet old boots from the Salvation Army, perfect size and everything, no holes, and warm too, like new!"

"That old fart is always giving you handouts, man, what's up with that?" Maurice said. "A little sumpin-sumpin cooking there?"

"Yeah, Champ . . . *hhsssp*," Lawrence added, "he must, like, like you or something, dude. You better . . . *hhsssp* . . . watch out for them old geezers like that."

"Come, on, holmes," Champ replied, "it ain't nothing like that. Old dude just knew my papá once, tries to help me out sometimes. It's cool, it's cool."

"Yeah, okay, but really, what the hell are you talking about, Champ . . . *hhsssp*?" Lawrence scoffed. "Look at your raggedy ol' shoes . . . *hhsssp* . . . they're filthy and they're leaking oil, dude!" He laughed, pointing at Champ's black sneakers that were caked with dirt and mud, one shoestring tied in numerous knots to hold together, the rubber sole on the other just a paper-thin strip.

Maurice laughed too. "Yikes! You crazy Mexican, if you bought those shoes for two-fitty you must be back in Mexico and smokin' some donkey-piss weed on the tequila farm or something! Them shoes are messed up!"

Champ eyed them with disgust. "Not *these* shoes, you a-holes. You idiots don't have a clue, man. Some *other* shoes, bro, some other boots, right? Dude at the Army sold me a cool pair for my two dollars and fifty cents, a bargain, know what I'm sayin'? Winter boots and the tag said six-fifty, man, no bull! And I told you, I ain't Mexican, you know, how many times I gotta tell you I'm Dominican, man. Dominican Republic represent!"

Lawrence looked at Champ like he was from outer space. "Well, you talk Mexican and you buy shoes like some dumb-ass Mexican too . . . *hhssssp.* But you wasted your money on those crap no-Cons right there . . . *hhsssp!*"

Maurice added, "And whatever you are, homeboy, those dirty kicks you're wearing are definitely representing the facts, loud and clear, that you're a crazy Mexican, or Dominican, or whatever, and your dang feet are gonna freeze tonight, know what I'm tellin' you?"

"You're both screwed, dudes, *fubar,* you hear me?" Champ said. "I *sold* those other boots to Raymond. His feet and mine are the same size, like a coincidence, you know. Well, you know, really, I actually swapped those boots with Raymond, man, no moolah changed hands."

"Well, lay it on me, brother man," Maurice responded. "What did you and Raymond barter for those amazing boots, which I ain't ever seen? I'm just sayin', why the hell did you trade those amazing boots to the sorriest drug dealer on the West Side, Raymond Donahue, who you know mixes dried-up old herbs and real grass with his ragweed to sell to crazy-ass rich-douche reefer-heads who wouldn't know great smoke from the kind blowin' up and through their booties, you know what I mean?"

"Damn, Mo." Lawrence peered at Maurice with pure awe, and in the moment forgot all about playing his toothless mouth instrument. "You shoulda been a poet or politician or something, boy. Your rap is greatness as anything I ever hear on TV at the Y."

"Both of you are wigging me out, really spazzin'," Champ said. "Come on, now, I'm gonna show you what I got from Raymond for those boots. Ray-Ray told me he mixed in some extra-special dust into this one here. You know it's good, homeys, Ray-Ray ain't shit but he don't lie to me."

Champion reached the fingers of his dirty right hand up and under his cap and into a fold in his Dominican do-rag, pulling out a dark-brown joint, not even half as thick as a No. 2 pencil. Champ displayed it proudly with his thumb and forefinger. "We gonna get high tonight, boys, you know what I'm sayin'?" he declared in a reverential tone.

To which both Maurice and Lawrence exploded with laughter.

"What the hell's *that?!*" Maurice guffawed. "A doobie for a dwarfie? A baby phattie for baby rattie?"

"Aw, hell no!" Lawrence joined in. "It's a toothpick joint, in case our dinner steaks and lobsters get stuck in our teeth . . . *hhsssp* . . . well, you-all's teeth, anyway!" Which set him off laughing hysterically, so much so that he choked on his own final, "*Hhsssp . . . hack-ack!*"

"Quick!" Maurice faked a shout, holding his hands megaphone-like over his mouth. "Call in the troops, call in the FBI, call in the FDA, the NSA, NIA, CIA, and all them other IAs—Champ's got hisself a major drug deal going down tonight, lemme tell you, boy!"

"And mind that special dust from Mr. Donahue!" Lawrence called out as well. "Special dust in da house!"

"Yeah, yeah," Mo added. "Keep them vacuums cleaners away, beautiful ladies and gentlemens, cuz we got us some special dust in this here special joint . . . the Champion Joint Smoke is what it is, Champ's Champion Joint Smoke!"

"Funny, fellas, funny for real," Champ said. "Well, you know, if that's how y'all feel about it, guess I havta enjoy this little toke all on myself, you know, all on myself." He waved the joint at the others. "Say bye-bye to the spliff, jokesters. This little baby's all mines."

That stopped Lawrence. He still hadn't shown his own stash, didn't want to show his stash, and *no way* wanted to share his stash with anyone, even his homeys. "Man, come on, Champ dude . . . *hhssssp,*" he said, stifling his giggles. "You know we playing. Right, Mo? Just . . . *hhssssp* . . . playing."

"Yeah, Champ, chill." Maurice had his own two joints, but the more high the merrier, he always said, especially if he didn't have to work for it. "We gotta have us a laugh once in a while, right, man? Street homies need to get some laughs any time we can. Otherwise, what are we, dudes? We just like them folks working nine to five, know what I'm saying? One foot in the grave, one foot in the poor house, man, and another foot up our asses. Day after dang-dog day. Come on, we gotta chill and laugh with each other, at each other, whatever. Just chill and laugh."

"Dude's right on, Champ. *Hhssssp.* Speaking the truth as always, Maurice," Lawrence agreed.

"Yeah, dudes, I hear you, all right," Champ relented. "Okay, maybe I share a little bit, as long as we all are. Just don't laugh at me no more . . . AND QUIT CALLIN' ME A MEXICAN!"

"That's what I'm talking about," Maurice said, a baby-blue BIC lighter magically appearing in his hands. He flicked the BIC and held the small flame to the already burnt end of the joint now clasped gently between his yellowed teeth. "Light 'em if you got 'em, boys."

Maurice squinted his eyes as he gently inhaled, long and steady, holding the marijuana smoke deep in his lungs. When he finally stopped, a third of the blunt had burned away. Still squinting, he then held the joint's red ember tip to his mouth and with his last spare lung-space sucked in the wispy smoke trail.

"Gettin' high like ching chong, Mo, massive hit, bro." Lawrence smiled, reaching out nonchalantly for Maurice to pass him the Mary Jane. They had done this many times over the last month or two—they didn't always share, but if they had enough to go around they usually did, no questions asked either way. Tonight Mo passed Lawrence the lit joint.

Lawrence raised his eyebrows with a quick "Thanks, dude." He sucked on the jay in three rapid inhalations, filling his lungs with the thick and pungent reefer smoke. Lawrence smiled at Maurice, exposing the gap in his teeth, then cocked his head slightly in Champ's direction; Maurice responded with a simple nod of his head—Lawrence understood it was okay to pass Mo's joint over to Champ for a toke. About an inch of the original joint was left.

"Thanks, fellas," Champ said, accepting the offering and placing the smoldering jay between his tightly squeezed thumb and index finger. "High Mo-amigo," Champ also said in his personal thank you, then took a long drag on the small butt. By the time he finished, only a tiny portion of the joint remained, an eighth of an inch or so. Champ's lungs, like the others', were used to taking long, full drags and holding the smoke deeply to allow the drug to fully work its magic. A doobie never lasted very long when the three of them shared it. And Maurice was right on too—the pot was damn good stuff.

Maurice expelled the reefer smoke he'd been holding in his lungs and reached into the front zipper pocket of his grimy

Adidas backpack. From there he pulled out a small silver medical clamp, now serving its pharmaceutical duty as a roach clip. "I'll take that roach, dude," he said, reaching across Lawrence, deftly accepting the joint from Champ, and locking the clip's teeth-lined jaws along the slightest edge of the butt. Pulling back, Maurice held the roach clip up as closely as possible to his lips without touching the sparked end of the roach, and, once again squinting his eyes, tenderly smoked the rest of the joint. Finally, with nothing left but a tiny scrap of rolling paper, he opened the roach clip and released the particle.

"All right, all right," Champ said. "That was some good puff, Mo, good start, know what I'm saying? What's next? Lawrence, what you got, bro?"

"Yeah, mo-fo Lo-Ro, whatchoo got, man?" Maurice asked, his eyes beginning to redden, his eyelids drooping slightly. "You got us a treat, High Lo?"

"Aw, man, you know how it is, fellas . . . *hhssssp,*" Lawrence began. He held his up his hands, palms facing out, wiggling his fingers. "Ain't got no smoke, dudes . . . *hhssssp.*" Lawrence was lying; he was holding out on an eighth-ounce of Grade-A skunk weed, and felt no qualms about doing so.

"Aw, brother man," Maurice cried out, "you messing with us or something, dude? Hell, you just smoked my ganja and now you tell us you buddels?"

"What the hell, Lawrence, you gotta be more weedsponsible than that, homeboy," Champ chimed in. "We oughtta kick your butt up and down the creek for pulling that crap, you know."

"Well, you guys are my street buds, right?" Lawrence replied. "I told you I was light earlier, remember . . . *hhssssp?*" But then, smiling, he reached into his coat pocket and pulled out a full pint of booze. "All righty then . . . *hhssssp* . . . tell you all what, you can kick my butt after we drink this here bottle of José Gold. Sí, sí, amigos?"

"Aw, man, thass cool!" Champ laughed. "I knew you wouldn't hold out on us, Lawrence! Nothing goes better with getting stoned than getting drunk!"

"Hell, I'll drink to that!" Maurice said, and when Lawrence passed him the bottle that's exactly what he did.

The pint didn't last too long, enough for just two rounds of glugs and guzzles.

Maurice finished the last sip, then tossed the empty bottle into the tangle of bushes on his right. "You crazy, drunk, high idiots, let's quit BS'ing around and spark up my other joint."

In just over ten minutes, the three homeless friends, sitting atop the creek's crumbling retaining wall in the gloom of early night, had smoked a pretty phat joint and polished off a pint bottle of tequila. They were feeling no pain. This, however, did not stop Maurice from using his BIC to blaze his second joint. The smoking, passing, and sharing resumed at a more leisurely pace.

"Damn," Maurice sighed, caressing his mountainous belly with both arms. "I got the damn munchies."

"Yeah, me too," Champ agreed, patting his stomach.

"No, dudes, hear what I'm sayin', man," Maurice said. "I mean I always got the munchies, but this time I really got the munchies."

"Mo," Lawrence said, "just don't think about it, man . . . *hhssssp*. We gonna get some food later."

"Yeah, right," Champ said. "From where? You hear what I'm saying?"

"Hell," Maurice wailed again, "I'd do anything for a burger and fries."

"Don't say that." Lawrence glared at his homeys. "Don't ever say you'd do anything for anything. Ever."

There was a moment of silence while they each contemplated this advice. Either that or they were still thinking about hamburgers, fries, and tacos.

Champ broke the quiet. "So, real question: like what *would* you homeboys do for a regular place to stay, every day, regular food coming too, man? Like every day?"

"Shit ain't gonna happen," Maurice responded immediately. "So I ain't answering."

"Yeah," Lawrence said. "*Hhssssp* . . . Why you asking, Champ, you ain't asked stuff like that before."

Maurice and Lawrence looked at Champ with their puffy eyes, red and bleary from partying, hunger, and feeling so dang tired.

Champ then explained about Gordon and the school at Laney, the school for homeless kids, dropouts, and fuck-ups. How Champ could get into that school, even have a place to stay, maybe a part-time job. And more than anything: how he could get off the damn street.

His two stoned street buddies thought he was crazy.

"Come on, Champ," Maurice scoffed. "You? Back to school? Think about that, go back to school after all this? Come on, man."

"What," Lawrence added, "you think they gonna hand all that shit over to you for free? *Hhssssp! Sure, sonny, come to school and, hey, live here too, and don't forget your three squares a day—no cost, no payment. Just for you! . . . hhssssp.*"

"Right," Maurice said. "Sounds like prison to me. Don't it sound like prison, homeys?"

"No, it ain't prison," Champ replied. "It's some government program. And why *not* me? I can do it. I wanna do it. I didn't even tell ol' Gordon, but you wanna know what I done? I called that school. I spoke to the head dude! And we met at the school, man. Coach Gelman was cool, man, he told me I could do it!"

"Uh-oh, here we go again," Mo shook his head. "Another homo-erecto freak, lookin' for some Champ-action, yeah? What is it with these old dudes and you, *amigo?*"

"Come on, Maurice," Champ answered, "it ain't like that, you know. Not at all. Dude, Coach Gelman's gonna deal with the details, I just gotta show up there Wednesday morning. He told me that."

"Wednesday morning? At the college? *Hhsssp.* You gotta be totally messed up! You're dreaming, Champ, look at you, dude . . . *hhssssp!* You're a mess! You? In college? Yeah, right. And I'm going to the White House next Monday, meeting with the first lady and the prez! Maybe they gonna fix my teeth too . . . *hhssssp.*"

"Nah, see, I shoulda known," Champ said. "I thought you guys were my homeboys, but you ain't shit. Screw you both! Believe me, man, I'ma take care of my business, ain't living like this no more. Coach Gelman even gave me his card—with his direct number and the day and time I'm meeting with him."

Champ pulled a business card from another do-rag hiding place, holding it up close to his eyes to read it in the evening shadows. "See? Right here: *East Campus, room 324.* Gelman's card, dudes. Says here: *Tom Gelman, Track Coach and Director, Home Place School of Education, Laney Peralta College.* Laugh at me all you want, but that's where I'm going."

With that stalwart declaration, Champion DeLeon Cromarté tapped his tightly closed fist against his heart three times in a solemn promise to himself. He pointed his finger and shook his head contemptuously at the others. *Damn 'em,* he thought, *I'm better than that. I'ma live up to my name—I'ma be the Champion.* And he reached for his special joint—Champ's Champion Joint

Smoke, as Maurice had named it. He pulled a matchbook from his pants pocket, and sparked the reefer between his lips with a big, bright flame. Before he inhaled, his thoughts flashed that this flame signified his own big and bright hopes for the future.

Champ squinted his eyes like Maurice had earlier—high like ching chong—as he sustained a long, drawn-out hit, two, maybe three times longer than any Maurice and Lawrence had taken. The other two watched with amazement and desire burning in their dull-lidded eyes as this monster toke demolished that Champion Joint Smoke. It was the MVP award–winning Champion Doobie Puff of all time! And Maurice and Lawrence held their own breath as their friend utilized years of experienced reefer smoking and overall drug abuse to draw that weed directly into his burnt-out lungs, along with whatever special dust had been added. They watched in ignorant appreciation as the doobage, bartered seemingly ages ago for a pair of used winter boots, quickly disappeared: one-quarter gone, one-third, one-half, two-thirds, then slowly—charred—completely away.

Champ closed his eyes momentarily as the last spark disappeared. The other two saw him relax his shoulders, holding the pungent smoke deep in his lungs for full effect. Suddenly, Champ made a snorting noise with his nose as he felt the hot, thick smoke begin to burn. A wilder snort erupted as a wispy smoke trail escaped a corner of Champ's lips. He raised a finger to block the smoky exodus, but then his eyes flew open wide as, finally, he could hold his breath no longer. He groaned, letting out raspy, heaving coughs as the remaining smoke rushed from his lungs, flying up into the chilly darkness of the night. The dark pupils of Champ's eyes raced wickedly back and forth across the scene—from Maurice to Lawrence, from Lawrence to Maurice—as his coughing fit continued, spewing jagged, painful rasps. And at exactly that moment when Champ simultaneously caught both of his street friends' astonished stares in his own, he fell from the crumbling concrete wall, collapsing to the ground in a heap. Champ thrashed in agony for three counts, his body seizing up in massive, racking convulsions, his breath coming in gagging gasps. And then, in a flash, his body suddenly lay limp and quiet.

The special dust that Raymond Donahue, the sorriest drug dealer in West Oakland, had added to that Champion Joint Smoke was very poorly manufactured fentanyl, the so-called King of All Opiates. The drug, fifty times more powerful than 100 percent pure heroin, may have been king on the streets, but in the cheap and deadly way it had been produced, distributed, and smoked, it was the Killer of Champions.

When the chemical in smoke form had seeped into Champ's lungs and entered his blood system, he'd immediately convulsed and vomited, the puke mixing with his saliva, gushing quickly in reverse down his esophagus, and flooding into his lungs. Champ had begun choking to death instantly. His heart, already vulnerable from years on the street and hundreds of bad choices, couldn't handle the potency. He had suffered a mammoth spasm, then crashed. No time for reflection, no time for regret.

"What the—" Maurice whispered, stunned.

"Holy shit," Lawrence said, barely audible.

Their fallen street bud's body lay on the ground, a few feet away. Maurice and Lawrence slowly got down from their concrete seats, faces masked in dumbfounded, dazed expressions—equal parts weed, booze, and shock. Maurice slowly reached out a toe in a dirty shoe and pushed it into Champ's shoulder. Nothing.

"Shit, he's dead, Lawrence."

"Holy shit," Lawrence repeated.

Maurice reached to pick up his backpack without taking his eyes off the body. He threw the pack over his pork butt–sized shoulder. "I'm blowing Dodge before the cops come," he said. But massive Maurice hesitated, slowly and carefully bending down and pulling off Champ's dirty knit hat and then his do-rag. "I'm taking this," Maurice said, either to Lawrence or to no one. And he rambled off, keeping close to the concrete wall, quickly swallowed up by the dark tangle of overgrown bushes and thick weeds. In a moment, he was gone.

Lawrence stood completely still. Without turning his head, his eyes followed his friend, quickly losing sight of him. Lawrence dropped his gaze to the lifeless body on the dirty cold ground; he realized he had but one choice to make.

He squatted down beside Champ and touched the dead kid's left hand, which still clutched that business card. Lawrence pulled it from Champ's fingers, straightened up, and tucked it in his jacket pocket, all in one motion. With a last furtive glance in the direction Maurice had gone, Lawrence turned and loped off the opposite way, into the darkness, into the cold Oaktown night.

CABBIE

BY JUDY JUANITA

Eastmont

March 21, 2009

T he last day in the life of Lovelle Mixon turned out to be a big holiday in Oakland—the Day of Reparations. Too bad no one knew. Everyone could have prepared, the way they do for Columbus Day or Halloween. Macy's could have sent circulars with 50 percent off. Even the coolie-hatted immigrants recognize holidays as an inappropriate time to dredge for bottles in the recycle bins. Too much clamor for the homeowners in the hills (not so deferential to us in the flatlands). Weekdays they make noise, Sundays they let people sleep. Mystically, they know which holidays to trample on. I call it the commotion-sensibility quotient. For instance, Thanksgiving—they know everyone's too tooted up to be bothered by container-hustlers.

Some newspaper called Mixon a cowboy, but he wasn't. Drug cowboys run weed from Arizona and New Mexico up through California. Lovelle Mixon was a gun runner. Dope dealer is an occupation. Gun runner is a different occupation, but he didn't make it as a dope dealer. He went to UC, the University of Crime, and found there were openings at several levels. Lovelle came out of jail with the ability to make new connections. They told him, *Why you wasting time dealing weed and coke instead of products that move faster and are more profitable?* Like guns, illegal weapons, flesh. The new criminal doesn't have to deal dope. And he's not going to get into gambling, fraud, or cybertheft because he's not trained for it.

I intend to put Lovelle Mixon in my book, the before-and-after-I-started-cabbing book. Of course, it doesn't exist outside of the parameters of my thick skull, packed with these streets. But what a spot it holds there.

New Year's Eve, 2008

My baby brother Terence was broadsided by a hit-and-run as he rounded 66th Avenue and Foothill. Crazy fool didn't even stop, just clipped his Toyota and kept going. Terence's son, my nephew, barely two, was sitting in the backseat, strapped in his car seat. Terence said, "I wouldn't give a damn except that drunk motherfucker in his Humpty Dumpty–looking Benz coulda killed my kid." When State Farm said they wouldn't pay a dime unless he could identify the driver, Terence was so pissed he started a block-by-block search on his off days. Everyone else was carrying on over Oscar Grant getting shot by the BART cop on New Year's Day, except Terence, who was fuming over his car.

It took a few weeks. Right after a Martin Luther King Day celebration, he spotted it on 74th Avenue. Terence said he sat there, angrier by the minute, waiting for the driver to come out. The car, a green Mercedes-Benz G55 AMG, was dented on the right passenger side. Some of the Toyota's maroon paint was on the dent like blush on a woman's cheek. Twenty minutes go by. Terence had to get to work at Kaiser. Nobody came out so he took down the license plate number. As he drove to the corner, he saw through the rearview a burly man come out, get in the car, and pull away. It was the hit-and-run driver. He wanted to confront him, but now he had the license number. He drove back and got the house number too. I know that house, a notorious drug den. I've picked up fares there. *No bueno*—bad actors in and out of that place. I told Terence, "Don't give your info to the insurance people."

But Terence is hardheaded. He yelled at me, "Man, I'm not paying for what some hopped-up junkie did to my car!"

"Listen, lil' bro: you mad, you sad, you all that. But if the police or insurance give him your particulars, his crew will come by your house and do a drive-by. And they ain't gon' be mad or sad, just taking care of biz. No emotion. Just *boom, boom, boom*, blow you and whoever's in your house away. Forget it. End of discussion."

My bro stewed for two months, like a pressure cooker about to blow if the jiggle-top gets popped too soon. He was intent on driving back by that house on 74th Avenue, where he saw the Benz. The day he chose to go there was the Day of Reparations.

March 21, 2009

It was after three p.m. Terence goes to 74th Avenue and runs into a hundred cops, a crazy scene. He told me there was nothing he could do but stand outside his car and watch. I can't believe he didn't hear on the radio about Mixon and the first two cops he shot. But that's Terence—he goes to work listening to jazz, mows his lawn listening to jazz, watches his kids play listening to jazz—he's the most predictable guy in Oakland.

By the time Terence got there, the cops were frantic, all over MacArthur Boulevard. Terence said it looked like nobody was in charge. The cops started going house to house until they knew Mixon was at 2755 74th Avenue—right in the part of Oakland that is under relentless siege by the po-po. Then they zeroed in, like bees to the queen. That black boy was queen for a day. Otherwise known as a clusterfuck. Terence said it was almost like a party and the people in the streets behind the barricades were talking shit, taking bets on when the po-po would go in like stormtroopers. There's no such thing as a standoff in Oakland. We don't have that kind of patience on either side. Either the po-po are gonna let it fly, or the target will. This ain't a TV show like *Law & Order*—this is town biz. Terence said the cops were angry, confused, and frustrated, running back and forth. But the street was not even nervous, not hot or bothered.

Terence had been so worked up over his car. But all that went away, he said. Everybody there—police, onlookers, all of East Oakland—turned like a kaleidoscope. He felt like he'd taken LSD, and Terence doesn't do drugs, not even Novocain at the dentist. But there he was in the middle of hell, with his poker face and the ghosts of Emmet Till, Nat Turner, and Huey Newton all looming larger than billboards. He found himself cheering for the brother, for Lovelle Mixon, for Oaktown, for the convict, for the guy who had murdered a cop, and by the end of the day would take out a total of four.

March 21, 2009, 1:08 p.m.

The first cop that Mixon shot knew him, and knew he was a gun runner. It was a routine traffic stop, but it's unlikely the cops knew his level of desperation. Every cop generally knows, on a first-name basis, the criminals on his beat, and the head criminal knows who's short on the money. They're in it together, this one pays that one, that one pays this one. That's why there are so many street deaths in prison, acts of retribution. I think Mixon was buying time. He wanted to bag up money and weapons, go to LA, and disappear. A great many people in the inner cities have no ID, no SSN—they're nonentities. You think you fingerprinted everybody, but you can't fingerprint the entire population. He probably knew that some of his schemes would lead him back to jail, where he was already a marked man. So that brings up—how did they know precisely where he was and who they had stopped? One of his known refuges was his sister's apartment, where the second battle took place.

Incarceration was not the major problem for Mixon. He was trying to avoid retribution. For an African or Latino man from the hood, incarceration is not the worst thing that can happen. You find friends, associates, and mentors in the prison system. It's just another neighborhood when you're sent to jail, leave one hood and move on to the next. Three squares and a rack on the inside, three squares on the outside. He didn't kill the first two cops because he was afraid to go to jail, he had decided to affect his own retribution. Understanding the end was near, he did not want to depart this world alone. He knew those cops had been sent by his superiors; he was just a pawn in the game now, traded off for something else. How many pimps are killed so that someone can acquire their hos? In the arms trade, how many runners are killed so that someone can acquire their guns?

In the Warsaw ghetto, how many Jewish husbands were turned in so the snitches could take their wives? It's an old story, been going on for hundreds, thousands of years. Squeal on somebody so you can get their land. Mixon's death was part of an old script, not such an individual thing as people thought. The things that didn't add up, though, are *Who did he know?* and *When did he know them?*

March 21, 2009

For people whose Saturdays start at four a.m., like mine, that Saturday was a day like any other in Oaktown. Weekend commuters tunneled north and south beneath the stretch of earth called Richmond–El Cerrito–Albany-Berkeley-Oakland–San Leandro–Hayward-Fremont before going into the long, submerged BART tunnel in San Francisco Bay. At intervals, the snake pops up and offers a tour through the backside of Oakland and its lower bowel, East Oakland, from which those looking east can glimpse the Mediterranean hillside that runs for eighty miles. Tourists making their way to the airports pass under downtown Oakland, speaking in German, French, or Japanese about the wine country, the mud baths, and the crooked street in San Francisco which they navigated in rental cars, with pedals on the left instead of the right. But if they see East Oakland, it's because of Ron Dellums—or in spite of Ron Dellums. As a young Berkeley councilman, Dellums argued for putting BART underground so the residents of his lovely town wouldn't have to see the snake crawling through it. So here's some cabbie wisdom for you: past, present, and future all exist in the same moment. Berkeley got BART underground, every other place got it aboveground, and my man Ron ended up the mayor of Oakland. Folks like to knock the boss, I don't care if they're white, black, or Mexican. *That Dellums, he's asleep at the wheel.* Folks, Jerry Brown had already sold off downtown Oakland. He said he would get it built up like Rio de Janeiro, tall buildings downtown, flatlands the same. Nothing left for Dellums to do. End of discussion.

People say Lovelle Mixon's going to hell because he killed four people. Hell must be a helluva place. There's death on practically everybody's hands, one way or another. The police chief of Seattle said recently that soldiers follow orders, police officers make decisions, and police officers are not soldiers. Something happened when the police heard that the first two cops had been gunned down that Saturday. That's when the clusterfuck started. That same police chief said we're a nation of 300 million guns. When they put on the Kevlar vests, you knew the SWAT teams were about to come in the DMZ. The police stopped being police and turned into soldiers. But who was giving them orders?

The po-po, cabbies, neighbors—they all knew 2755 74th Avenue. Notoriously, a woman was found strangled with her own drapery cord. Police knew it was her ex, but they classified it as suicide. I never heard of suicide by drapery cord. I rode her around a lot. She could buy out a dollar store with a twenty and still have cab fare left over. She didn't take her own life. Murder, yes. Suicide, no. But the po-po say what's convenient and let the badasses roam wild.

Here's a parable: I call it the Parable of the Two Brothers, both dead now. Before Brother #2 died, having been a drug dealer, user, convict, hustler, parolee, he went around in his last days to see his kids, grands, and say goodbye. Even went to his social worker, caught up to her on his old stomping grounds, heard her telling a user, "If you can, stop using between tests and not just the day of the tests." Brother #2 told her, "Scolding won't work. Give him something he can't get out here." She didn't know what that could be. Brother #2 said, "You can't give money, or drugs, or women. Give him praise. That's what you gave me."

Brother #1 was dying, same period. Drugs, they shorten your lifespan, don't matter if you're a rock star or a hustler. Brother #1 hustled me out of three hundred dollars twenty years ago, so you could say I'm biased. But in his last days—he had AIDS—he kept travelling to Africa, back and forth, back and forth. Word is he had women over there under his ladies' man spell. I didn't buy that. It's just that AIDS is so out of control there that he didn't face a stigma.

Brother #1 and Brother #2, different paths to the grave, one got more wisdom than the other, but he had done more dirt on the whole. They went the same, six feet under. Which one's going to the crowded place?

March 27, 2009

Here's the definition of awesome. Twenty thousand police and citizens converging in Oaktown for the funeral of those four dead cops. They came from all over the country. Even the Royal Canadian Mounted Police. And all 815 OPD attended, according to the *Chronicle*. So who was minding the shop? Fifteen law enforcement agencies from Alameda County, CHP's, and local police departments. Bagpipes, a twenty-one-gun salute from a military cannon, and of course a couple dozen helicopters buzzing overhead, more than the usual four circling the hood. Ah, man, and the OPD told Dellums, *Shut your black mouth and sit your black ass down.* They wouldn't let him speak. *If we have to let you be here, then be unheard.* Word is that the mayor had mispronounced the officers' names at a previous memorial. The PBA didn't want that again.

Yeah, a likely story. Remember lynching, back in the day? Crackers went for the black middle class, the shopkeepers, the folks who were coming up in the world. Envy, pure and simple, it's human. But what you do with it is the right or the wrong. One week before 9/11, Colin Powell was at an international conference on racism in South Africa. He said the US wasn't about to apologize for slavery if that apology involved reparations, and the United States delegation got up and walked out, in front of the whole world. What a meathead.

New Year's Eve, 2010

I dropped my last fare of the day downtown and stopped at the Bank of America near Lake Merritt at two thirty p.m. Later that night the bank showed up on the TV news. It was the scene of the last homicide of the year—at three twenty p.m. That meant I had dodged a bullet by forty minutes. Witnesses said two Latino males and two African American males had a parking lot altercation. The Latino used an ethnic slur, and one of the black guys pulled out a gun and shot him. The two blacks drove off. Bruno, who was from Brazil and delivered pizza, for God's sake, died on the spot.

May 5, 2013

I drove a white Lovelle Mixon home one night from the Oakland Arena. Rolling Stones concert. You could hear Mick all the way to the BART station. I went to pick up this white kid, twenty-two or twenty-three, high as I don't know what. Gets in my cab and my dispatcher says, "Take him to Sebastopol"— that's a four-hundred-dollar ride. His father called in the fare. This kid is high out of his mind, all the way up there, and it's in the middle of nowhere. But we get about a mile from his house and he sobers up enough to give me clear directions. The kid stumbles out, the father pays me double fare, and then he pulls out two more hundred-dollar bills. And thanks me for my troubles. White, black, same stupid kids, different outcomes.

The guy that's teaching me dispatching says I'll never be unemployed, right up to the end of my life, because there's always a need for good cab dispatchers. I know, though, that dispatchers don't have to see what cabbies see. Nevertheless, I like security as much as the next guy. I've seen enough to last me.

TWO TO TANGO

BY JAMIE DEWOLF

Oakland Hills

Love is a straitjacket you're waiting for someone else to tighten.

Oakland, 2004: I'm fresh out of the ground zero of a break-up with apologies stitched vertically on my left wrist. I move out of my ex-girlfriend's house before she gets evicted; just another waiter with a misanthropic streak and cheap tattoos he buys with tips. I'm saving up by sleeping on any couch I can beg for, or any bed I can charm my way into. I'm homeless, living out of my backpack, hopping couches and BART stations. I have an appetite for destruction that wants dessert.

The night I meet her is a slow night at Van Kleef's on Telegraph, and the saxophone player is six drinks in, slurring blues to the empty street. I'm writing poems on bar napkins but the ink keeps bleeding through with whiskey. I can't afford a psychiatrist, but Jameson picks up the slack. The future is laid out in front of me like a railroad track I tied myself to. I have no idea what's gonna fix anything, besides a deposit, two months rent, and anything that will make me forget today.

And in walks my future—Bettie Page in combat boots, damage in a dress. I smell her perfume before I see her, cinnamon mixed with cigarettes. She takes the empty stool next to mine. She doesn't look like the other girls in the bar, with their thrift-store fashion sense and flower prints to complement the pretty umbrellas in their drinks. This girl has eyes dark as a black hole, lips red as an opening curtain.

She orders a whiskey neat, but a meathead stumbles into her, spilling her drink. She turns with her fists out, but he's already moved too far past the sucker punch that had his name on it. She meets my eyes straight on and apologizes for the spill. I tell her it's all right, she asks what I'm writing. I hold up the ink-blurred napkin—it's my autobiography drenched in whiskey. Art imitates life.

She asks about the scorpion tattoo on my arm. I tell her poison should always be labeled. She's a Scorpio herself, tells me her name is Syd, short for something she doesn't want to tell me. She was just in the neighborhood, back home from a year alone in the mountains. She takes kickboxing classes and is working on a photography portfolio. She asks if I want the next round here or in a mansion alone with her. Easy question.

Fifteen minutes later we're driving up in the Oakland Hills and she pulls up to a house at the top, buzzes open the gate, and I'm walking up the plush staircase past seascape paintings. Daddy's liquor cabinet has got Scotch an Irishman can't pronounce and sherry glasses. She pours us a Cognac, takes me to the basement, shows me her portfolio. Every picture is a self-portrait on a timer where she's standing naked on a box with the words *Whore* and *Slut* scrawled across her in lipstick. She says this is how the world sees her, as if the Scarlet Letter was an entire alphabet written across her flesh.

She holds up the largest print, a photograph of her blindfolded in front of a mirror. She says this is how she sees herself. She says she loves how photographs take weeks to finish, like watching a scar heal.

In the living room, I toast to the ashes of the past. She says, "We can be as loud as you want," and smashes her glass against the wall. It shatters across the living room, then she grabs my hand, puts it around her throat, and tells me: "You won't break me. But I want you to try."

She kisses me like anger is an aphrodisiac. We hit her carpet, our bones crashing into each other like a wet car wreck. After, she blows smoke rings at the ceiling, says, "You can stay here, you know. This house is too big for me and I can't stand it alone at night."

I was the right blend of poverty and horny. When you're drowning, a partner can make you feel like you're swimming instead.

The next night she cooks me a blood-rare steak, cracks open a bottle of champagne. A week later we've drunk half the liquor cabinet. We toss the empty bottles out of the third-story windows into the pool. We live every night like we broke in.

Every evening starts to get more physical. She shows me how she trains at her gym, swinging fists into my hand in combinations. Then she wants to wrestle and throw me against the wall. Syd rakes nails across my back until it bleeds, scratches her name into my chest until I can still read it the next day. We hit the walls so hard paintings fall. She wants a knife to her throat, she wants me to say things to her I'd never repeat. She wants me to love her like I want to kill her.

Self-destruction is lonely; she's made it into a duet.

One night we lie there after and her hands trace my rib cage. She traces where she'd cut out my heart and keep it with her. I tell her this is moving a little fast. She says restraint is for hospitals and cops—don't hold myself back.

I need a breath, a break. I tell her I gotta work double shifts for three days, and I don't have a cell phone yet so I don't have to worry about ignoring her calls. My friends haven't heard from me in weeks. A buddy asks me why I keep picking poison. I tell him it's because I learned to love the taste. I need to try something else.

I go on a date with a librarian, a quiet girl who wants to discuss Dostoevsky and Dickinson. She paints in watercolors, writes poems about trees, about weeping willows. We go to a café; she wants to kiss over a cup of tea. I see a life of yoga in the mornings, of easy nights reading in bed.

But I tell you, I was still hungry for the girl in the mansion who could make every night feel like my last one on earth. I kiss the librarian goodbye, tell her I have to go. I catch the BART to Oakland and Miss Matte Black is waiting at Van Kleef's, smoking and smiling as I walk in.

"I knew you weren't going anywhere but back to me." She grabs my leg and says, "Just don't do it again."

Three rounds later and I'm back at her house, she's pouring champagne down my chest. It feels like back to high times again until she breaks a wineglass and begs me to cut my name in her chest, brand her, make my words become flesh. She tells me the flesh is weak, but love is permanent. This isn't love, this is a tango that's turned into a mosh pit. The deeper we go, the harder it's going to be to find the surface.

This time I vanish for a week, go back to waiting tables, and then the hostess tells me I have a new table in my section.

There she is, smiling, with a bandage on her arm. She unwraps it; a scorpion tattoo exactly like mine.

"I had to draw it out from memory but it's pretty close, isn't it?" She holds it next to my arm. "See? Now we're a reflection of each other. You said poison should always be labeled."

I tell her I'm not going to Oakland tonight. She says, "Don't worry, I got us a hotel room. There's a champagne bucket waiting for you." She puts a bag on the table. "Open it."

Inside is a pair of handcuffs. She says, "Come commit some crimes with me and when we're done, you can arrest me."

What kind of crimes?

She says that'd be premeditation. "It's nothing you haven't done before."

I'm thinking, *I haven't even told you what I've done.*

If she's my reflection, then I wonder what I'm afraid to see. I ask her again what kind of crimes, but she says it'll ruin the surprise.

She's quiet on the ride there. We pull up outside a café, she turns the car off and points inside. "Now you can stop a crime about to happen."

I look through the café window—the librarian girl I kissed a week ago is sitting at a table, sipping tea. "What the fuck is this?"

Her eyes flash. "You can stop a beating if you want to."

"What are you talking about?"

"Well, it's simple: you could have stopped this girl from a beating if you didn't kiss her last week. But you did, and now here we are."

"You *watched* me? When?"

"It was by a window, you know. You weren't exactly being sneaky about it."

"You drove here from Oakland? You were fucking *stalking* me?"

"I missed you, that's all, and you didn't want to see me. And you didn't see me. But I saw *you*. And her." Her fists clench on the steering wheel.

"You're just gonna walk in there and attack her? In the café? In front of everyone?"

"Unless you stop me. Just tell me you love me and you don't love her. And you'll stop a crime."

I stare at her. "Tell you I love you. And then we'll leave?"

"And then we'll leave."

I tell her I love her. I lie. Her fists come off the steering wheel.

I'm in a game I don't know the rules of anymore. She drives away from the café, the librarian vanishing in the rearview. We're back at the hotel, champagne in an ice bucket. She throws the handcuffs on the bed and says, "Good job, officer. Throw the book at me."

I realize we're alone in this room. No one knows where I am.

I open the champagne instead, start chugging until it froths down my shirt. Someone could die in here. She gives me that smile again over her shoulder. I feel sick. She's a spider in skin.

She tells me that anyone can learn to love anyone, it just takes time. Then she tells me my time is running out. I pour the rest of the champagne on the floor and hold the bottle by the neck. I tell her, "I'm walking out of this room, and don't follow me. Don't show up at my work again."

She doesn't stop smiling but her eyes are blinking at a weird rhythm. Like a TV starting to fritz. "You'll come back."

I don't see her for a month and I can't believe I still miss her. I miss the champagne, the pornographic prologue turning into a horror film.

A month later, she walks into my birthday party, says she was just in the neighborhood, didn't even know it was my birthday. She sits in the back corner while I'm going round for round with my friends.

She moves closer, joining conversations, buying me drinks. After the fifth round her hand slides up my leg and I don't stop it. It's closing time, my friends are offering me a couch to crash on, but she whispers in my ear, says a birthday boy should stay in a bed.

No, I'm done with that madness.

She says just for old time's sake. I tell her no.

"Okay then, I'm sorry. How about a ride to your friend's house at least?"

I slam back the last of my drink. "All right. It's a ten-minute ride—but nothing more than that."

"Nothing more than that."

As soon as the doors lock to her BMW, I know I've made a mistake. But she's got child locks, and I didn't think of that. Thirty seconds later she's driving 45 mph down a 25 mph street and has a slur in her voice I didn't notice before—maybe I didn't let her talk long enough, maybe I didn't ask the right questions.

But then her voice gets real cold and quiet.

"Anybody can learn to love someone, it only takes time." She's not even looking at the road, just at me. I tell her to slow down. We hit a speed bump so hard my head smashes against the ceiling. She's listing off the reasons why if I knew myself, I would know I was in love with her. I would love to debate this paradox of me not knowing what I should know, but all I hear is the gas revving, horns blaring. I realize I'm going to have to jump out of a moving car. Every action movie I've ever seen is replaying in my head, like how the hell to roll once you hit the ground.

She blasts through a traffic light like it just wasn't red enough.

"Slow down," I plead.

She's says, "What, am I taking it too fast for you? You want me to slow down? Tell me you love me!"

A man pushing a shopping cart leaps out of the head-lights.

She doesn't even notice. A three-way intersection is coming up fast ahead of us.

"Tell me you love me!" Syd screams.

"I love you, all right? Stop the car!"

"Love doesn't stop."

I watch a stoplight fly past above us. I put my forearms out in front of me.

We smash headlong into a sedan that goes spinning into the crosswalk, glass shattering across the street. There's the sickening screech of metal grinding, the windshield cracking in pieces, the hood crunching into a twisted mess, then just broken glass twinkling down to the asphalt. I sit heaving for a second, hands on my face, moving my toes in my boots. Everything is spinning. My forearms are wet with the spit that flew out of my mouth on impact.

The other car is twenty feet away, spun out on a crazy axis. A black woman is at the wheel, holding her head, checking herself for damage. I turn to Syd. There's blood trickling down her forehead.

"I knew it. I knew you loved me."

I slowly unclasp my seat belt. Metal scrapes and glass falls into the street from across the intersection.

"What happens now?" she asks me.

"What happens now? There aren't many choices here. What happens now is the cops come, you get a DUI, and you go to jail. Or you can try to run, but that woman you just hit doesn't look like she's gonna let you get too far."

The other woman is outside in shock at the wrecked metal of her sedan.

"No, what happens now between *us?*"

I want to wipe the blood off her forehead but I'm afraid to touch her. Now the other woman is outside Syd's window. She has her phone in her hand. There's a fight about to go down in the street. I know well enough how hard Syd can hit, but I don't think she would win this one—the other woman is yelling already: "Are you crazy, woman? Girl, what the hell you doing? Get out the car!"

Syd undoes her seat belt and unlocks the child lock. I get out, making sure my ankle isn't broken. One of the headlights is busted. Syd steps out on wobbly high heels. The woman in the smashed car is livid.

"Bitch, is you drunk? You better have insurance, bitch!"

Syd isn't even looking at the woman, she's got her eyes locked on me. "I knew you loved me. I always knew it." Sirens are approaching from a few blocks away. "Help me."

I can't. I back up slowly as blue and red lights come around the corner. I'm fading into the shadows past the streetlight. I walk ten blocks, turn, and circle around, long enough to see Syd in handcuffs in the backseat of the cop car.

She leaves me a message from jail that morning, tells me she loves me, says her parents are flying back. She leaves another message the day she gets out. I stay away from the old bars. I don't go to Van Kleef's for a year—the game is over.

It's ten years and three girlfriends later. I've been paying rent on a house at 53rd and San Pablo for a decade. A friend gives me a free pass to a yoga class. I usually train at a kickboxing gym but I blew out my knee during a sparring match so want to try an easier route. I'm stretching out my tattoos and scars on a mat, enduring the slow meditative music, ready to sweat out years of toxins. The clock hits eight p.m. and the instructor walks in.

It's Syd, now impossibly toned and tanned, her hair cut short. She's wearing all black. Our eyes lock. That smile comes across her face. She looks away, starts the class. I can see the scorpion tattoo faded on her arm. I follow her instructions up to the point where she asks everyone to close their eyes for deep breaths—I keep mine open and she stares at me in silence. The class ends, everyone rolls up their mats. I'm ten feet out the door when I hear her say my name. She's standing there with her keys.

"Want a ride?"

I take a deep breath.

She smiles. "Nothing more than that." She points at her car. It's a station wagon with two child seats in the back, and she holds up her wedding ring. "Just kidding, there's no room."

I laugh. "Yeah, I live nearby anyways."

"You still writing suicide notes on napkins?"

"No. Now it's to-do lists."

"It's all a choose-your-own-adventure. I hope you get the ending you want." She points at her tattoo. "Poison's always labeled."

I tell her I'm sorry; she was right. We were reflections of each other, and I've learned I can't look away anymore.

"We were young. We just weren't the right antidote for each other."

She clicks her car open and I keep walking. I don't look back as her headlights pull away behind me, just another car going the opposite direction.

PART III

A View of the Lake

SURVIVORS OF HEARTACHE

BY NAYOMI MUNAWEERA

Montclair

I moved to Montclair in 2014. I was going through a divorce that had me gutted like a fish. Three years before I had married an artist. He was from Sri Lanka too, and finding him in San Francisco where I had not met another Lankan in years had felt like coming home. I had believed him when he said I was the only one who could save him from the demons: six ecstasy tabs on his thirtieth birthday, sex without a condom in the seediest parts of San Francisco after openings, and the like. He had been deadly depressed and courting death, he said, but then I had arrived like a princess in a flowing white dress and wrestled his life back from the dark. I had loved the idea of myself as savior, and then muse, and therefore I had believed him.

We had a large and expensive wedding in the fanciest hotel in Colombo. Then we returned to San Francisco, and for two years we built a life in the foggy city. At first he sketched me endlessly. I looked at the drawings and laughed, "I'm not this beautiful," and he said, "To me you are." He had rendered me perfect—the arch of my brows, the curve of my cheekbones, the angles on my hips far lovelier than the reality. A year later there were fewer drawings. When I snuck a look at his sketchbooks toward the end, I found myself a pendulum-breasted, hook-nosed hag.

That was around the time he realized I wasn't his muse at

all. The real angel of his salvation was a blond twenty-four-year-old nude model. After this revelation, we resided in hell. He didn't know if he loved her enough to leave me; I didn't know what to do with my life without him. One terrible midnight I held onto his ankles and sobbed, begging him not to go. The humiliation of this memory still scratches at my skin. Despite everything that happened, this is the only regret that lingers from that grotesque time.

What saved me? A few different things. Friends, of course. And a soft landing across the bay in a town called Montclair. When it was clear that the divorce was imminent, I tried to understand how to begin life anew. I couldn't stand the apartment that had been the witness of my humiliation. I would leave it to him and therefore I needed a place to live. Friends said, *Come to Oakland, it's better here, the rents are cheaper, the people more diverse.*

Oakland? I thought. *The murder capital of America?* I had lived in San Francisco for a decade and grown up in Florida before that. Oakland was just a few miles away, over the bridge flung across the glittering bay, but I had barely ever been there. There were guns all over the streets, people said. Young black kids were getting shot by racist cops all the time, we heard. From the soft, hilly embrace of San Francisco, Oakland sounded like a war zone.

My friend Chloe had lived in the Oakland Hills for more than a decade. Her house was impossible to get to without a car so I had never visited her. Instead, in the years of our friendship, she had always come to me, and every time I had opened the door of our San Francisco apartment to her, she stood there in shorts, a T-shirt, and sandals. I'd let her in and she'd say through chattering teeth, "It's warm and sunny in Oakland right now, you know." I didn't really believe her. How was it possible that just miles away the sun was blazing?

Now, in the midst of my divorce ravages, she invited me to rent a room in the house where she lived. A roommate was moving out so it was perfect timing. She said, "You'll love Oakland. Anyway, you won't find a place you can afford in the city anymore." She was right. I dragged my heartbroken self from open house to open house, but during the three years of my marriage, rents had skyrocketed. Tiny apartments with no light and moldy bathrooms were going for exorbitant prices; people lined up to fill every available vacancy; landlords could afford to be assholes.

The first time I drove to her house, across the bridge and into the hills, the sun burst through the fog and the temperature rose. I felt ridiculous in my jeans and thick sweatshirt as a misty sweat broke on my skin. I followed Chloe's directions, winding higher and higher, thinking, *What the hell is this place?* The roads got narrower and snakelike, the foliage got thicker, there were hundreds of flowering plants. I glimpsed the bone white of eucalyptus, caught the scent of pine through the window. The trees were different, of course, but the place reminded me of nothing more than the upcountry of Sri Lanka. There was the same sense of driving precariously into the sky, of entering a place both magical and mystical.

There were houses set right on the cliff's edges, and between them I caught slivers of the sea and the Bay Bridge. Even farther away the Golden Gate stretched into Marin. The city nestled between the bridges with a blanket of fog settling into its crevices. I drove past the address Chloe had given me, parked on a sharply steep climb, and walked back along the tree-fringed road to the house. She threw open the door and said, "Welcome to Montclair."

Just like that I found myself in a new life. I lived in a room with red walls. Originally I had thought I'd repaint it a hue less intense, less womblike, but soon it felt like exactly what I needed to birth a new life. I had very little: a mattress on the floor, some clothing, and books on anatomy. This was everything I had salvaged from the shipwreck of my marriage.

I saw them from the window first—two little girls in the lavish backyard of the house next door. Around six and eight, though I don't know much about kids and am terrible at estimating ages, so they could have been older or younger. Of course, later I would come to know everything about them, but at that time they were just two normal kids.

They were running around with their dog, a great fluffy white thing. They were blond, playing Marco Polo. The older girl was blindfolded, she reached her arms out, thin pale arms like the eucalyptus branches above, and stumbled forward blindly feeling for her sister who slipped just out of her grasp. The leaves crunched under their sneakers. I watched for a while. It was a lovely tableau of childhood joy. I felt a pricking under my skin, a terrible and fierce longing. Then I turned away and went back into my new life.

The house we lived in had five bedrooms. There were four of us—Chloe, Shahid, Dina, and me. Chloe had "inherited" it from a friend who had moved to Zimbabwe, gotten married, and settled there. The friend didn't care that she could rent out the house for four times the price we paid. She didn't want to bother with locating renters, and this is how we found ourselves able to afford a house in a neighborhood where Governor Jerry Brown lived a few streets away. We were the odd house out—a collection of ragtag, single people of color in a neighborhood of predominately rich white families.

One day at breakfast Chloe asked, "You've seen the neighbor kids? The dad's name is Michael, he's some kind of computer genius. Have you met the wife? She's like a Romanian Marilyn Monroe."

I didn't tell her that I saw them often. Through a sliver of curtain I could watch the two children, the beautiful wife, and the computer genius. With the intimacy of people who have not met but who live in silent proximity, I knew which car belonged to him, which to her, the times they came and left, who picked up the kids on which days. I watched them in the summer months, him serving breakfast, her in wraparound glasses, the kids and dogs gamboling about.

It was some months later that we first noticed trouble. There were noises from next door; sometimes it sounded like shouting, sometimes screaming, sometimes his or her car would screech away down the hill. The kids barely came out anymore and when I did see them, they were pinched looking, as if what little color they had had drained away. They didn't chase each other, didn't play Marco Polo, they just sat on the bench and whispered to each other as if hatching plans, plotting. Sometimes they looked up and I could swear they were staring straight at me. I pulled away from the window, my heart thumping.

Then the dog started barking. At first it lasted only a short time and we were able to ignore it. But one night it went on and on, until the sound penetrated the very walls and ricocheted all around us. It felt like we were trapped in a cage of noise. At times the animal screams would stop and silence would fall, thick and welcome. But just when we had sighed and turned over in our beds, the agonizing noise would resume. At midnight, after the dog had been barking for three straight hours, we gathered in the living room.

"What should we do?"

"I called them. No one picked up," Chloe informed us.

Shahid said, "What the hell? I have to go to work in the morning."

"Let's put a note on their door," I suggested.

I wrote, *Your dog has been barking since 9 p.m. None of us can sleep. Please make it stop. Your neighbors at 482*, and offered to put it on the door. And then, in my sweats, armed with the note and bit of sticky tape, I walked out. It was November again. A year had passed since I'd moved in. The air was sharp, the trees dark and crowding overhead, the dog's anguished voice filling the night.

I pulled my hoodie over my head and walked onto the street. Their door was down steps, shrouded, and no automatic light snapped on, so I was guided not by sight but by my feet on the steps, my hand on the railing. I felt my way to the door, my palms made contact, and with a sigh of relief I reached for the knob. Then there was a different, subtler sound. I spun on my heel and saw a figure towering at the top of the steps and coming quickly toward me. My blood screamed; in a quavering voice I said, "Hello?"

It was the wife, I realized in relief. But then her voice rose: "Who is it? Who's there? I can see you! Stand right there or I'll call the police." A light shone straight into my eyes. "Fucking kids, you people come up from Oakland and think you can just break into our houses. I'm calling the police!"

"No! No, I'm your neighbor. Your dog was barking. I just came to tell you."

A fumbling with her phone. "What?"

"I'm just your neighbor. Your dog was barking. Look, here's my note!" I thrust it forth like a guilty school kid caught in the hall after classes have started.

She shone the light at it, said, "Oh . . . okay. I see . . . There have been so many break-ins recently. I thought . . ." Her eyes were still suspicious as they took in my skin, my black hoodie.

* * *

Thanksgiving arrived, the first one after my divorce. Chloe and Dina had both invited me to their family meals, but I said that I wanted to spend the day watching Netflix. It was only after they left that I realized I was terribly, awfully lonely. The house was empty, and my room felt claustrophobic, so I fled into the living room, which was cold, though I didn't want to put on the heater because our bill was already too high. Then the doorbell rang, and somehow I knew it was Michael before he even introduced himself. He was taller than I had thought. He wore a red plaid shirt and was even more handsome up close.

"We saw your car in the drive, and we wanted to say sorry. For the dog. Will you come to dinner? It'll just be Galina, the kids, and me."

I saw then that as much as I knew their comings and goings, they too knew which of our cars was which and that I was alone on Thanksgiving. I nodded. "I'll come. Thank you."

I went at six, carrying the fanciest bottle of wine I could find in the house. Galina opened the door, smelling of jasmine and musk. When she leaned in close to pat me on the back, I inhaled deeply. She said, "Welcome to our home," and swept me into the dining room. The floor plan was similar to ours, but this house was much bigger. While we had bits of furniture salvaged from thrift stores, things left behind by an endless succession of roommates, theirs was all luxury, light, and warmth. A fire danced. The entire back wall was huge windows opening onto the lovely garden and the woods beyond, past which was a glorious view of the bay. The children sat at the dining room table like stiff little adults. They seemed even more pale and thin than the last time I'd seen them. Their eyes recognized me, followed me.

Michael came in and said, "Ah, the conscientious neighbor." He swept an arm toward the window, "Look. We have fixed the problem."

I went to the glass. In the yard the dog circled and pawed at leaves. It opened its mouth and I got ready for the incessant cacophony. Instead it flinched and went mute, and I realized that its collar was shocking it. The muscles in my throat constricted. It had only wanted to express its primal loneliness and they had taken away its voice. Surely there was some more humane solution?

As if reading my thoughts, Michael said, "It was the *only* way. He was stubborn, and he refused to be trained." I felt a flush of shame. Was it my fault that they had silenced the creature? Meanwhile, a blessed quietness fell around us. Michael said, "Enough of that, come. Galina has prepared a feast."

We sat. Galina brought in the turkey. It was delicious and opulent, and everything was overwhelming. Later, when the turkey had been reduced to a cave of bones and the children had been dismissed, Galina sipped wine as dark as a gorgon's blood. She looked at me and said, "Have you seen the wild turkeys that roost in the woods?"

I nodded.

"Beautiful, aren't they? Big and ungainly but also beautiful. Prehistoric. You watch them and you know what the dinosaurs looked like. It seems such a strange thing to appreciate their beauty and then eat them."

I said nothing.

"Living here, it's like living in the midst of paradise. In the summertime we had the doors open and two fawns wandered in." I must have given her a look of disbelief because she said, "No, really! The children were thrilled and we stayed quiet as they trotted all around the house. They must have been searching for water because it's been such a dry year. But they came into the house so easily, as if they were curious. As if they wanted to know how the humans lived. They were like creatures out of the fairy tales I grew up with. They walked all around this room." She spread her hands wide. "And then their mother was at the door and made this noise and they ran out. Their hoofs left marks but I had them erased."

I asked, "How long have you lived here?"

"Fifteen years," Michael replied.

Galina tapped her bloodred nails against the crystal of her wineglass. "Back then this was a safe neighborhood. Now there are all sorts of criminal elements coming up the hill—poor people, black people. They can't find work so they resort to crime. The house at the end of the road got broken into last month. That's why I was so upset when I thought you were one of them."

She didn't apologize. She was not a woman used to apologizing.

I brushed it away. I was as curious as a cat about them so I asked how they had met.

He said, "That's a funny story," and pulled her to him, kissing the side of her luminous face. She made the tiniest movement then, so subtle that he missed it. But I recognized it. It was how my husband used to move, ever so slightly, away from my kiss. I hadn't thought about it for months but now a hairline crack reopened on the surface of my mending heart.

"I wanted to marry. I was ready. So I went to Romania looking for a wife."

She said, "He wanted a mail-order bride."

"Really?"

"Why not? I was sick of meeting women here and having it go nowhere. I knew what I wanted, and I knew where to get it. Dating in America is a terrible thing."

I turned to her. "And you . . . were the mail-order bride?"

"No! I was the interpreter."

"I took one look at her and here we are," Michael finished the story.

I stayed late as they got drunker and drunker. She sat on his lap and they kissed as if I was not there. Then I too, like the children, was dismissed. I walked the short distance to my own door, went into my red room, and shivered all night on my mattress. I was alone, abandoned, unloved. It was the worst night since my husband had told me we were finished.

I got close to them after that. They needed someone to watch the kids and I was right next door. What could be easier? They had this idea that the girls were attached to me. I bought them toys, courted them in the way you are supposed to do with children, and they—used to a succession of brown-skinned nannies, Costa Ricans, Guatemalans, Mexicans—did not complain. I had lost my job some time before and was glad of the money they tossed my way.

I watched the girls while they played in the garden and at the park. We went for walks in the woods with the dog. There were trails everywhere. Huckleberry Trail, Redwood Regional, and Tilden Park were close. One could walk for miles and not run into a soul. Once the dog led us, panting, straight to the carcass of a stag. It lay at the edge of a cliff on its side, its antlers tangled in the undergrowth, its hoofs pointed at us. Its stomach had been slit and there were organs strewn in a jumble next to it, a bloated mint-green sack, dark viscous puddles of blood.

The children squatted, their eyes large. "What did this?" they asked me. Something big, I thought, something voracious. We looked at it for a while. Then they got bored and wanted to leave, and I walked after them.

In all that time, the kids kept getting thinner, paler. No one could understand it. They ate at mealtimes, their mother hovering over them, cooking their favorite foods, begging them to take just one more bite. But however hard she tried, the girls did not thrive. She watched them like a hawk, she said. They did not throw up, they did not purge, and yet the shadows loomed large under their eyes, their limbs got more sticklike. It was uncanny.

It was months later that I came upon Michael in his study. The girls were in their bedrooms putting away toys. I had heard his car arrive and went looking for him. His hair was bedraggled, and when he saw me he waved me into a seat and said, "I need to talk to you." I sat. He paced up and down the room behind his desk, running his fingers through his hair. I kept silent until finally he spoke: "I don't know how to say this . . . Have you ever . . . seen Galina do anything to the kids?"

I was shocked. "What?"

"They get sick all the time. I think it's Galina. I think she's sick in the head, I think she's hurting them."

"Why would you think that? And no, I've never seen her be anything but good to them."

"I don't know what to think. We've taken them to every doctor, done every test. But you see how they are? The doctor asked me if it might be her. He said sometimes mothers . . ." He paced some more. "But why else would they look like that, like little ghosts?"

Then he sat at his desk, leaned his head back on the leather, and I watched as tears ran out of the corners of his eyes and along the planes of his face. When he spoke again his voice was broken: "She's fucking someone else. I know it."

He put his head on his arms and sobbed in great, painful

gulps. It was startling to see a man express pain in this way, but I knew exactly how he felt. There is no dagger more cold than betrayal. There is no wound more terrible than the thought of your lover with their lover. The idea of their two bodies together takes over, becomes the entire pulsing world.

It got worse after that. They had screaming matches; they threw things. They sobbed and hurled accusations. Some of it happened in my presence because by then I had become indispensible. I'll spare you the details—everyone has gone through heartache, everyone knows what the end looks and sounds like.

In December I needed a break so I went to my parents' place in Florida for some weeks. My folks were happy to see me. We hadn't been together since my wedding in Colombo, and we had a pleasant and uneventful visit. When I got back to Montclair and went next door, she was gone.

"Where's Galina?" I asked.

"She's left me. She's gone back to Romania," he replied.

"Really?"

"Yes, really."

"What about the children?" I asked, because that's what you are supposed to say in these sad circumstances.

"They're with my mother in Houston. They'll be okay."

I looked into his handsome face and said, "I went through a divorce. At first you think it's the worst thing in the world, but it really isn't. It might even be the best thing."

"You know, you might just be right." He smiled then, and I felt the hairline crack in my heart begin to knit itself together.

There was an investigation, of course. You can't lose a rich white woman in America and not have an investigation. They suspected Michael. There was a trial, and it took a long time, but he had expensive lawyers and finally they cleared his name. There was no body and you can almost never convict without a body, so I knew it would be okay.

I see Chloe, Shahid, and Dina every now and then, but I don't really talk to them. My life is different now. We don't have anything in common anymore, so what would we even speak about? The girls live with their grandmother in Houston. It's a more stable environment for them. She says they're putting on weight, the shadows under their eyes have receded. They are normal kids now. I'm so glad. I never had anything against those girls.

It was easier than the first time. My husband's lover had been young and fierce. She had fought me until I managed to stick the needle into her neck and push the plunger. Did I forget to tell you what my job was? The one I lost in the midst of that terrible year? I was a nurse. At San Francisco General, where the motto was, *As Real As It Gets*. The things I saw there, they were real. If every now and then I helped a tortured soul to their rest with a certain cocktail, who could blame me? If you were suffering and miserable in your final hours, would you not welcome an angel of mercy?

Anyway, that's not important. I lied when I said I hadn't come out to Oakland before I moved here. I used to come and hike the dark trails all the time. I drove my husband's lover to a cliffside close to here and pushed her into a ravine. It was a spot not far from where we stumbled upon the dead stag. Whatever it was that ripped the deer open must have taken her too, because she was never found.

It was easier with Galina. She wasn't strong and she wasn't sober. We went Christmas shopping for the children on a dark December evening. On the way home she sobbed about Michael and drank from her flask of whiskey. I drove up the hill and stopped the car. I jammed the needle into the flesh of her elbow, and then, to be sure, I put a plastic bag over her head and gripped my belt around her neck while it inflated and deflated. There was a struggle and then she was gone. I pushed her out of the car, into the deep growth, and that was that.

When I moved in, the first thing I did was take the shock collar off the dog. At first he cringed away from me. But then, in the way of sweet creatures, he opened his canine heart wide and let me in. He's fiercely protective of me now—even Michael is a little nervous of his teeth and his size—but I won't let anyone collar him ever again. He's sitting by my feet as I write this. The fire is blazing; Michael will be home soon. I have finally found my place, my house, my love. I rest my feet against the dog's furry side. Both of us, survivors of heartbreak.

PROPHETS AND SPIES

BY MAHMUD RAHMAN

Mills College

Waiting for Keisha to show up at his door, Gholam regrets he isn't more into kink. He would have had the proper accessories—handcuffs and a ball gag. It would be easy to truss her up, and it would keep her from screaming. So he'll just have to be sneaky, act fast before she wakes.

He improvises: Inside his toolbox he finds plastic cable ties of different lengths and selects the longest ones. He worries they will cut into her wrists, he doesn't want her to feel unnecessary pain. Grabbing an old T-shirt, he cuts the fabric and wraps it around the ties as a cushion. One piece he rolls into a ball to stuff in her mouth. He considers a roll of duct tape, but it would stick too strongly. Masking tape makes better sense. Carefully, he puts everything inside the nightstand drawer, stuffing it behind the condoms, lube, and silk ribbons, and while he waits for Keisha, he cradles a heart about to burst.

On the gated campus, where the hills slide into the flats of East Oakland, the fall semester had begun four months ago amid meadows manicured by a small army of Mexican laborers. New students wore excited faces, returnees were happy to reunite with friends, and faculty geared up to start a new year. Only the staff who worked year-round were ambivalent, some among them blue that the summer of an empty campus had ended too soon.

Not Gholam. Tasked with keeping the computers humming on campus, his job takes him everywhere. He meets interesting people and enrolls in a class now and then. In a literature class last spring he had met Keisha, a resumer student. They had a blast working on a project together, and over the summer they cemented into a couple.

The pair spent their Labor Day weekend together, one day at the beach, another on a Berkeley excursion, the third at home, mostly in bed, their lovemaking mixed with conversations over tea. On weekends Gholam keeps a samovar going, with a ready supply of tea, sugar cubes, and mint. They eventually fell asleep, thoroughly exhausted.

When the phone woke him, Gholam's eyes barely opened. The clock read 1:13 a.m. Calls this late scared him. Such a call had brought news of his father's death. And that of the execution of a boyhood friend in Evin Prison. If his placid life here in Oakland was yin, his past in Iran was yang. Always a phone call away.

He picked up the phone and swung his body out of bed. When he needed to jot something down, he reached with his free hand to switch on the nightstand lamp. In the soft light, Keisha's red-brown face glowed. Though he kept his voice low, she woke up. She didn't understand Farsi but her eyes reacted to the tone of his voice—first quizzical, then alarmed, eventually patient.

Hanging up, he stroked Keisha's arms. "I have to go back."

"For good?"

He shook his head. "For a visit. Mother's in the hospital. I'll go during winter break."

"Shouldn't you leave sooner?"

"That'll be soon enough. Let's go back to sleep." He put his head down on the pillow.

"Promise me you'll be safe."

He turned, pulled her close, and whispered, "One never knows. But more than anything else in the world, I want to come back to you."

"Inshallah then," she said, hugging him tight.

He nodded, but as he drifted back to sleep, he thought how people used that phrase to suggest hope, but it meant more like, *It might take a miracle.*

In the morning, Gholam drove to work in a meditative state. At eighteen, lurching from life as a teenager in Tehran to a foreign student in Detroit, he had wanted nothing more than the fall of the shah. Twenty years after the revolution, its dreams hijacked by the mullahs, his own yearnings for a socialist outcome long buried, Gholam now wanted nothing more than the love of a woman.

Midmorning, he trod out of his office to answer a call about a jammed printer in Reinhardt Hall. In the computer lab, a stocky man with a shaved head greeted him. With a class starting soon, he needed to print a dozen copies of a document. The man wore a black T-shirt that screamed out, *Don't Mess with Me—I'm from Detroit.* He could have been more badass if he wore the hard-core version. While Gholam labored on the jam, the man introduced himself as Michael T., a visiting lecturer. The college had put him up in this residence hall that housed graduate students. He said he was fine with it, which meant he wasn't.

"I'll let you work," he said, as he walked to the living room. Gholam heard the television go on and soon Michael T. broke out into full-throated laughter, chased by snorts and chuckles.

The printer fixed, Gholam walked over to Michael T. The visiting lecturer pointed to the television screen. "Dude, ever see anything like this? I'd totally forgotten you had this here in Oakland. I used to catch them late night in Detroit. They called it *Soulbeat Oakland Detroit*."

"You really from Detroit?"

"Went to college near there, and grad school. I'm finishing my dissertation."

So he attended Michigan, lived in Ann Arbor, and went slumming into Detroit. Maybe he didn't even do that, satisfying that urge by watching WGPR-TV 62. Gholam knew the channel—it specialized in music videos, religious programming, late-night Italian B-movies, a dance show imitating *Soul Train*, and yes, late in the night, there had been a *Soulbeat* slot. It usually featured folks jabbering away outside a sun-soaked mansion that must have been in the Oakland Hills.

Learning that Gholam had lived in Detroit, Michael T. asked if he would hang around while he finished printing. They talked about Gholam's Detroit days, and Michael said Gholam might find his "manifesto" interesting.

"I need to get back."

"I can e-mail you a copy. The contents are delicate. You use PGP?"

"Sure."

"I could tell you're one of us." He winked while ripping one of the mangled sheets of paper in two. They exchanged e-mail addresses and PGP encryption keys.

It ended up being a busy day: more printer jams, virus infestations, and one hard drive crash.

At home Gholam finished dinner and checked his e-mail. Michael T.'s document had arrived. Gholam had acted as if he used PGP all the time but it had been years since he'd needed to encrypt or decrypt anything.

The title read, Y2K: *Time to Throw Down*. The document aimed to provoke discussion about preparing for a social collapse. It was now September 1999, only months short of the end of the century. Decades prior, government and corporations had chosen to code years in two digits instead of four—70 instead of *1970*—citing the expense of computer memory. It had since become clear, however, that this shortcut was spectacularly shortsighted. When the calendar advanced to the year 2000, the two-digit coding could make systems assume it was now January 1, *1900*.

The corporations and state were dithering. T's manifesto boldly predicted that at midnight on New Year's Eve, computer systems would fail, power grids would come down, ATMs would lock up, planes might crash, and nuclear plants could face meltdowns. Without money, heat, or power, people would resort to looting and mayhem. The state would respond with force.

The population needed to prepare, although it might already be too late. Michael T.'s document proposed that his class work to develop an "action plan" appropriate for Oakland.

The manifesto slammed Gholam back some ten to twenty years. When the revolution broke out in Iran, he had been an engineering student at Wayne State. In his free time he devoted himself to "revolutionary work"—writing articles, engaging in debates, communicating with comrades back home. Their student federation shattered into factions, each believing the mullahs' seizure of power would not last and that soon it would be *their* comrades' turn.

It wasn't just Iranians. When the 1980s began, many believed Something Big was about to happen. Gholam remembered a poster that went up everywhere: *The '80s will make the '30s look like a picnic*. In multiple tongues—English, Spanish,

Farsi, Arabic, Amharic—pamphlets spoke of "sharpened contradictions." And what did the world end up with? In the US and UK, Reagan and Thatcher. In Iran, Khomeini.

Still, some held out. If you were desperate to believe, you could always find signs auguring Something Big. Otherwise, disillusionment seeped in. Some counseled that people needed to become better students of history. Despite casualties, most managed to cope. Gholam embraced this one piece of advice: he began studying ancient worlds, and learned to measure history, not in years or decades, but in centuries. In the meantime he had to make a living. He wasn't going anywhere as an engineer, but he had learned his way around computers. When the Internet age dawned, he headed for the promised land, the Bay Area, and secured a job on this Oakland campus.

It took him four years to settle down, though it had brought him to Keisha, another refugee from the Midwest. She was fleeing a family she could no longer be near without doing harm to her spirit. She worked a couple of part-time retail jobs while finishing up a BA in liberal studies. She was smart, her dimpled smile could light up a room, and she was fierce the way you'd expect someone to be if they grew up in the heart of Cleveland. The campus drew in folks like her. Until he met her, Gholam's life—sex, camaraderie, friendship—had been rather empty. With her, he felt recharged.

He replied to Michael T.'s e-mail: *You really believe this shit? Or is this an academic exercise?*

Gholam never received a reply.

A few days later when he went to eat lunch in the plaza behind the student union café, he found his regular table occupied by Michael T. and a couple of students.

"My savior!" Michael T. shouted, beckoning him over. "Join us." He introduced Gholam as the guy who'd helped him impress his class on the first day. The two others with him were from the class, Tracy and Rachel.

As Gholam chewed his hamburger, popping fries into his mouth, he listened to their conversation. Michael T. was describing his dissertation topic. He was studying humanity's responses to apocalyptic moments, like stock market crashes, bank runs, massive disasters, and revolutions. He pointed toward Gholam. "He's lived through such a moment but doesn't believe in the Y2K crisis."

The spotlight made him uncomfortable, but Gholam had to respond. "Things don't always turn out the way you think." He described the aftermath of the Iranian revolution.

Tracy asked, "So you give up?"

"I'm not 100 percent sure about Y2K, but surely there's sense in being prepared."

Tracy said, "A handful of us being aware isn't enough. Those with resources may be okay, but what about the poor people in East Oakland, right outside our hallowed gates? Everyone's supercharged by the dot-com boom, but it's precisely when your expectations are high and then there's a collapse that you could have revolutionary implications. Here we are in Oakland, home to the Panthers. This shit could sink deep roots here."

Michael T. nodded. "This is what I love about being here. I did a semester in Kansas and I could hardly get a conversation going. The other day at a coffee shop downtown, I sat next to someone who moved here from the boonies because of the Panthers. Another time I met a woman at a bar who campaigned against apartheid in high school. Random encounters, but both were loaded with so much meaning."

Their youthful energy reminded Gholam of his younger self, but, he reminded himself, there's history and then there's myth. One needed to appreciate the difference.

Tracy said, "Getting the message out has to be our priority."

Pointing to Michael T., Gholam laughed. "He should get a slot on *Soulbeat*."

Tracy lit up. "Why do you think that's funny? It might be low-budget, but it's African American–owned and provides both entertainment and enlightenment."

"I think that's a terrific idea. We need media access," Michael T. said with a smirk.

Rachel turned to Gholam. "We're going to host lectures and a rally. You should come."

"The voice of a skeptic—we need that too," pointed out Michael T.

Gholam sighed. "I'd like to believe you all. I work enough with computers to know there is a problem. But there is an army of programmers out there working on Y2K. Some things here and there might fail, but it'll be a blip. On the other hand, I'll make sure to have a full tank of gas and take out some cash before the New Year."

"Such faith in the corporate elite," Tracy scoffed. "You'll take care of your own self. What about the rest?"

Gholam rose to leave but couldn't resist a parting remark. "I imagine you folks can take care of the others. Best of luck."

In a few weeks, Gholam discovered that Michael T. had managed a weekly spot on *Soulbeat*. It pissed him off. They had joked about the channel, and now he'd wormed his way in there. Gholam wasn't going to engage with these people any longer. A campus could be a bizarre place sometimes.

Gholam's life settled into a routine. During the week he saw Keisha in passing, but on weekends they usually spent one night together. Sometimes he visited her at the huge Victorian behind Highland Hospital she shared with a couple of roommates, but mostly they spent their nights together at his apartment.

His mother's condition had stabilized, and they'd spoken a few times. Through a travel agent he purchased a consolidator ticket to Tehran via Frankfurt. The only ticket he could find at a reasonable price had him flying out on New Year's Eve.

The afternoon he booked the ticket, he returned from a service call to find Keisha waiting outside his office. She said she'd stopped by just for a minute. "I got my thesis proposal approved. Dr. Browning loved my ideas."

"That's wonderful, I didn't have any doubts."

"I needed the affirmation."

"I have some news too. I just bought my ticket." He showed her the printout.

She slammed her backpack on his desk and shouted, "How could you do this?"

"What?"

"You're flying out on December 31? You'll be in the air when it turns January 1. Do you have a death wish?"

Y2K had never come up in their conversations, but apparently a few days ago Keisha had attended one of the lunchtime meetings. She was usually a grounded person, but there was a side of her drawn to the beyond-rational. Like many in California she readily took to the "spiritual not religious" tag. That meant layering her Baptist upbringing with flakes of Buddhism and Hinduism, some references to Islam, and an added coating of radicalism. Something about how she blended her philosophies fascinated Gholam. Normally it was all talk, but now something seemed to be shifting.

"Walk with me to my car."

Gholam agreed, and while they headed to the parking lot, Keisha quoted Michael T. as if she'd memorized his manifesto. She sang his praises: how deep he was, how he could break things down to the essentials, how disciplined he was . . . et-cetera, etcetera. It nauseated Gholam to see her fall under his spell.

Once they reached her Honda Civic, she popped open her trunk to show that she meant business. She had made a trip to Grocery Outlet to stock up on bags of rice and pasta, bottled water, beans of a dozen kinds, crackers, cereal, and a mountain of canned goods.

"When the new year comes, I'll be ready, and I'll be damned if I let you fly out the day before. You'll have to change your ticket."

"It's not changeable."

"You . . . we . . . will have to find a way."

He shook his head. "I don't think much will happen. Sure, there could be a few glitches, but there are enough people working on the problem that widespread disruption is unlikely."

"That's just your opinion. How closely have you studied the subject?"

"I read a few articles."

"Michael T. has studied the problem in depth."

"Why don't we get dinner somewhere and talk it over?"

"There's a lecture at the Greek Theater at five thirty. Why don't you come?"

He thought for a moment. It no longer seemed possible to ignore the Y2K crowd. "Okay, but I have to get back to work now. I'll see you there."

When Gholam arrived, the event had just begun. The discussion focused on Octavia Butler's novel *The Parable of the Sower*. The organizers couldn't bring in Butler but had lucked out with a PhD student from Berkeley who was researching her fiction.

About thirty students came. Most sat at the bottom of

the theater and others moved down after being asked to come nearer. The speaker didn't refer to Y2K; she merely talked about how Butler had written this novel set in the immediate future based on an assessment of current trends: gated communities, homelessness, and drugs.

Michael T. followed by summarizing points from his manifesto. Then Tracy took the platform. She said the power of Butler's work was that she could project where things were headed. In the book, Lauren Olamina coped by creating her philosophy, but otherwise she was unprepared. Wouldn't it be better if the Laurens of the world were better prepared when chaos breaks out? That was the purpose of the Y2K Campaign: preparedness. Survival kits with cash, water, food, fuel, stoves, tents, sleeping bags, and other essentials needed to be assembled.

Rachel spoke about broadening their outreach. They had distributed flyers around the city, Michael T. had a weekly slot on *Soulbeat,* and the next step would be a postering campaign downtown and in high-traffic areas—Fruitvale, MacArthur BART, Grand Lake. She held up a poster they had designed. On gold paper, in bold red letters, it read:

Y2K: Are You Ready?
ATMs shut off, bank savings go poof!
Power fails, gas lines run dry!
Transportation halts. Airplanes grounded!
Chaos on the streets?
It's time to prepare!

The poster also called for a rally at the campus student union on November 18.

Rachel appealed for postering team volunteers, and Keisha marched down right away and signed up. As she and Gholam left the meeting and headed toward their cars, he asked, "Is this something you really want to do?"

"I was going to ask—why is this something you *don't* want to do?"

He remained silent.

"Yes, this is something I really want to do. I believe in the cause. I should put something on the line."

"I think something will happen, but I'm not convinced it will be a big thing."

"On this, we'll just have to agree to disagree." She sounded disappointed. "I thought it'd be fun to do something like this together."

It was an ongoing grievance, and she had a point: they didn't do much together other than sharing some meals, a few trips to the beach, a movie now and then, and sex. He wished he could go with her on this.

"I'd do it if I was convinced of the cause, but I'm not. I'm willing to come hear what people have to say. I won't argue you out of it—if you believe in it, you should do it."

She threw her hands up. "I don't know why I even hang with you."

It was chilly and Gholam suggested they continue talking in his car. Once inside, they went back and forth without resolution.

Finally she said: "Every relationship faces a test. This might be ours and it looks like we're failing. Gholam, I like you, but you think you know everything. I was ready to buy you a new ticket, but I've lost the desire." She turned away from him and clutched her backpack.

He was stunned to see her belief so strong, moved by such a generous expression of love. She didn't have that kind of money to spare.

She opened the car door and was about to leave when he reached out and caught her arm. "Okay, count me in. This might be fun."

They went out midweek just after ten p.m. Before Keisha picked him up, Gholam fortified himself with a shot of bourbon. The arrangement was that Keisha would stay in the car, he would paint on the glue, and Rachel would slap up the posters.

Two teams headed downtown. Their territory was east of Broadway to Harrison, from Grand Avenue down to 14th Street. They covered blocks in lightning strikes, encountering only homeless people or other youngsters who gave them words of encouragement. One kid joined them for half a block.

Only once did a police car come their way. They had prepared for the contingency: Rachel and Gholam dropped their bucket and posters on the ground, stood next to the car, and began arguing loudly about a movie while Keisha pretended to mediate. When the police car slowed to observe them, Rachel explained they'd just come from watching *The Bone Collector* and their differing reviews had become a bit heated. The cops bought it. It helped that she was white and acted earnest.

Once they'd finished, Rachel declared she was ravenous. Could they stop at Sun Hong Kong in Chinatown? Gholam and Keisha locked eyes. Keisha said she just wanted to get to bed, Gholam said he was exhausted. Though Keisha lived closer to Rachel, Keisha said she would drop her off first.

"Wouldn't it make more sense to take Gholam home first?" said Rachel. When there was no response, she said, "Oh, I see."

After they dropped off Rachel, Gholam and Keisha had their hands on each other's thighs in the car, their fingers sliding ever higher. As soon as they were inside the apartment, they stripped off their clothes, rushed to bed, and made fierce love.

Afterward, Keisha said, "See, we should go out postering more often."

Gholam smiled. It had been a good night but as they drifted off to sleep, he felt soiled by the knowledge that he had joined Keisha out of love and lust, not any faith in the cause. By morning, this feeling consumed him and he felt like a total fraud.

So sordid did Gholam continue to feel that he cooked up an excuse to not show up for the Y2K rally at the student union, telling Keisha his mother had been hospitalized again and he needed to call home.

Keisha came over late, brimming with excitement. The rally had succeeded beyond anyone's dreams. More than a hundred people had shown up. Michael T.'s appearances on *Soulbeat* had brought several dozen people from the community. Students had come from a number of other schools. A supermarket owner had promised discounts for emergency packs of food and water.

"And your friend Michelle was extremely helpful," she added.

"My friend Michelle?"

"Yeah, she said she went to college with you in Detroit, an engineer."

"What does she look like?"

"Full-figured black woman, light complexion, probably your age. Smartly dressed."

Gholam was puzzled. He didn't know a Michelle and there was no one in the area he knew from his Wayne State days. He questioned Keisha some more, but all she could say was how helpful Michelle had been with potential contacts and new ideas about how to reach the mainstream media.

It would take one more night for the mystery to be solved. As he got ready for bed, the phone rang.

"Is this a good time?" an unfamiliar female voice asked.

"Who is this?" said Gholam.

"Your old friend Michelle. You don't remember me?"

"No."

"Your classmate from database theory with Professor Lee, the Chinese guy."

"No, I don't remember you. What do you want?"

"Can we meet in the morning? Say nine a.m., on the walkway around the lake, across from the cathedral?"

"If you're not telling me more, I'm not coming."

"Oh, you'd better come." She hung up.

He wasn't going to go, but the edge in her voice suggested it would be risky to ignore her.

Gholam noticed a woman on a bench fitting Keisha's description. As he approached, she said, "There you are. Come sit."

Gholam scrutinized her face. He was certain he'd never seen her before. "We've never met. Who are you?"

She opened the book in her hands and fished out an old photo of two men on a bench: Gholam, a bit more boyish looking, with a white American in a suit. "Remember Leicester Square, 1989?"

Gholam felt a stab in his chest. In his life he'd done some stupid things, and here was a reminder of one. On his way back from Iran that year, his first visit since the revolution, he'd met some old comrades in London. One of them had talked him into meeting with this man. He was probably from some US intelligence agency, and the man had pumped Gholam for information about his visit. He had not shared much.

"We need a favor. We'd like you to maintain my cover. There's something dangerous going on and we want to make sure the kids here don't do anything crazy." She showed the photo again, tapping the image of the American. "A shame Bill's cover was blown. Now he's recognizable and he had to be pulled back stateside."

Gholam understood the implicit threat. If this photo was ever shared with Michelle's counterparts in Iran, Gholam would be marked as an American spy.

It had been a long time since he'd felt fear so close. He walked home and lay on his bed, beginning to sweat, although it was not a particularly warm day. Then he felt chills. He tried music; jazz usually soothed him. Today it annoyed him.

There had been a time when fear was a daily companion. When they were active against the shah, Iranian students weren't safe even on American campuses. The shah's secret police had kidnaped some of their leaders, and Washington cooperated by deporting them. Gholam was too unimportant to be noticed in Washington, but there were even spies in Detroit. For the last ten years he had built a life away from engagement with Iran, and fear's grip on him had weakened, only returning when he visited home. There he had to be extremely careful who he visited. He rarely took chances.

If he chose now to never return home, he could maybe walk away from this, but he had to see his mother, perhaps for the last time. He couldn't jeopardize this visit.

Buoyed by their rally, the Y2K folks decided to host one last event in December. With students dispersing for winter break, they wanted to make sure the community members mobilized for December 31.

Juggling her final projects and these activities, Keisha didn't have much time for Gholam. They met up for tea now and then at the cafeteria. He'd hoped they would spend Thanksgiving together but she had begged off, saying she needed marathon study sessions. She did invite him to the final rally and to an after-party at a family apartment on campus. It would double as a planning meeting for the run-up to December 31. Gholam told her he wasn't sure he could make the rally, but he'd come to the party. She didn't try to change his mind; he worried he was losing her.

When he arrived at the apartment, there were only six people there: Michael T., Keisha, Tracy, Rachel, Michelle, a woman named Isabel, and the hosts, Raphael and Allison. Everyone acted as if they were at a funeral, and Gholam quickly learned why. The rally had only brought out six people beyond this core group. Not even the other students in Michael T.'s class had shown up.

Gholam was relieved: now they *had* to face reality. But he had forgotten how the human mind works.

He would have expected Tracy to make the proposal, but no, it was Keisha. She believed the drop in their numbers meant more radical action was required to rouse the people. She related anecdotes from her work distributing flyers at Eastmont Mall, Bayfair, and the 12th Street BART. Everywhere, people had been sympathetic, and when warned about what would happen on December 31, they were incensed.

"Just to save a few bucks, they toy with the lives of millions. We can't let them get away with it."

The conversation turned to action ideas. A debate broke out: symbolism vs. substance. There would be no rising of the masses, so they could only prepare for the coming chaos on their own. Should they do something spectacular to make people notice, or should they do something to help others prepare? Take over a TV station? Hijack a food delivery truck and distribute the food to the poor?

Isabel felt this was stupid. Decades back she'd come to the

Bay Area to join the Symbionese Liberation Army. Back in Gallup, New Mexico, this had seemed romantic. By the time she arrived, the SLA members were either dead or in jail. She ended up meeting some Marxists, who convinced her that violence without the masses was not revolutionary, they'd be better off working for the longer haul. She'd tried it, but even that had gone nowhere. She'd come tonight to see if this group had any fresh ideas—but clearly they didn't. She gathered up her coat and walked out the door.

What followed made Gholam's heart sink. Michelle, who'd mostly been silent, came over to Keisha's side. She was smooth. She struck a skeptical posture, she asked leading questions, and she allowed Keisha to persuade her. Falling for her provocations, Tracy and Keisha competed to present the most radical ideas. The choice came down to robbing a bank to gather funding, or commandeering a food truck to distribute groceries.

When Gholam tried to interrupt, Michelle cut him down: "There was a time when Gholam was courageous, but he's lost the spirit of his younger days."

Tracy muttered, "Sellout."

Keisha looked confused.

Gholam understood Michelle's game. Here was a group of overzealous students and one ABD, and sure, in the hothouse of a campus, students and would-be professors might easily fantasize about apocalyptic or utopian scenarios, but come final exams, things would usually fizzle out. Unless, of course, espionage agencies sent instigators in to stir the pot.

Gholam caught Michael T.'s attention and said he'd like to speak to him outside. Michelle gave him a warning look.

They stood out on the landing.

"Look, this is getting out of hand. It's time for you to tell these people this was all just part of your dissertation, an exercise to see how people react. It's not real."

"I can't," Michael T. responded. "I've set it in motion, I need to carry this to the end."

"Even if it means you guys end up in jail?"

"I'll make sure there are no weapons involved."

"But the other side will have weapons. You can't risk people's lives and future."

"They're adults, free to make their own choices."

"Damnit, Michael, you're not being much of an adult."

He could have spilled the beans on Michelle but his own self-interest restrained him.

When they went back in, Michael T. informed the group that since Gholam didn't agree with taking action, he should leave. Only those who wanted to be involved should help with the planning. Gholam saw confusion in Keisha's eyes once again but she remained paralyzed. Michelle was smug.

Gholam desperately sought a way to stop this disaster in the making. He tried to engage each of the players. Tracy was contemptuous, Rachel shut him down, and Michael T. was unreachable. Keisha stopped coming over but they met once for tea after her last final exam. She wouldn't say what they were planning but was insistent on her duty to act.

"What about *us*? Is it over?"

"No. But if you cared for me, you'd join me. The least you could do is change your plane ticket."

Gholam tried to contact Michael T. through e-mail. He offered detailed arguments, providing scenarios of how Michael T. could pull these students back and still maintain respect. When he received no reply, he concluded these people were beyond reach.

Still, he could not let Keisha come to harm. He had to find a way to get through to her. Gholam decided to forfeit his plane ticket, and bought a new one for a flight leaving on January 2. It cost him twice as much. He called to tell her, but he had to leave a message, so instead he wrote a passionate e-mail. He knew she was busy New Year's Eve—but what if they had one night together on December 30? He was headed to the other side of the globe. If something did happen on January 1, he wouldn't be able to fly out, but if he did fly out and then something happened back home, would she not want to see him one last time?

Somehow this desperate plea worked; Gholam didn't have to come up with an alternative plan.

When she arrives at his door, there's a tentative look on her face, as if she's not sure why she's here. Her face brightens when she sees the spread he's laid out. He's even lit candles. Gholam's about to open a bottle of wine but she says no, she needs a sharp mind for the following day. That's her only mention of the next day, and she seems relieved when he doesn't press.

After they finish eating, they play Scrabble. Then they make love slowly and fall asleep. He wakes her one time and they have another go.

Gholam hardly sleeps and wakes before dawn. When he slides out of bed, she's still lightly snoring. He quietly opens the drawer and takes out his accessories. With the silk ribbons, he loosely ties her ankles to the bed frame. He can tighten them later. With one of the cable ties, he carefully clasps a wrist to the headboard. Before he can use the second tie, however, Keisha wakes up.

"What . . . are you doing?" She has a curious smile. She

doesn't seem surprised, perhaps because there have been one or two times they've used light restraints in bed.

"Hush." He kisses her left nipple. She moans and closes her eyes, he sucks harder, and in her moment of confused pleasure he clasps her other wrist to the bed.

"Gholam, not now. Maybe after you get back." She pulls her hands and realizes it isn't just ribbons holding her wrists but something tighter. "What the fuck?"

Before she can get another word out, Gholam stuffs her mouth with fabric. Now Keisha's eyes are open wide. She's scared, confused, and hurt.

He sits next to her, one of his hands on her belly. "Don't be afraid. I can't let you go today. You don't know what's waiting out there, so I have to keep you like this for the rest of the day since I don't know what you guys have planned. I'm really, really sorry, but I have to tell you the full story."

Her eyes fill up with pain, tears, and blazing hatred. No matter what story he tells her, he doubts she will forgive him. He doubts whether he will forgive himself, for it is his cowardice that led to this.

Gholam extends his mind ahead. In ten, twenty years, what will he remember? What will she? Will it be a story of him as a savior, a betrayer, or both? Whose story will stick longer? Will it depend on what happens when the calendar turns and the prophecy fails . . . or proves true? Or are the myths that survive built much deeper?

He needs at least one certainty. In the wreckage he's created, he doubts he can get on a plane. Unless, of course, he obtains forgiveness. Only tomorrow will tell if he has a chance.

"Inshallah," he whispers.

BLACK AND BORAX

BY TOM MCELRAVEY

Haddon Hill

Sean swallowed the hard fact that being the doorman at the Nitecap wasn't the most lucrative position he could get in Oakland. So he supplemented his income as a small-time dealer of low-grade narcotics—never inside the bar, but the gray area outside left him overlooked although not invisible.

Thoughts of bottom-shelf tequila shots soothed the endless supply of his cutthroat bump-and-grind, although this gave him access to the local clientele, most of whom ended up drunk and interested in increasing their high. He was the man.

The jazz clarinetist inside improvised Davis's "So What," as Sean swayed in his seat and watched the stage lights blinking above his head. *Funk Town Arts Street.*

"Everything you've got, motherfucker! You did that, baby . . ." Danny's laughter beat the musicians back into their two-dimensional heaven while Sean picked himself off the sidewalk.

"Piece of shit! What'd you do that for?"

"Cuz you an easy target."

"I didn't hear you walk up."

"You lucky I didn't run up. What were you doin'? Dreamin' of that girl you don't have or somethin'?"

"More like . . . remembering yours from last night." They gave each other that TV dinner grin—half plastic and no meat.

Sean changed the subject: "So, supwitchu?"

"What you think, man? Same shit, same ol' shit." Danny dragged his vowels like he dragged his spliffs. He paused a moment, lighter in hand, and cupped the end of the stoge. He had just finished rolling another one and it bounced between his lips. He handed Sean the last of his spliff. "Lemme know when you ready to get your ass whooped. I'll be back," Danny said, stepping inside.

Sean inhaled, shifting his attention toward the mural across the road, back into his daydream. The spiff burned his fingers with the second drag, and he tossed it toward the gutter.

The music slipped through the doorway like greasy fingers with painted nails, red and chipped from the wrestling match between tunes. A chill went down Sean's back as applause drowned his daydream with the first lines of "St. Thomas." He rocked the barstool, shoulders supporting his lean body against the stone wall, head cocked against the window.

The clink-clank-bling of bangles snapped Sean back to attention. He sat up and gave a quick half-smile to Hershe. She was neighborhood royalty, commanding an impressive air of confidence as her footsteps popped sharply on the cement. Her Diana Ross do bounced lightly, contrasting with the heavy jewelry hanging from her wrist and neck. The studs on her leather jacket glistened as she passed in and out of the shadows.

"Honey! It's been too long!"

It hadn't been that long, maybe a week, but Sean reveled in Hershe's affection. He stood to greet her, blushing. She swayed her heavy bag with practiced instability in her matching Gucci heels, leaning down to receive his kiss.

"It *has* been too long! I used to see you twice a week at least! Where've you been? You'll never believe what happened around here the other day. Tommy, you know Tommy, came in blind drunk—"

"That's wild, honey!" Hershe interrupted. "As to where I've been, I've been through it. Good thing I can always count on a kiss from my favorite doorman."

"Well, I'm always here."

"I wouldn't want it any other way. I'ma go talk to our favorite proprietor, don't go far now."

Another kiss, and she disappeared into the dark bar.

He listened to the eruption of friendly greetings as she walked toward Ms. Shirley, who took her arm as they disappeared to the back office. The Thursday shift was usually slow and full of regulars and tonight was no different. Sean looked forward to shooting a couple games of pool with Danny and talking business.

Sean stayed within his means—he never sold larger than dime bags, half-grams, and Norcos. It was his principle to keep his head down and he'd yet to have trouble with the local hoods. Danny was his connect, one and only. They never passed goods close to the area, but they did talk inventory over a game of pool and friendly gambling.

"Fuck it, I'm off tonight."

"Man, you ain' never on when I'm around. Bring it back."

The colorful balls rumbled down the chamber, and a resentful crack sounded as Sean forced the eight into the center of the triangle. Danny cocked his cue for the break.

"Hershe lookin' fly as fuck."

"You think you're real clever, huh? Rerack that shit."

"Just thinking out loud. I'ma make you play it though, ball touched a rail."

"You hustlin' ass cracker. Fine, I'll play and I'll still win. Double or nothing."

Hershe and Ms. Shirley emerged from the office. Both had

the looks of actresses, insincere and pleased with themselves. Ms. Shirley took her seat where the bar bent. Hershe catwalked to the pool table.

"Gentleman playing fair?"

"You know Sean can't shoot, 'specially when you around. Poor kid's distractable."

"He's got taste is all. How're you faring, honey?"

"'Bout to come up twenty bucks." Danny let out an over-zealous "Ha!" earning a scowl from Sean.

"Just another night."

"Another night when you buyin' my drinks! Where you been, girl? I h'ain't seen you in a minute."

"I been layin' low, you know, focusing on myself. It's not just beauty here, a girl's got to stay sharp to get ahead in this world. Can't be spendin' all my time in bars like you men."

A sleek black '87 Cadillac pulled up to the front door and honked twice.

"That's my ride, gentlemen, see you two later. You don't go takin' *all* the baby's money. Be safe now."

Sean stared at her ass while she strutted to the car, her strong thighs shifting with hip-shaking grace.

"That woman really is something. What does she do, any-how?" Sean asked. "I known her for years and never got a straight answer."

"Man, would you ask me what I did? Mind your own damn business," Danny replied with a knowing smile. "A beer says I run you out."

He did as he said. Sean swore as his opponent sunk the eight ball for the third time. Now twenty in the hole, Sean re-luctantly returned to his position at the front door.

Danny beamed. "I'll take that beer anytime."

Back outside, Sean took a pinch of tobacco from his pouch

and stuffed it into a rolling paper, shaping the cigarette into a small cone. The smoke floated into his eyes, blinding him. As he blinked through the tears, the pain began to recede. Sean held his eyes closed to expedite the process.

"You sleeping on the job?" came a stern, melodious voice from his right. "What I pay you for anyhow?"

Ms. Shirley had an interesting sense of humor, though her employees were rarely subjected to or included in the comedy. Sean was caught off-guard and froze, looking like he had a pocket full of wallets. He smiled, attempting to interpret whether this was one of those rare occasions. She smiled back, confirming his doubts and setting him at ease.

"Taking off, Miss Shirley?"

"I'm the boss." She smiled ferociously. "Get back to work," she chided, and swaggered to her car.

He shook his head, confused again by their interaction. Several minutes crawled by before he heard an engine growl to life. She took the intersection at a dangerous speed and drove toward East 18th, not bothering to stop at the light.

Ms. Shirley was a reckless, intelligent, self-made, and self-ish Korean woman in her forties, known throughout Park Boulevard as a shrewd businesswoman, a "dragon lady." She was genuine, not generous, and could diffuse a disagreement with simple totalitarian logic: *My bar, my rules.*

She was also mindful of her patrons. Sean had seen her help more than one "fly who lost his job" or "friend of fly who needed work," considering it was mutually beneficial. She was well connected; receiving in return an owed favor, a new body added to the roster of regulars, and more cash in the register.

Sean was considered a "fly who lost his job."

Six months back he had hit bedrock, his shit job washing dishes at a greasy burger joint making just enough money to cover rent and buy smack. Repeat. Until a scratcher won him five hundred dollars. Cash in hand, he walked straight to the dealer, buying enough black for a two-week spree, enough to disregard responsibility and lose his job. With the change he went to the bar. A week later he woke up facedown under the "borax king's" train of plastic donkeys in F.M. Smith Park, the late-afternoon sun pressed against his thick field jacket. A plaque within arms' reach became a crutch as he struggled to his feet: *Mules in Oakland?* The letters danced across the information board—a brief history of the commercialization of borax. Describing F.M. Smith's mule teams as they marched to the center of the Mojave and back, so he could be rich

This image of tired mules trudging to their sorry destination forced Sean's exhausted body three blocks to the bar. He vividly remembered falling into the swinging door with force enough to make the walls shake.

Ms. Shirley was tending the bar, a factor he hadn't considered. Her disapproving scowl glared up from the well. Slurred, incomprehensible words dribbled from his mouth, and he watched her face distort into perturbed sympathy. She shook her head no, igniting a passionate rage. He flew from his stool, shouting incoherently until a local fly threw him to the floor and gave him a singular punch to the nose. Submitting, the large man picked him up and pushed him out the door. He lay against the wall outside, drunk and defeated.

"I like you." Ms. Shirley's voice had a reverberating effect as thick blood pounded in his ears. "But you especially stupid lately. Come back tomorrow when we're open, or never come back." She gave a final huff and opened the bar door. "Go home!"

He stumbled toward the "shortcut," an overgrown staircase designed to connect Oakland's old trolley system, now forgotten. His final memory of that afternoon was gazing at the city skyline from the top of this stairway, attempting to pick the pocket lint from the last of his black.

The next morning Sean awoke, guts aching; he lay in bed attempting to recollect the evening before. Ms. Shirley's threat reverberated through his skull. He glanced at the time before pulling on his cleanest clothes. It was two thirty p.m.

The Nitecap had been open for an hour before he timidly pushed his way inside. Ms. Shirley looked up when the door creaked open and greeted Sean with a solemn nod. He slunk to the seat adjacent to her and waited. She dramatically finished polishing a glass, held it up to the light, and said, "Johnny quit. We need a new bouncer, you it. Clean up and come work. You have one week. No show, no work."

He agreed to the terms, spent a week sweating in bed, and began his new career.

His pipe had one hit left, maybe two if he scraped the bowl. Sobriety made him feel, and weed dulled that edge. It was twelve thirty a.m.: he didn't want to stick around any longer. The night had been painfully slow, not a full gram sold, not a single argument escalated. Bored and profitless, he felt like a waste of space. An evening like this would keep him awake until daybreak.

A black Lincoln Town Car stopped in front of the bar and turned on its hazards. It wasn't unusual to see a luxury cab pick up an individual from the Nitecap. A fair number of professional drivers used it for respite, shooting pool and drinking between shifts. Sean shouted through the door, asking if anyone ordered a ride. A small chorus of "No" came back so he remained in his seat, arms crossed. Both passenger doors opened and Ms. Shirley, escorting a gentleman he didn't recognize, stepped out.

Flashing a crocodile smile, she walked past Sean without intro-
ducing the guy. Repeating this tactic as they walked through
the bar, they strode confidently into the back room. The door
shut quickly, fanning an air of intrigue throughout. Sean never
asked Ms. Shirley about the significant other that supposedly
had part ownership, but he had at least met him, and the gentleman in the office was not her blue-collared Irishman.

The bartender whistled for Sean's attention. "Th' fuck was
that about, you think?"

"What'm I s'posed to say? Ms. Shirley got friends. Not really my business."

"She's never brought another man since I've been around.
Just seem like something's up."

"I don't know, dude, just ask her later."

"Hershe and her were in there earlier."

"You mean like, whenever Hershe stops by? C'mon, man.
Look, tonight is dead, lemme go. I don't have shit to do, but I'd
rather not do it here. Fill me in tomorrow?"

"All right, get out of here, I will. G'night, Sean. Everyone
say g'night to Sean, lucky bastard's off."

He headed toward the door and tossed up his hand, an im-
personal goodbye to the few voices that obliged the bartender.

It was too early to go home. The antiquated Casio wrist-
watch he wore beeped one a.m. as he walked past the Parkway
Theatre, an old 1925 movie house still boasting a Wurlitzer and
intricate décor. It had been unused for years, leaving a feeling
of urban blight in a neighborhood the city recognized as "up-
and-coming." The sign board that used to list what was playing
now simply read, *We l-ve you Oakland*. The feeling didn't seem
mutual.

He turned right on East 18th and made for the "gem" of
Oakland—Lake Merritt. It had been recently polished, the wa-

ter glowing as it reflected the string of Christmas lights hanging between old-fashioned streetlamps. They illuminated the fresh landscaping and two-year-old Kentucky bluegrass. It was a pleasant aesthetic: paid for by *us* to be enjoyed by *them*.

Three years ago those lights, had they been there at all, would have shown the bloated corpse of a retired champion pit bull, half-submerged in the shallows by the shore. They also could have revealed the young hood who once snuck up behind Sean and drove a fist into his kidney, a hit that threw him into the dried dirt and used prophylactics. He walked away from that episode with a broken wrist and without the server's generous fifteen-dollar donation. That type of thing didn't happen anymore, which he supposed was a positive. It also drove up his rent.

He reached the lake and turned right; he had his beat. Before he was a junkie, the walk would take him past several bars while he meandered home. After he started using, it took him to Hanover Hill, where you could always score. The top of the little hill held a public restroom which no one used but the addicts. It was a storefront the city occasionally attempted to lock, and the doors were scarred from countless boots which had broken the blockade. Sean's favorite joke: *It houses the world's most effectual plumbing design.* He grimaced as the polluted memories bubbled into consciousness, quickening his pace to avoid an imagined silhouette of the dealer. A Town Car passed as he stepped off the curb and crossed Lakeside Drive. He would walk to the tip of Adam's Point, sit on his bench, and roll a cigarette. It was a fifteen-minute stroll, time spent attempting to breathe through addiction and loathsome nostalgia. His self-developed methods forced him to have patience and a ritual.

The odd Greco-Roman structure which marked the Point was shining in the moonlight, growing brighter with each footstep until it was washed in the pale, artificial glow which soaked the interior. The heels of Sean's boots echoed closely behind, like an assassin's. Emerging from the other side of the covered embarcadero, he came to a stop in front of his bench—a coated figure lay across it. He was snoring. The first snore brought relief—Sean held an unpleasant notion that every body outside after two a.m. was a dead body; the second brought disgust. It was *his* bench, *his* cigarette, *his* ritual, ruined by this odious breathing overcoat. He gave the bench an angry kick as he about-faced, settling for one of the more exposed and less comfortable spots which lined the promenade.

The excited clamor of a startled flock of geese could be heard from the unlit interior of Lakeside Park, a final frontier for activities that appreciate the cover of darkness. Further listening divulged a muffled argument.

His cigarette burned to the butt, Sean stood up. Back down the promenade and homeward bound. As he approached the intersection of Brooklyn and Lakeshore, a flock of geese burst from the darkness and flew, shrieking, into what was left of the evening. He looked up to watch them form a ghostly chevron, the flashes of white from their exposed chests blinking like so many eyes. Crossing the street drenched him in fluorescent light from the now-closed Quikstop, and he quickened his pace till he reached the softer light of the streetlamps.

He began the ascent up Haddon Hill. A Venetian child tailed him for twenty feet, skipping behind his steady gait. He turned around to catch a glimpse of a romantic city built over water, threatened by an innocent leaning tower. "Leaning Tower of Pizza," he said aloud as the mural ended.

It was a childish and misguided piece of art that always captured his imagination: hope, romance, anonymity; a fresh start that guaranteed success. He would never get there. "Santa

Lucia" spilled from his pursed lips and carried him to the hill's peak. He wheezed as it leveled, cutting the song short. The terrain began to slope in his favor, restoring the energy needed to roll another cigarette.

The traffic light which marked the intersection changed and then changed again: stop, go. An inane ode to structure and authority at such an untrafficked hour. The squeal of tires announced another presence, and Sean jumped over the low concrete wall of Smith Park, out of the way where he was able to watch the show. The car spun a donut and roared toward the hills. He applauded the driver's reckless abandon and turned; Smith Park was empty and unlit.

Walking through the moist, dead grass, he glanced over his shoulder, imagining the sounds of a potential assault. There was a picnic table in the center of the park. A quiet place to lie and look at the city's few stars. Sean's refuge for his last cigarette and final bowl of the night. Sitting down and rolling up, he sparked his nightcap. A shining object reflected the moon, diverting his attention. *Fast money,* he hoped.

Instead he found a single stiletto, useless to him and everyone else, not worth a dime without its partner. He picked it up anyway. Fuck, it was Gucci. If he could find the other one he could make an easy twenty-five dollars.

Sean scanned the grass around him using the light from his phone. Looking up, he saw he was near Smith's plastic mules, locked in their perpetual train to the Mojove. Then he noticed that he was not alone; there was a sleeping body lying comfortably in the dirt behind the mules, with a small bundle near its head. This bundle could contain the missing shoe.

Sean crept toward the body and braced for a reaction, but there was none, so he bent down and dragged the package to a safer distance. He reached inside, immediately jerking his hand out in violent surprise and falling backward. He scrambled to his feet. It was soaked, sticky, and warm. Gathering his wits, he waited to see whether his reaction had disturbed the sleeping individual, but it had not. Regaining confidence, he approached again, this time inspecting his mark thoroughly.

Her legs barely stuck out from under the overcoat, and just one black-stockinged foot covered the other—which held the missing shoe. Sean froze. He then listened for breathing, and hearing none, he gave a hard shove on her shoulder. As the body rolled over, the overcoat fell off. Sean stood shocked; he recognized that face. Or what was left of it.

"Hershe!" he cried, shaking the body. It was cold—she was dead.

He looked for her purse and found it under her knees. It snapped open with genuine Gucci ease. Pulling out the matching clutch, he removed its cash contents; as an afterthought he looked at the ID.

Lic. No. D400-7686-1285
D.O.B. 08/13/1979
Expires: 08/14/2001
Issued: 08/24/1995
Karl Malone
1846 Fifth Ave. Chicago, IL 60612
Male 6'1" 189 lbs. Brn. eyes

"Karl."

A moment of hesitation gave rise to a strong, sickly emotion which he suppressed. *I was a favorite, she'd understand*, he thought. Tossing the wallet back near the body, he began to run in the direction of home. His knees collapsed. Doubling over, he vomited through choking sobs. It didn't make sense, he'd seen her hours before, broadcasting her contagious charm throughout the neighborhood. *Her* neighborhood. There wasn't a soul in their lowly underworld who didn't like or respect her. Sean gathered his wits and rose to his feet, forcing them once again in the direction of home.

At the foot of the old staircase he changed his mind, crossed the street, and dashed down a road he hadn't used in six months. Taking a sharp right up the driveway of a solid old Craftsman, he found the hole in the fence and crept through, heading straight to the neighbor's recessed garage. Greg was awake, at the very least half-alive, and Sean needed his advice and company.

Greg was an old friend, a moderately successful artist whose philosophies stank of France. Sean pounded the door with the bottom of his fist, hearing a snap of rubber and a groan from the tired mattress, followed by the soft opening of a drawer.

"The fuck?! It's three o'clock. Who is it?"

"Sean, Greg. It's Sean. You need to let me in, some fucked-up shit, man."

"I haven't seen you in months, you're square, right? We're square? I'm not opening this door till you promise you're not here to steal my contentment."

"I promise, Greg! It's nothing like that. Fuck you, man, open the door!"

The dead bolt clicked and Sean pushed his way in. The place hadn't changed—a pack of needles lay next to the sheetless mattress on the floor, along with tinfoil and a half-burned candle. Greg's silver spoon hung on the bleach-white plaster wall by two rusting nails, one of which held a corner of his latest piece: *A Chaotic Nightmare of Purples*. He stepped over the mess of strangled tubes of acrylics and fell into the lone piece of furniture, an ugly old yellow rocking chair with shredded upholstery, and began to sob.

"Shut up! Shut the fuck up!" Greg moaned, picking up a heavy brush and firing it into Sean's chest. "What is *wrong* with you?"

Sean choked his pitiful version of the recent events through a refried cig he'd found on top of a beer can.

"It's Hershe, man. She dead. Face all smashed to bits, teeth missing. Damn, I've never seen anything like that before. She's wrapped in a giant coat under the donkeys. I went to the park, you know, for a nightcap, maybe see a star or two. Anyway, I found this shoe—her shoe, I guess—and went looking for the other. I found it. I wish I hadn't."

"Shit" was all Greg said for several minutes; by the fourth minute Sean was growing impatient and began frantically asking what they should do.

Greg gave him an annoyed look, silencing his outburst, and looked back down at his feet. "Did she have anything on her?"

"Like clothes? She was definitely wearing those . . . Uh, her bag was between her legs, full. I grabbed her wallet, Greg. License said *Karl*. She only had eighty bucks in there, I have that here."

"The wallet? You took her fucking wallet?!"

"No, no. The cash. See?"

"Christ! A bizarrely rational reaction. Still kind of fucked, though . . . Then, it wasn't misplaced tranny-bashing. Nothing, we can't do anything."

Sean was appalled. "We can't just leave her there, man, can't you call someone? Can't we give an anonymous tip to the cops? Something?!"

"No, idiot. First: there's no such thing as anonymous anymore; and second: this was a hit. You don't get involved in a hit."

"A what? What'd she do?"

"She was big-time. Damn, you're slow. Big-time Chicago. Her and Ms. Shirley been doing big business in the neighborhood for years, and you don't do big business without making enemies."

Sean again looked appalled, and dropped his head into his hands—contemplation wasn't his strong suit. He didn't change position until he heard the snap of rubber. Greg had just tied off and was attempting to light a pine-scented candle while his right arm still had motor function. Sean watched the lighter spark with each attempt until it finally took. He stared into the flame.

"Can you spare any black, Greg?"

"What? No, Sean, I knew you were after my contentment. You're clean, remember? I'm just gonna take this hit and try to mute all the fucked-up shit you walked in with. *You*, go home."

Sean watched the white powder dissolve into a silver pool of serenity. "Please, Greg, I know it's been a fucked night, I'm the one that found her. Look, I'll buy it from you, I have money."

"You really are fucking screwy if you think I want stolen money from a dead friend. Fuck you, you know where it is." Greg pushed the plunger and fell slowly into his mattress.

Sean opened the drawer and unwrapped a moderate-sized rock. He laid the requisite tools at the foot of the chair as he sat back down and cut a piece of foil. Everything set, he tipped his plane and chased the dragon.

He awoke just after dawn. Greg was snoring painfully, and Sean moved the needle from the bed to an overflowing Schlitz bucket. He pinched another small rock from the drawer and tossed a tenner in its place. Cops were swarming the park as he walked up the short hill. He could just make out the now-covered body of Hershe through the throngs and police tape. The sight made him pause for only a second. He was exhausted, terribly confused, and still very high. The night had been too much, the following would be worse, and he would have to disguise his using again. He fingered the rock in his pocket as he unlocked his door, stumbling up the stairs and into bed.

The alarm went off at five thirty p.m. *Just a small hit*, he thought, finding his foil and lighter where he'd left them, between the bed and wall. His shift started at six thirty—an hour of oblivion before he talked to Ms. Shirley. He figured the news had already saturated the block. A car alarm went off in the distance, rousing him enough to begin clawing away the sheets. Accomplished, he got dressed and locked the door behind him.

Sean trudged down the block toward the bar, heavy legs sticking in the black. As he turned the corner the clarinetist looked him dead in the eye and played a single, long note that followed him into the bar, ending when he was greeted with an unfamiliar, "Hello there!" He waited for his eyes to adjust. A man, the same man Ms. Shirley had with her yesterday, sat at the bar with Danny.

"You must be our beloved doorman. I'm Rich, new owner, pleasure to meet you."

Sean shook the hand held before him and without a word sat on Danny's other side. This was too much, too soon. Danny looked at him with a gentle, knowing gaze and asked if he'd heard about Hershe. He responded with a solemn nod.

"What happened to Ms. Shirley?"

"She came back last night after you left and told me, told us, that she was taking an impromptu visit home, dead aunt or something. She didn't mention she'd sold the place though, I found that out when I walked in the bar about a half hour ago. Cops are saying it's a hate crime, just another tranny killed because—"

"Fuckers."

"Anyway, Shirley must've made a tidy profit from the sale. I'm surprised though—her and Hershe had a good thing going, and after all these years I never would've guessed she would . . . Well, this is New Oakland, I can't even guess anymore."

WAITING FOR GORDO

BY JOE LOYA

Hegenberger Road

O
n May 1, 2016, Hazard&Transgressions.com *received
from an anonymous source the attached two copies of
actual court trial transcripts. They appear to be police
audio surveillance of Mexican mobsters in East Oakland.*

*The first transcript follows two men, John Bañuelos and
Rudolfo Gomez, after Gomez picks up Bañuelos from a sheriff
substation following his release from custody. The second transcript
records Rudolfo Gomez and Harry Gong-Lerma in conversation at
the Gomez residence in Oakland, California.*

*During the month following we received twelve additional
recordings of surveillance events leading up to the violent episode
captured here.*

*Sincerely yours,
Student Gallette
CEO and Founder, Hazard&Transgressions.com*

```
1.    SUPERIOR COURT OF CALIFORNIA, COUNTY OF LOS ANGELES
2.                        —oOo—
3.        THE PEOPLE OF THE STATE OF )
4.        CALIFORNIA, )
5.                              )
6.        Plaintiff(s), ) Case No. 01x45728b
7.        vs. )
8.        RUDOLFO "PRETTY RUDY" GOMEZ )
9.        Defendants(s) )
10.       _____ )
11.
12.
13.                        AUDIOTAPE
14.           AUTOMOBILE CONVERSATION BETWEEN
15.          JOHN BAÑUELOS, aka "JETHRO JOHNNY,"
16.           RUDOLFO GOMEZ, aka "PRETTY RUDY,"
17.       and HARRY GONG-LERMA, aka "SILLY CHINO,"
18.              8:30 PM, January 5, 2016
19.
20.
21.
22.
23.
24.       Transcribed by:
25.       POMPTON X. GALA REPORTING SERVICES
26.       9694 San Fernando Road, Suite C
27.       Los Angeles, California 90057
28.       Telephone: (323) 555-1287
29.
30.
31.
32.
```

1. (CAR ALARM BEEPS. DOORS OPEN, SLAM SHUT.)
2. JETHRO JOHNNY: (plastic bag rustling) Better be some Dev-
3. il's Lettuce in this motherfucker. I wanna be higher than giraffe
4. balls within the hour.
5. PRETTY RUDY: I threw a Snickers and Dr. Pepper in there
6. with your phone. Gordo gots the other shit.
7. JETHRO JOHNNY: We ain't gonna eat here at Denny's, right?
8. PRETTY RUDY: Fuck Denny's. Gordo says he's bringing his
9. jefita's tamales for us.
10. (CAR STARTS.)
11. JETHRO JOHNNY: Can't we swing by my *chante* first? I
12. gotta wash this holding-cell funk off my body. San Leandro Sher-
13. iff Substation can suck a dick.
14. PRETTY RUDY: Gordo says we got to meet him first. Don't
15. get your thong in a bunch.
16. (MUSIC ON RADIO.)
17. JETHRO JOHNNY: I saw you limping. You got some leg disease?
18. PRETTY RUDY: Nah. Slipped and shattered my (unintelli-
19. gible) kneecap.
20. JETHRO JOHNNY: Wrong, homeboy. You got a bad case of
21. dick-do.
22. PRETTY RUDY: What the fuck is dick-do?
23. JETHRO JOHNNY: Medical condition. Where your belly
24. sticks out farther than your dick do. (chuckles) You know it
25. wouldn't hurt to miss a meal, Sancho Panza. Guarantee your
26. knee will thank you.
27. PRETTY RUDY: I can't hear you, homeboy, you're mumbling.
28. Pull your pants down.
29. (LAUGHTER.)
30. JETHRO JOHNNY: What the fuck is this contraption?
31. PRETTY RUDY: I put my iPhone on there like this. Then I
32. can listen to my music.

1.   JETHRO JOHNNY: Oh, check you out. All modern an' shit.
2.   PRETTY RUDY: Gotta keep up with innovations to survive,
3. *qué no?*
4.   JETHRO JOHNNY: Right, right. The world is changing fast.
5. No bullshit there.
6.   PRETTY RUDY: Yeah, but the new world don't always know
7. 'bout the old tricks.
8.   JETHRO JOHNNY: Can't always see who's hiding in the cuts.
9.   PRETTY RUDY: Pleased to meet you. Hope you (unintelli-
10. gible) my name.
11.   (LAUGHTER.)
12.   JETHRO JOHNNY: Devil's one ambushing motherfucker.
13. Gets my sympathy.
14.   PRETTY RUDY: We ain't puzzled by the nature of his game.
15.   JETHRO JOHNNY: What puzzles me is what the fuck's up
16. with the world? I get locked up three months and terrorists hit
17. Paris, San Bernardino, and them clown white boys're holding fed
18. property hostage in Oregon.
19.   PRETTY RUDY: They're on Facebook asking people to send
20. them care packages of zoo-zoos and wham-whams.
21.   JETHRO JOHNNY: Remember when we would send out SOS's
22. like that from prison?
23.   PRETTY RUDY: Fuckin' Donner Party 2.0. Them stupid
24. motherfuckers. People calling them Vanilla ISIS.
25.   JETHRO JOHNNY: (laughs hard)
26.   PRETTY RUDY: No bullshit. Joking that these hillbillies gon-
27. na implement Shania law.
28.   JETHRO JOHNNY: (coughing, laughter) Fuck! Funny moth-
29. erfuckers out here.
30.   PRETTY RUDY: Working with good material.
31.   JETHRO JOHNNY: So why didn't you get off at Golf Links
32. Road? We're going to the airport Marriott, right?

1.   PRETTY RUDY: Nah, I said *by* the airport Marriott. Fran-
2. cesco's parking lot across from the warehousemen's hall. And
3. I'm getting off at Keller, gonna get a Quality Doughnut.
4.   (SOUND OF HORNS HONKING.)
5.   JETHRO JOHNNY: That'll work. This Snickers is good, but it
6. ain't no chocolate sprinkle doughnut.
7.   (MORE HORNS HONKING.)
8.   PRETTY RUDY: GET THE FUCK OUT THE WAY, STUPID
9. MOTHERFUCKER! Look at this sleazy slope trying to turn left
10. from the right lane.
11.   JETHRO JOHNNY: These Panda NON-Express drivers turn-
12. ing the East Bay into chink-chink Beijing. Makes me miss my
13. *cuete*.
14.   PRETTY RUDY: YEAH, THAT'S RIGHT, BITCH! BACK THE
15. FUCK UP!
16.   JETHRO JOHNNY: I'd blast some Kung Pow BLAM BLAM
17. right in her mascara. Put her out of YOUR misery.
18.   PRETTY RUDY: Hold on—back to Y'all-Qaeda. Obama says
19. that bullshit is a local law enforcement issue, not FBI?
20.   JETHRO JOHNNY: Clever fucker wants to avoid another
21. Waco or Ruby Ridge. Those white boy cops ain't gonna do noth-
22. ing but turn off the water and power, then sit and wait out the
23. winter.
24.   PRETTY RUDY: If I were Obama I'd drop in a planeload of
25. life-sized cutouts of a twelve-year-old black boy with a BB gun—
26. do it so they all land standing up, staring at all them white cops
27. surrounding the joint.
28.   JETHRO JOHNNY: You got a morbid mind.
29.   PRETTY RUDY: Think about it. Get them lazy-ass cops all
30. twitchy-fingered. Think of like a thousand of these motherfuck-
31. ing cutouts of a menacing little armed nigger staring at them.
32.   JETHRO JOHNNY: Yeah, the militia would see them too,

1. know they were 'bout to be blasted or even droned! They'd rush
2. out that building hands in the air, be all like, *Don't shoot! Don't*
3. *shoot!* Like them Black Lives Matter kids last year. Ironic like
4. shit.
5.   PRETTY RUDY: Think if 150 armed Black Panthers took
6. over an office building in Yosemite the feds would call it a local
7. issue?
8.   JETHRO JOHNNY: I ain't no friend of the nigger, but them
9. motherfuckers ain't got no play in this country. Not one fuckin'
10. drop of play.
11.   (MUSIC . . .)
12.   JETHRO JOHNNY: Remember how we used to go get that
13. seafood pasta at Francesco's after every hit?
14.   PRETTY RUDY: Thought we were all fancy and shit.
15.   JETHRO JOHNNY: Tradition stuck. When we start that
16. anyway?
17.   PRETTY RUDY: Sailor Boy, I think.
18.   JETHRO JOHNNY: That was when?
19.   PRETTY RUDY: I'd just got out of Folsom the third time.
20. Beetle Bailey OD'd two days later. I needed (unintelligible), so
21. Lil' Samson recommended you.
22.   JETHRO JOHNNY: '96?
23.   PRETTY RUDY: Yeah. Day before Christmas.
24.   JETHRO JOHNNY: Fuckin' Sailor Boy.
25.   PRETTY RUDY: You mean *fuck* Sailor Boy!
26.   JETHRO JOHNNY: You mean *fuck* his *firme* wife.
27.   PRETTY RUDY: Hey, what she didn't know couldn't hurt her.
28.   JETHRO JOHNNY: Virgie Ledesma. Smokin'-fine rack. And
29. you got to rub your shitty little dick between 'em.
30.   PRETTY RUDY: He who smokes a worthless piece of shit
31. gets to dick down his smokin'-hot wife.
32.   JETHRO JOHNNY: Lucky dog.

1.   JETHRO JOHNNY: Sailor Boy didn't go easy.

2.   PRETTY RUDY: They rarely do. Body wants every last

3.   breath.

4.   JETHRO JOHNNY: Dude fought till the end.

5.   PRETTY RUDY: (unintelligible) Gotta respect the life force.

6.   JETHRO JOHNNY: Hey, Burckhalter Elementary. Got my

7.   edumacation there. First tongue kiss too.

8.   PRETTY RUDY: Yeah? What was his name? Hey, here's Qual-

9.   ity Doughnuts.

10.   JETHRO JOHNNY: *Her* name was Marta Muñoz, and you're

11.   buying me a glazed. I'll stay in the car.

12.   (CAR DOOR SLAMS. CELL PHONE BEEPS.)

13.   JETHRO JOHNNY: Hey, so you got that for me? . . . Good.

14.   Wait till we've been there a minute, then bring the bag. Hide the

15.   gun in the bottom. Stay on point. This is the big leagues, young-

16.   ster . . . Okay, listen, I gotta go. You do this, you earn your bones.

17.   (unintelligible) Just make sure you're there!

18.   (MUSIC . . .)

19.   (CAR DOOR OPENS. BEEPING. DOOR SLAMS.)

20.   PRETTY RUDY: Here's your doughnut.

21.   JETHRO JOHNNY: Hey, you remember that time you were in

22.   Corcoran and I got the green light to take out Boxer?

23.   PRETTY RUDY: Boxer from Varrio Nuevo? Or Boxer from

24.   Logan Heights?

25.   JETHRO JOHNNY: You Alzheimer's motherfucker: Boxer

26.   from White Fence!

27.   PRETTY RUDY: Oh yeah. And?

28.   JETHRO JOHNNY: I made that move with my homeboy Si-

29.   lent from Stockton.

30.   PRETTY RUDY: What a fucked-up *placaso!* Who lets them-

31.   selves be nicknamed Silent?

32.   JETHRO JOHNNY: Um . . . ya know . . . men with fragile-ass

names like Pretty Rudy shouldn't trip down nickname lane with attitude.

PRETTY RUDY: Pretty Rudy works cuz I've got twelve bodies buried around the state, most of 'em in prison cemeteries. But Silent, c'mon, even you gots to know that's a jacked name.

JETHRO JOHNNY: Dude was a killer too. The name works for that, right?

PRETTY RUDY: The name don't inspire fear. (Assumes announcer voice) *Hi, my name is Silent and I kill silently . . . like mold.*

JETHRO JOHNNY: Why you bustin' my balls? I didn't give him that name. His older homegirls probably nicknamed him when he was a *chavalo.* Couldn't say no.

PRETTY RUDY: Fucked-up Snow White dwarf nicknames: Dinky, Blinky, Smiley, (unintelligible) Dopey. What next? Nice Eyes? *Sensitivo?* (Laughs into coughing fit)

JETHRO JOHNNY: Awright, I get it. You didn't like Silent.

PRETTY RUDY: Hey, is it true his crew didn't know whether to nickname him Silent or Baby Powder Scent? (Laughing, more coughing)

JETHRO JOHNNY: Can a motherfucker finish a story?

PRETTY RUDY: Yeah, go for it. *Dispensa.* (Still chuckling)

JETHRO JOHNNY: You got it out of your system, Giggles Gomez?

PRETTY RUDY: Yeah, yeah. Done.

JETHRO JOHNNY: Okay. So like I was saying, after we waste Boxer, you know, I'd already done Francesco's with you after every hit like four or five times by that point.

PRETTY RUDY: Making someone dead makes me (unintelligible) hungry.

JETHRO JOHNNY: So I want to go to Francesco's, you know, per usual.

1. PRETTY RUDY: Right.

2. JETHRO JOHNNY: So I tell Silent, you know, Francesco's or
3. bust.

4. (MUSIC . . .)

5. PRETTY RUDY: Fuck this song. Don't even know why it's on
6. my playlist.

7. JETHRO JOHNNY: What the fuck? Bowie's a legend.

8. PRETTY RUDY: What are you talking about? (Assumes
9. falsetto voice) *This is not America. Sha-la-la-la-la.* Bowie and
10. Metheny make this song like two clicks away from a Boy George/
11. Kenny G duet.

12. JETHRO JOHNNY: All your taste is in your mouth. You don't
13. know nothin' 'bout classic rock.

14. PRETTY RUDY: Whatever. Finish the story. After Boxer, you
15. need to go get your grub on. And?

16. JETHRO JOHNNY: That mutherfucker says, nah, he ain't in-
17. terested in seafood pasta. Has his own ritual.

18. PRETTY RUDY: Wait. It was your hit, right? The Council
19. gave you the order?

20. JETHRO JOHNNY: That's what I'm saying. Gordo made that
21. *my* fucking hit. So Silent's post-hit ritual can suck a sweaty nut
22. sack as far as I'm concerned.

23. PRETTY RUDY: That what his ritual was? He wanted to lick
24. your lozenge?

25. JETHRO JOHNNY: I told you, homeboy, I ain't gay. And my
26. boyfriend can verify that shit.

27. (LAUGHTER.)

28. JETHRO JOHNNY: *En serio.* Dude tells me he wants to go get
29. a massage, then go dancing.

30. PRETTY RUDY: A *massage* massage?

31. JETHRO JOHNNY: That's what I ask. *You mean like a rub-
32. and-tug massage?* No, he says, a legit massage.

1.   PRETTY RUDY: Whaaat?

2.   JETHRO JOHNNY: That *chapete* had just helped me stab

3. Boxer like forty-five times, and now he's proposing we go get our

4. *Saturday Night Fever* on.

5.   PRETTY RUDY: You sure pick 'em, homes. So what'd you do

6. with his sugar-in-the-tank mutherfuckin' ass?

7.   JETHRO JOHNNY: Dropped dickhead off at his car. But I was

8. (unintelligible). Like I wanted to kill again. I didn't even want to

9. go to Francesco's, like he'd fucked up seafood pasta for me.

10.   PRETTY RUDY: I get it. So what'd you do?

11.   JETHRO JOHNNY: I got some In-N-Out. One by Panda Ex-

12. press, other side of the 880.

13.   PRETTY RUDY: Next best thing.

14.   JETHRO JOHNNY: Animal style, like a stylin' motherfuckin'

15. animal.

16.   PRETTY RUDY: I fuckin' love In-N-Out.

17.   JETHRO JOHNNY: I was so fucked up inside. I ate so fast I

18. barely tasted that burger on the way down.

19.   PRETTY RUDY: Almost never the wrong time to throw down

20. a Double-Double.

21.   JETHRO JOHNNY: Thing is, I tasted all of it when I threw it

22. up on some poor slob's Camaro in the parking lot. Felt like that

23. motherfucker's softness jinxed the pleasure of murder for me.

24.   PRETTY RUDY: Wait . . . So you . . . ? Nah . . . you didn't . . . ?

25.   JETHRO JOHNNY: Yeah, I did.

26.   PRETTY RUDY: *En serio?*

27.   JETHRO JOHNNY: Gospel truth!

28.   PRETTY RUDY: Same night?

29.   JETHRO JOHNNY: Right there in San Leandro, not far from

30. the sheriff's substation where you just picked me up. In an alley

31. behind where he got his massage. Waited by his car.

32.   PRETTY RUDY: Did what you had to do.

1.   JETHRO JOHNNY: He kept asking me, *Why, why, why?* I
2. didn't say nothing. He didn't have that coming.
3.   PRETTY RUDY: Sometimes you never see it coming. Never
4. get to know why your ticket got punched.
5.   JETHRO JOHNNY: Tell you what—Silent didn't go silent into
6. that night. That motherfucker shitted himself, ass loud like a
7. cracked diesel engine.
8.   PRETTY RUDY: (laughing, then choking) You're a sick fuck,
9. homeboy. Practically choked on my gum.
10. (MUSIC . . .)
11.   PRETTY RUDY: Hold on, I gotta stop here and buy some shit.
12. You need anything?
13. (ENGINE STOPS. MUSIC STOPS.)
14.   JETHRO JOHNNY: You going to the CVS? Couldn't wait to go
15. to Trader Joe's in your hood?
16.   PRETTY RUDY: What? You writing a book? Leave my chap-
17. ter out. Better yet, let me fuck you in the ass and make it a love
18. story.
19.   JETHRO JOHNNY: (chuckles) I mean, you can't wait? You got-
20. ta stop off right here, at the shitty Eastmont Mall CVS, right next
21. to the police station, to buy your tampons and some almond milk?
22.   PRETTY RUDY: So what if I'm lactose intolerant and I wear
23. a tampon to staunch the occasional flow? That don't make me a
24. bad guy, right?
25.   JETHRO JOHNNY: Staunch the flow. You motherfucker.
26. (chuckles) Nah, it don't make you a bad guy. In fact, it don't
27. make you a guy at all.
28. (BOTH LAUGH. CAR DOOR OPENS. BEEPING.)
29.   PRETTY RUDY: So nothin'?
30.   JETHRO JOHNNY: Yeah, get me a toothbrush, medium. And
31. some condoms, jumbo girth. Battleship-gray if they got color
32. options.

1.   PRETTY RUDY: No fuckin' hope for humanity.

2.   (CAR DOOR SLAMS. CELL PHONE BEEPS.)

3.   JETHRO JOHNNY: Hey, babydoll, it's me. Ready to ride the

4.   high hard one? . . . I'ma tear that pussy up . . . Gotta take care

5.   of some bullshit first, but I'll bring dinner, okay? . . . Yeah, I'll

6.   see you soon . . . Go play with that pussy, get it ready for Big-

7.   Dick Daddy from Cincinnati, okay, sweetheart? . . . Okay, see

8.   you soon.

9.   (CAR DOOR OPENS. BEEPING.)

10.   PRETTY RUDY: Here, I got you baby powder–scented

11.   rubbers.

12.   JETHRO JOHNNY: Yeah, so, uh, go ahead and rub 'em in

13.   your chest.

14.   (BOTH LAUGH. CAR ENGINE STARTS.)

15.   PRETTY RUDY: So Gordo called and said his meeting's going

16.   late. Says just wait for him in the Francesco's parking lot.

17.   JETHRO JOHNNY: Still don't know why it's so urgent.

18.   PRETTY RUDY: Just to debrief, you know. That was a big

19.   move you made in there. Big shit could go down if that ain't

20.   handled right.

21.   JETHRO JOHNNY: I've been locked up for three months.

22.   Fighting my case while living with a bunch of hygiene-hating

23.   motherfuckers. I just wanna be knee deep in my girl's pussy for

24.   like three minutes, bust a heavy nut.

25.   PRETTY RUDY: Whoa! You got a broad?

26.   JETHRO JOHNNY: Yeah, I got someone to sometimes knock

27.   the dust off. But you got me fuckin' bumpin' gums with you and

28.   Gordo instead.

29.   PRETTY RUDY: Hey, if it'll make you feel any better, I prom-

30.   ise I'll take you for a massage and dancing afterward.

31.   (BOTH LAUGH HARD.)

32.   PRETTY RUDY: For fuck's sake, chill out. Everything's cool.

1.   (MUSIC . . .)

2.   JETHRO JOHNNY: I met this crazy white boy inside, from

3.   Emeryville. Richie Rich strung out on dope. This fish was a trip.

4.   Smart youngster. 'Cept he thought he could beat me at chess.

5.   PRETTY RUDY: So wasn't too smart already.

6.   JETHRO JOHNNY: Yeah, *blanquitos* from Emeryville come

7.   into County with all their Ruy Lopez and King's Indian openings,

8.   acting like they the only ones ever memorized Bobby Fischer–

9.   Boris Spassky matches.

10.   PRETTY RUDY: Underestimating your opponent's intelli-

11.   gence in battle's the fastest way to end up with a dry fist in

12.   your ass.

13.   JETHRO JOHNNY: I did what I do. Lay in the cut. Play pos-

14.   sum. Act more interested in the titty mag on the bunk. Then I

15.   dropped the hammer. Took his milk money.

16.   PRETTY RUDY: Best moment! See the face when they're

17.   like, *Oh fuck, there's more treacherous animals in the jungle.*

18.   JETHRO JOHNNY: They wanna sup with the Devil, but they

19.   never bring a long enough spoon.

20.   PRETTY RUDY: So that's it? You sharked a youngster at

21.   chess? That ain't impressive.

22.   JETHRO JOHNNY: Nah, after I showed him how his chess

23.   skills sucked, I listened to him talk about crime and shit and

24.   realized this kid was like some evil genius. Just budding, barely

25.   beginning his career. Coming at it all sideways, but clever.

26.   PRETTY RUDY: Huh, now you got me all up in suspense an'

27.   shit.

28.   JETHRO JOHNNY: (unintelligible)

29.   PRETTY RUDY: What's up?

30.   JETHRO JOHNNY: Man, all of a sudden I got this itch in my

31.   boot.

32.   PRETTY RUDY: Scratch that motherfucker!

1. JETHRO JOHNNY: What do you think I'm trying to do,
2. homes?
3. PRETTY RUDY: It's Silent, homeboy. In heaven. Holding a
4. voodoo doll of your likeness in one hand and a needle in the
5. other. Stabbing the fuck outta your ankle.
6. JETHRO JOHNNY: Ahhh! Better. (unintelligible) OH! And
7. that fucker ain't in heaven. Best believe that!
8. (MUSIC . . .)
9. PRETTY RUDY: So, you were saying about this evil genius?
10. JETHRO JOHNNY: Yeah. Kid asked weird questions, like if I
11. started all over again in crime, what would I do different?
12. PRETTY RUDY: Easy call for me: no heroin. Probably no tat-
13. toos either, gives too much away.
14. JETHRO JOHNNY: Kid had this game he called Ten Bullets.
15. You get ten bullets to start. One bullet to assassinate a national
16. figure. So you got to figure out, what ten murdered Americans
17. would fuck up the country the most?
18. PRETTY RUDY: You mean how Martin Luther King's assas-
19. sination torched the country, all them riots? Fucked it up that
20. way?
21. JETHRO JOHNNY: Exactly. What ten people wasted by a bul-
22. let would kick off big-time damage to society? Like that.
23. PRETTY RUDY: Does it have to be racial shit? Or *any* kind
24. of retaliation shit? Like that NRA dude, LaPierre. Shoot him and
25. plentya people gonna get shot.
26. JETHRO JOHNNY: Yeah, like that. I used one bullet on Rush
27. Limbaugh. Thinking, a bullet back of the head while he's shovel-
28. ing pancakes down his gullet at Denny's, and it's on like Donkey
29. Kong. Some dittohead pops a cap in your boy Al Sharpton?
30. PRETTY RUDY: *My* boy? Fuck you! But that is some out-
31. there criminal shit, tell you that.
32. JETHRO JOHNNY: See what I mean?

PRETTY RUDY: Like if Anonymous had a crew of rogue killers. That's like the shit I could see them pulling off. Anonymous could go treacherous real quick and change up the crime game big-time.

JETHRO JOHNNY: Clever stuff, huh? Try to pull the covers off all that moral-superiority shit Americans talk about themselves.

PRETTY RUDY: Wonder if there's money in smoking dudes like that.

JETHRO JOHNNY: Or broads.

PRETTY RUDY: Yeah, guess so, or broads. Ann Coulter like a motherfucker.

JETHRO JOHNNY: All those asshats on TV talking politics this and that, man, they were like pop stars to youngblood. Kept track of their influence and shit. Even called them high-value targets, like they were military strikes.

PRETTY RUDY: Was he an anarchist? Like does chaos give him wood? Or did he see some way to extort money out of it?

JETHRO JOHNNY: Who knows what the fuck motivates a tweaker trust-fund college dropout? But I played that game with him every day for like a week.

PRETTY RUDY: Ah shit, Whitey turned you, huh? Next thing you know you're gonna tell me you're all into Dungeons & Dragons and shit.

JETHRO JOHNNY: Huh, funny you say that. That kid was way into (unintelligible) game Risk, about world domination. Know it?

PRETTY RUDY: Never played it. But those white boys in prison obsessed over that game back in the day. *Gavachos* obsess over the freakiest shit.

JETHRO JOHNNY: That was youngblood. Would sit and explain his strategies like he was some bat-shit crazy monk in a cave sharing the secrets to illumination. Weird focus. And I

1. swear, sometimes it was like he knew what I was up to.
2. PRETTY RUDY: What?
3. JETHRO JOHNNY: One morning we're talking game strategy
4. and he says that to gain advantage over an opponent, you should
5. sacrifice one of your own then blame the enemy. You know, to
6. rally the troops.
7. PRETTY RUDY: Scheming prick. I like his style, drives me
8. wild . . . But nobody knew how things would change up. Not me.
9. Not Gordo.
10. JETHRO JOHNNY: That's what's weird. Maybe he's the one
11. gave me the idea.
12. PRETTY RUDY: Either way, cops are dumb fucks, but they
13. ain't retards. If he was a snitch planted there to set you up, you
14. ain't giving up shit to a fish.
15. JETHRO JOHNNY: Got that right! Well, Gordo's a cop and he
16. ain't no dumb fuck.
17. PRETTY RUDY: Who'da thought we'd have one of our own in
18. the Oakland PD?
19. JETHRO JOHNNY: I see a lot, but I never saw that one com-
20. ing. Gordo. Council member—also a righteous cop?
21. PRETTY RUDY: So who won the game?
22. JETHRO JOHNNY: Wasn't that kind of party. It was more
23. like war games, spin out every scenario . . . You saw how those
24. DAs were killed in Texas last year?
25. PRETTY RUDY: Yeah, just like that prison warden in Colo-
26. rado. Answers his front door and *blam!* Shot dead. Don't fuck
27. with the Aryan Brotherhood.
28. JETHRO JOHNNY: Payback's a bitch. And that cycle just got
29. kicked off. You know law enforcement and the AB ain't done kill-
30. ing each other yet.
31. PRETTY RUDY: Preachin' to the choir, homeboy, you ain't
32. got to tell me. Bullet retaliation is as American as a fried

1. stick of butter at the Iowa State Fair.
2.   JETHRO JOHNNY: That's a real thing?
3.   PRETTY RUDY: Fucking A.
4.   JETHRO JOHNNY: That some fuckin' gross shit. Why you
5. got to malign all-American butter lovers?
6.   PRETTY RUDY: You know that having your dick sucked is
7. illegal in the Midwest, but it's okay to make out and masturbate
8. with margarine all day long?
9.   JETHRO JOHNNY: Stop, stop! I always told you watching all
10. that porn would fuck you up.
11.   PRETTY RUDY: I think you can legally marry margarine in
12. Kansas and Oklahoma.
13.   JETHRO JOHNNY: Sick shit.
14.   PRETTY RUDY: Twisted fuckin' world.
15.   JETHRO JOHNNY: Know what's sick? Check out that nigger
16. hooker right there. Broke from the neck down.
17.   PRETTY RUDY: Looks like she had a rough paper route.
18.   JETHRO JOHNNY: My homeboy Pie Face told me this joke:
19. What has six tits and eight teeth?
20.   PRETTY RUDY: I give up.
21.   JETHRO JOHNNY: Night shift at the local Waffle House.
22.   PRETTY RUDY: Ah, that's fucked up. My road dog's a racist,
23. breaks my heart.
24.   (MUSIC . . .)
25.   JETHRO JOHNNY: You know my fucked-up parents had me
26. read all those dead white men as *chavalón.*
27.   PRETTY RUDY: Your parents were pieces of work.
28.   JETHRO JOHNNY: It was one line from a dead white broad
29. always stuck with me.
30.   PRETTY RUDY: I know, I know, I got it: (clears throat, imi-
31. tates Clark Gable) *Frankly, my dear, I don't give a damn.*
32.   JETHRO JOHNNY: That's from the movie, not the book. But

234 // Oakland Noir

keep quoting *Gone with the Wind*, see how that works out for you.

PRETTY RUDY: Don't dog the movie. Rhett Butler's my idol.

JETHRO JOHNNY: That pussy-whipped motherfucker? Coughs up a nut sack at the end of the flick, finally kicks Scarlett to the curb, and we're supposed to cheer?

PRETTY RUDY: Whoa! Hold on.

JETHRO JOHNNY: Fuck him. He was a punk. Rhett Butler's on nigger pipe.

PRETTY RUDY: Man, you know nothin' 'bout love.

JETHRO JOHNNY: Oh, and you do?

PRETTY RUDY: If you had a girl you'd know what I'm talkin' 'bout. Now that I think about it, I ain't seen you with a broad for a couple years.

JETHRO JOHNNY: I just told you I'ma knock the dust off with my broad in a minute.

PRETTY RUDY: Nah, that's some suspect shit.

JETHRO JOHNNY: Whatever.

PRETTY RUDY: Being a stone-cold killer ruined romance for you, I see that now.

JETHRO JOHNNY: What do you know that I don't?

PRETTY RUDY: Riddle me this, loverboy: if—and this is a big fuckin' if—but if you ever REALLY get a girl, how would you know when she's climaxing?

JETHRO JOHNNY: What?

PRETTY RUDY: You heard me: how could you tell when your girl is climaxing?

JETHRO JOHNNY: Climaxing, what the fuck? You know what? You got me. How?

PRETTY RUDY: You'd see my car parked in her driveway. (bursts out laughing)

JETHRO JOHNNY: That's fucked up, homeboy. Serious egregious shit right there.

1.   PRETTY RUDY: Don't get all butt hurt. Anyway, we both
2. know you got no real girl, so she's fake-safe anyway.
3.   JETHRO JOHNNY: That brings me all the way back to the
4. point I was gonna make.
5.   PRETTY RUDY: What's that?
6.   JETHRO JOHNNY: This broad wrote this story about these
7. killers who snatch up a family with one talkative old bitch
8. hostage.
9.   PRETTY RUDY: Remind you of anyone?
10.   JETHRO JOHNNY: Huh, never thought of that connection.
11.   PRETTY RUDY: Right?
12.   JETHRO JOHNNY: Anyway, one killer finally shoots that
13. loudmouth bitch dead. Says the coolest line ever uttered by a
14. killer in books: *She would have been a good woman if there had*
15. *been somebody there to shoot her every minute of her life.*
16.   PRETTY RUDY: That's a good line. I know people that would
17. apply to.
18.   JETHRO JOHNNY: We all do, that's the point. That's why
19. God invented bullets. To stop people from talking.
20.   PRETTY RUDY: We talking Bandit now?
21.   JETHRO JOHNNY: He didn't go by no bullet, but yeah, his
22. mouth turned him cold.
23.   PRETTY RUDY: Why Bandit? I mean, your job was to smoke
24. a nigger and fuck up the bullshit prison peace treaty. You didn't
25. worry there'd be consequences for going off script?
26.   JETHRO JOHNNY: Long game, homey. Plus, Bandit was
27. closer than any *mayate* shot-caller I could get to. County is
28. mostly segregated now.
29.   PRETTY RUDY: Makes sense. But what long game?
30.   JETHRO JOHNNY: Bandit was that typical convict who
31. thought he was tough cuz he had all that makeup on his muscle.
32. The bald head with the old-school bandito mustache.

1.   PRETTY RUDY: Yeah, but we need those idiots on our side.
2. They're our mascots, our logo, and our best recruiters.
3.   JETHRO JOHNNY: (laughs, then imitates announcer voice)
4. *There's strong, and there's convict strong. Join our army.*
5.   PRETTY RUDY: That's right. There's a reason the pecker-
6. woods in the AB all look alike, call themselves The Brand.
7.   JETHRO JOHNNY: Thug marketing.
8.   PRETTY RUDY: Why not? So . . . long game?
9.   JETHRO JOHNNY: I used to lie in my bunk and think: *If I*
10. *had a time machine I wouldn't go back and kill Hitler. I'd go*
11. *all the way back to the road to Damascus and kill Saul of Tar-*
12. *sus before he became St. Paul, the greatest missionary in all of*
13. *Christendom.*
14.   PRETTY RUDY: That's it! I'm driving you to the crazy house
15. right now. You just went all the way 5150.
16.   JETHRO JOHNNY: No, really. Think about it. No Christians
17. means no conquistadors fucking up the Aztecs—our peeps.
18.   PRETTY RUDY: I'm thinking about it, and I don't know what
19. that crazy *Star Trek* time travel shit has to do with you killing
20. Bandit, one of our own.
21.   JETHRO JOHNNY: I took out the guy who was gonna be the
22. biggest preacher of that fucked-up prison peace treaty gospel.
23.   PRETTY RUDY: You telling me he was pushing that hard inside?
24.   JETHRO JOHNNY: Converts make the greatest zealots.
25.   PRETTY RUDY: Bandit never needed a reason to be a loud-
26. mouth. And he did have the full backing of the Council in Pelican
27. Bay.
28.   JETHRO JOHNNY: Exactly. I figured we either tangle with
29. him now or tangle with him later, when he transfers from
30. county to Corcoran and is too big to get at.
31.   PRETTY RUDY: You think he suspected someone was gonna
32. try and fuck up the treaty?

1.   JETHRO JOHNNY: Never saw nothin' coming. He trusted the
2. wrong muscle. He would've been better served lifting a coupla
3. books about Julius Caesar than lifting all them weights.
4.   PRETTY RUDY: We beat 'em with history every time.
5.   JETHRO JOHNNY: Deserved what he got.
6.   PRETTY RUDY: Some people don't get enough of what they
7. deserve.
8.   JETHRO JOHNNY: I set up that *terrón* for the hit and waited
9. till a Mexican guard spread the rumor Bandit was killed by a
10. nigger—you saw the news, it lit that jail up.
11.   PRETTY RUDY: The little homies were on that bait faster
12. than a hobo on a ham sandwich.
13.   JETHRO JOHNNY: Got that right.
14.   PRETTY RUDY: Anyway, you made it work better than me
15. and Gordo expected.
16.   JETHRO JOHNNY: Cue the clusterfuck, *qué no?*
17.   PRETTY RUDY: The boys at Pelican Bay are already going
18. crazy trying to figure out who betrayed who.
19.   JETHRO JOHNNY: Punks. Broke weak with that peace
20. treaty shit.
21.   PRETTY RUDY: By the time the smoke clears there'll be bod-
22. ies for days. Gordo will have consolidated his shit. Then we're
23. golden.
24.   JETHRO JOHNNY: As my six-year-old niece says, easy peezy
25. lemon squeezy.
26.   (MUSIC PLAYS . . .)
27.   JETHRO JOHNNY: Hey, check out Francesco's. Looks the
28. same as twenty years ago.
29.   PRETTY RUDY: That should be their motto: *Francesco's,*
30. *since 1962. Ain't nothin' changed but the weather . . .* Hey, so
31. I'm gonna park here and go check in across the street.
32.   JETHRO JOHNNY: Local 6, there?

1.   PRETTY RUDY: Yeah. Gordo's in there. Got the longshore-
2. men on a lockdown vote.
3.   JETHRO JOHNNY: I'ma stay in the car and call my *jefita*
4. while you check shit out.
5.   PRETTY RUDY: Yeah, awright. Tell her I said hey.
6.   JETHRO JOHNNY: *Órale.* You gonna be all right getting outta
7. the car with your bum getaway stick?
8.   PRETTY RUDY: Don't worry 'bout me, *pendejo* . . . But all kid-
9. ding aside, you put in good work, homeboy. *Te aventaste.*
10.   JETHRO JOHNNY: Does that mean the massage and dancing
11. are off the table now?
12.   PRETTY RUDY: Call Ma Duke. I gotta check this out.
13.   JETHRO JOHNNY: *Gracias.* And leave the car running. I
14. wanna hear the music.
15.   (PRETTY RUDY EXITS CAR. DOOR SLAMS. CELL PHONE
16. BEEPS.)
17.   JETHRO JOHNNY: You see us drive up? . . . Cool. So when he
18. gets back in the car, walk over slow, hands at your side. You're
19. only wearing a T-shirt, right? . . . Tuck that shit in. I don't want
20. him thinking you're packing. Okay? Go.
21.   (MUSIC VOLUME RISES, DOOR OPENS)
22.   JETHRO JOHNNY: Hey, so you hurt your leg how again?
23.   PRETTY RUDY: Don't go there, man.
24.   JETHRO JOHNNY: No, *en serio.* You said something about
25. slipping but I didn't get what the fuck that means.
26.   PRETTY RUDY: Slipped on ice.
27.   JETHRO JOHNNY: Ice? What the fuck . . . Hey, there's my
28. homeboy Silly Chino.
29.   PRETTY RUDY: What's he doing here?
30.   JETHRO JOHNNY: Bringing me a boatload of cash in that
31. backpack.
32.   PRETTY RUDY: How'd he know we were gonna be here?

1. JETHRO JOHNNY: Don't get all panicky, homeboy. That's my
2. little homie. I called when you were buying tampons. Look at his
3. goofy-ass T-shirt, all tucked in and shit . . . How do I roll this
4. window down?
5. PRETTY RUDY: I control it—here, I got it.
6. (SOUND OF WINDOW OPENING.)
7. SILLY CHINO: Hey, Jethro Johnny, good to see you out. (un-
8. intelligible) Here's your backpack.
9. JETHRO JOHNNY: Thanks . . . Silly Chino, this is my road
10. dog, Pretty Rudy.
11. SILLY CHINO: *Mucho gusto.*
12. PRETTY RUDY: Yeah, me too.
13. JETHRO JOHNNY: Hey, so untuck that shirt, you look lame.
14. But thanks for this. I'll call in a few hours. Catch up on account-
15. ing. Awright?
16. SILLY CHINO: Awright. I'll be at the pad. Good to finally meet
17. you, Pretty Rudy.
18. PRETTY RUDY: Stay up, youngster.
19. JETHRO JOHNNY: So later, right?
20. SILLY CHINO: Yeah. *Te watcho.*
21. (SOUND OF WINDOW ROLLING UP.)
22. JETHRO JOHNNY: See, that wasn't bad.
23. PRETTY RUDY: Respectful youngster.
24. JETHRO JOHNNY: Kid's sharp. Couldn't tell right there but
25. he's got mack for days. He could talk a cat off a fish truck. Gots
26. long heart too. He'll be us one day.
27. PRETTY RUDY: So that's all cash in the bag?
28. JETHRO JOHNNY: Look for yourself.
29. (SOUND OF ZIPPER.)
30. PRETTY RUDY: That's a lot of *feria*, homie. Ah fuck, smell
31. that? Zip that shit up.
32. JETHRO JOHNNY: Money fuckin' stinks like a camel's crack.

1.   PRETTY RUDY: I don't even wanna know how you know
2. what a camel's crack smells like.
3.   JETHRO JOHNNY: *Fuck-an-Animal Digest*, the scratch-and-
4. sniff page. I used your copy at the crib, so don't look at me like
5. that.
6.   (BOTH LAUGH.)
7.   PRETTY RUDY: Sick puppy, homes . . . That stench reminds
8. me of the time I robbed a vault and dumped the loot on my bed.
9. Laid in it like a fuckin' little kid.
10.   JETHRO JOHNNY: What, you thought you were in the
11. movies?
12.   PRETTY RUDY: Over a hundred grand on that bed. All of a
13. sudden I smelled something so bad I swear I thought I'd stepped
14. in shit. So I jump up, check my shoes, but nothin'.
15.   JETHRO JOHNNY: Leftover camel sweat on your covers.
16.   PRETTY RUDY: Sniff sheets, pillow, shirt—nothin'. Finally,
17. going crazy looking for what's causing the smell—I figure out
18. it's the cash.
19.   JETHRO JOHNNY: Man, you gotta roll the windows down!
20.   (BOTH LAUGH.)
21.   PRETTY RUDY: Filthy fuckin' people. Wipe their ass cracks,
22. don't wash their hands, then put their funky fingers all over the
23. bills to buy a Big Mac.
24.   JETHRO JOHNNY: Fuck. Smells worse than a Tijuana whore-
25. house on dime night.
26.   (BOTH LAUGH HARDER.)
27.   JETHRO JOHNNY: So your knee? Mexicans ain't supposed
28. to be on ice, especially ones with obvious gland problems. You
29. know that.
30.   PRETTY RUDY: Look, your homeboy's coming back.
31.   JETHRO JOHNNY: Yeah, about that (rustling sound) snitch
32. motherfucker—

1.   PRETTY RUDY: So you're gonna shoot me? That's what's
2. happening?
3.   JETHRO JOHNNY: Gordo says your weak-ass rat game
4. earned you these bullets.
5.   PRETTY RUDY: Frankly, my dear, I don't give a damn.
6.   (MULTIPLE GUNSHOTS, THEN DOOR OPENS.)
7.   SILLY CHINO: Fuckin' gun jammed. C'mon. Before the cops
8. get here.
9.   (SOUND OF SOMEONE SPITTING.)
10.   PRETTY RUDY: Look at you. Thought you were slick. Now
11. you're just another fool, learned the hard way. Ain't no fun when
12. the rabbit's got the gun.
13.   (FOOTSTEPS RUNNING. CAR DOOR SLAMS. SQUEAL OF
14. TIRES.)
15.
16.
17.
18.
19.
20.
21.
22.
23.
24.
25.
26.
27.
28.
29.
30.
31.
32.

1.
2.   STATE OF CALIFORNIA,)
3.   COUNTY OF LOS ANGELES.)
4.
5.
6.
7.   I, POMPTON X. GALA, a Certified Shorthand Reporter in and
8.   for the County of Los Angeles, State of California, do hereby
9.   certify:
10.   That on February 11, 2016, thereof, I transcribed the text/
11.   electronic/audiotaped recording of the proceedings; that the
12.   foregoing transcript constitutes a full, true, and correct tran-
13.   scription of all proceedings had and given.
14.   IN WITNESS HEREOF, I have hereunto set my hand and af-
15.   fixed my Official Seal on February 11, 2016.
16.
17.
18.
19.
20.
21.
22.   _____
23.   POMPTON X. GALA, CSR #(d)-10-5942
24.   Certified Shorthand Reporter
25.
26.
27.
28.
29.
30.
31.
32.

1.
2. SUPERIOR COURT OF CALIFORNIA, COUNTY OF LOS ANGELES
3. —oOo—
4. THE PEOPLE OF THE STATE OF)
5. CALIFORNIA,)
6.)
7. Plaintiff(s),) Case No. 01x45728b
8. vs.)
9. RUDOLFO GOMEZ aka PRETTY RUDY)
10. Defendants(s))
11. _____)
12.
13.
14.
15.   AUDIOTAPE
16.   GOMEZ RESIDENCE CONVERSATION BETWEEN
17.   RUDOLFO GOMEZ, aka "PRETTY RUDY,"
18.   and HARRY GONG-LERMA, aka "SILLY CHINO,"
19.   4:00 PM, January 5, 2016
20.
21.
22.
23.
24.
25. Transcribed by:
26. POMPTON X. GALA REPORTING SERVICES
27. 9694 San Fernando Road, Suite C
28. Los Angeles, California 90057
29. Telephone: (323) 555-1287
30.
31.
32.

1.   SILLY CHINO: What's up with you, *tío?* Look like you just
2. saw your new girlfriend blowing Brad Pitt near the toaster.
3.   PRETTY RUDY: Nah, it's just there's this new thing where
4. I'm pouring water in coffee, or pouring anything really, then
5. something takes control of my arm, and I'm talking to my arm,
6. like, *Quit pouring that on the cookies,* or the counter, or what-
7. ever. Like my brain knows I'm not supposed to be missing the
8. mark that bad but my hand ain't got the memo yet.
9.   SILLY CHINO: Does your hand just keep pouring and then
10. put the water or milk back in the fridge on its own? Or does it
11. go back to the cup?
12.   PRETTY RUDY: The water slides back to pour in the cup, like
13. nothing happened. But not soon enough.
14.   SILLY CHINO: Weird. Must suck getting old, huh?
15.   PRETTY RUDY: Yeah, like it must suck being such a dopey
16. motherfucker.
17.   SILLY CHINO: Just sayin', that sounds serious, like that Lou
18. Diamond disease.
19.   PRETTY RUDY: Lou Gehrig's disease. Looked it up online
20. yesterday, degenerative shit. Lou Diamond's only disease is he's
21. a degenerate who stars in shitty flicks.
22.   SILLY CHINO: Lou Gehrig, Lou Diamond, who gives a fuck?
23. Whatever they call it, you still end up with old-timer's disease.
24.   PRETTY RUDY: Does make me think of Michael J. Fox,
25. though. Wonder if he started to notice a lot of tiny bad spills
26. before he went full-blown shaky?
27.   SILLY CHINO: You think when his body started to lose con-
28. trol he was like, *Fuck, I gotta do shit. My time's almost up?*
29.   PRETTY RUDY: Hell yeah. I'm spilling just a little more than
30. usual and I'm like already figuring out a bucket list.
31.   SILLY CHINO: I ever learn I'm gonna die soon, I'ma start a
32. fuck-it list. Just go do some crazy I-don't-give-a-fuck shit.

1.   PRETTY RUDY: Funny you say that. First thing on my
2. bucket list actually is a fuck-it list.
3.   SILLY CHINO: You wanna just say *fuck it* too?
4.   PRETTY RUDY: No, I wanna like literally fuck a porn star.
5. And not some stripper on the corner with a cam site. Like a
6. righteous porn idol from way back. Bring 'em out of retirement
7. if I gotta.
8.   SILLY CHINO: Like who?
9.   PRETTY RUDY: Kay Parker, Christy Canyon, Nina Hartley—
10. who's still in the game and ain't lost a beat—Honey Wilder maybe
11. too.
12.   SILLY CHINO: I don't know none of them names.
13.   PRETTY RUDY: 'Course not. You pull your pud to all that
14. slope anime porn, jacking off to fuckin' cartoons. Yours is a
15. loopy generation.
16.   SILLY CHINO: Them anime broads are perfect. No worrying
17. 'bout wrinkles, cellulite, and shit.
18.   PRETTY RUDY: You into pixels. I'm into real pussy with
19. bushy cavewoman pubes.
20.   SILLY CHINO: What else you got on your bucket list? Mount
21. Everest? Race-car driving?
22.   PRETTY RUDY: Fuck no! The thing's to try *not to die* while
23. doing your bucket list.
24.   SILLY CHINO: Then what?
25.   PRETTY RUDY: You know how they got names for sex posi-
26. tions? Like the Rusty Trombone? Dirty Sanchez?
27.   SILLY CHINO: Yeah, my favorite is the Tony Danza.
28.   PRETTY RUDY: What the fuck?
29.   SILLY CHINO: It's when you're fuckin' some chick doggy-
30. style, then when you're about to drop your load you punch her
31. in the back of the head and yell out, *Who's the boss!*
32.   PRETTY RUDY: (laughs)

SILLY CHINO: Or the Coyote Ugly. It's when you wake up with the ugly broad you banged the night before all cuddled up and asleep on your arm. So you gnaw that fuckin' arm off like a trapped coyote and leave it there.

PRETTY RUDY: I take it back. Your generation ain't half bad.

SILLY CHINO: So what about the sex names?

PRETTY RUDY: I want to nickname a sex act.

SILLY CHINO: Ha ha! For your bucket list? Ha! Why not?

PRETTY RUDY: Exactly. So the other night I was doing 69 with this broad, and she's really fuckin' chowing down on my schlong, and I'm thinking this cunt is a goddamn cannibal the way she's gobbling my meat. I mean, Sudanese refugees who ain't eaten in three weeks devour a meal less savagely than this fuckin' bitch on my pipe.

SILLY CHINO: Call it 69ing the Sudanese Refugee. Or better yet—the Walking Dead.

PRETTY RUDY: I said cannibal, not zombie, you dumb-ass. Nah, I'm thinking of naming it the Donner Party.

SILLY CHINO: (laughs hard)

PRETTY RUDY: Works, right? Num-num, all grubbing on groin and shit.

SILLY CHINO: I'm thinking of some *paisa* in TJ all *dame el Donner Party, con fuerza.*

PRETTY RUDY: *Dame, con hambre, chiquita!*

(HARD LAUGHTER.)

SILLY CHINO: Motherfucker, that's on point, *tío*.

PRETTY RUDY: Yeah. So I can cross that one off now, I suppose. Next, well, I'm not sure if losing weight is a bucket list thing or not.

SILLY CHINO: That feels more like a New Year's resolution thing. Like trying to quit smoking. Or maybe this year quit spilling food on every shirt you own.

1.   PRETTY RUDY: Wait. What you really saying?

2.   SILLY CHINO: Look at your shirt. What, the food at Burger

3. King was so good you had to bring some home with you? That's

4. your last six days: six different shirts.

5.   PRETTY RUDY: I know, I know. That's actually one reason

6. I wanna lose weight. No bullshit. Dry cleaning bill's killing me.

7.   SILLY CHINO: What's another reason?

8.   PRETTY RUDY: What?

9.   SILLY CHINO: You said stains on your shirts are one reason

10. you wanna lose weight. What's another?

11.   PRETTY RUDY: I was jacking off the other day, and right

12. when I was 'bout to bust a nut, my stomach cramped so hard I

13. thought my appendix burst.

14.   SILLY CHINO: (laughs hard) Stop! Stop!

15.   PRETTY RUDY: I was yanking my shitty little dick all bellig-

16. erent and shit, so my belly got all twisted up from my aggressive

17. reach-over.

18.   SILLY CHINO: That's why they got massage parlors, *tío*. You

19. shoulda retired your hand in the nineties.

20.   PRETTY RUDY: Sometimes the urge is stronger than logic,

21. kid.

22.   SILLY CHINO: What you do?

23.   PRETTY RUDY: What I do? Well, first I screamed out like a

24. broad. Then I laughed my ass off.

25.   SILLY CHINO: Hey, you know how you said when you walked

26. out the kitchen how your hand had a mind of its own sometimes?

27.   PRETTY RUDY: Yeah?

28.   SILLY CHINO: So when you're stroking yourself, your hand

29. ever like lose control and reach out to jack the cock nearest to

30. you? (bursts out laughing)

31.   PRETTY RUDY: Fuck, you smart-aleck punk, I should—

32.   SILLY CHINO: Nah, it's just, you know, you were sayin'—

1.   PRETTY RUDY: Fuck that. You can't clean that shit up.
2.   SILLY CHINO: It's just, you know, maybe I'm minding my
3. own business one day, then your hand starts giving me a slow
4. ride.
5.   PRETTY RUDY: Don't go there, youngblood.
6.   SILLY CHINO: It's just, I wanna know what's the protocol
7. for a rogue hand job.
8.   PRETTY RUDY: You got some balls on you, kid!
9.   SILLY CHINO: You see, that concerns me that you know any-
10. thing about the size of my balls. Should I be concerned? (laughs)
11.   PRETTY RUDY: That's it. Get me my gun. Let's go do this
12. before I shoot you right here and pick up my third strike, while
13. that mutinous motherfucker gets to walk the planet free.
14.   SILLY CHINO: Just keep your hands to yourself, that's all
15. I'm saying . . . And here's your Magnum. You want the revolver
16. instead?
17.   PRETTY RUDY: This'll do. Now remember, give *him* the gun
18. with blanks. And shoot him once in the head, twice in the chest.
19.   SILLY CHINO: I know! I know!
20.   PRETTY RUDY: The money's real good on this one. Your
21. aunt gets a better tombstone.
22.   SILLY CHINO: Let me hear it again.
23.   PRETTY RUDY: Nah, not now. We're about to go—
24.   SILLY CHINO: Now is the exact right time. We're gonna go
25. put this dude in the crypt. I wanna hear my Aunt Maggie's voice
26. again.
27.   PRETTY RUDY: Okay. Only 'cause you were her favorite.
28.   (RUSTLING NOISES.)
29.   TÍA MAGGIE: (on voice mail playback) *Hey, honey. Can you*
30. *please bring some of them Lorna Doone Shortbread Cookies*
31. *when you come back to the hospital? A nurse here let me have*
32. *one yesterday, reminded me I got some in the cupboard above*

1. *the fridge. Thanks, I love you. You're the best, babe. Tell Chino I*
2. *love him too. And kiss Pokey for me. And don't forget to give her*
3. *the medicine by her food bucket. See you soon. Mwah!*
4.   (CLICKS OFF.)
5.   PRETTY RUDY: Right. Let's go punch this punk's ticket . . .
6. Last thing I'ma say to him is, *Ain't no fun when the rabbit's got*
7. *the gun.*
8.   (FOOTSTEPS. DOOR OPENS.)
9.   SILLY CHINO: I was talking to Big Ralph, my old biker cell-
10. mate from Fresno. Says he wants me to join his crew. You think
11. I could be a Hell's Angel?
12.   PRETTY RUDY: Fuck them. You don't wanna be a Hell's An-
13. gel. Now, a Charlie's Angel? Fuck yeah!
14.   SILLY CHINO: Aaahhh! I don't know why I waste my time
15. asking you a serious question.
16.   PRETTY RUDY: No, really. You could be a Charlie's Angel all
17. day long. All the fellas at the bar say you got a pretty mouth.
18.   (LAUGHTER. DOOR SLAMS SHUT.)

1.
2.
3.
4.
5.
6.
7.
8.   STATE OF CALIFORNIA,.)
9.   )
10.   COUNTY OF LOS ANGELES.)
11.
12.
13.
14.
15.   I, POMPTON X. GALA, a Certified Shorthand Reporter in and
16. for the County of Los Angeles, State of California, do hereby
17. certify:
18.   That on February 11, 2016, thereof, I transcribed the text/
19. electronic/audiotaped recording of the proceedings; that the
20. foregoing transcript constitutes a full, true, and correct tran-
21. scription of all proceedings had and given.
22.   IN WITNESS HEREOF, I have hereunto set my hand and af-
23. fixed my Official Seal on February 11, 2016.
24.
25.
26.
27.
28.   _____
29.   POMPTON X. GALA, CSR #(d)-10-5942
30.   Certified Shorthand Reporter
31.
32.

THE HANDYMAN

BY EDDIE MULLER

Alameda

First time I set foot in Alameda, I moved there. Laurie and I had been searching all over the East Bay for an escape route out of San Francisco, and not long after emerging from the tube that links downtown Oakland to Alameda, we spotted a *For Rent* sign in the upper window of a place on Central Avenue. It was a late June afternoon, and the sun cast a warm glow across the majestic Edwardian-style structure and the gorgeous garden that bloomed out front.

There was a phone number on the sign, too small to read.

"Let's just go ring the bell," Laurie said.

We'd seen more than two dozen places that week and this was the first one that had made Laurie excited. She was out of the car before I could get my glasses on. That's crucial, looking back now. If I could have seen the phone number on the sign, if I had told her, *It's getting late, let's call tomorrow,* maybe everything would have turned out differently. Maybe not. I've thought a lot about how things might have turned out differently. It's all I do, really.

We crossed the garden to a pathway leading up to the entrance. A woman was leaving the house, an attractive African American in conservative business dress, with a young girl, her daughter I presumed, holding her hand. We smiled in passing. I dismissed the possibility that she was the owner, or the current tenant. She said to our backs, "You don't want that place, believe me."

Laurie was nonplussed, and I turned around, saying, "Why's that? Is there something wrong with it?"

"Yeah, *I* want it!" She tried to laugh it off, only it wasn't funny. "Oh my God, the place is *fantastic*," she said. "It's everything I ever wanted. And a good school just blocks away? I won't ever find a place like this in Oakland." She picked her daughter up and hugged her, appearing to be on the verge of tears. Grimly, she said, "You looking to rent this place?"

"Driving around, that's all," Laurie said quickly. "We just like to look."

"I could actually afford it. Maybe." She stroked her daughter's head. "But we'll probably never get in a place like this." She surveyed the lush grounds—a gorgeous Japanese red maple formed a canopy over a bubbling koi pond—then gazed at the house looming above. Finally she said, "C'mon, baby, we got to get home."

"Okay, *that* was uncomfortable," I whispered, climbing a few steps to the front door, which was still open.

We rang the bell, knocked, called out—that's how eager we were—and presently a tiny figure appeared, coming rapidly down the stairway: a petite Asian woman, her wiry gray hair pulled back into a bun. Hard to figure her age; could have been anywhere between fifty and seventy. She wore a simple denim smock and slip-on sandals. Stepping between us, she glanced down the pathway, squinting through delicate, wire-framed glasses.

"She gone?"

"Who?" Laurie said, playing dumb.

"The black. She gone?"

We shuffled awkwardly, coughing a few noises that weren't words.

"Single mother never good tenant. They bring home men.

Men make them do drugs, maybe gamble. 'Specially blacks. Black woman means black man. No trust. She pay rent, maybe he steal her money, gamble." She looked us up and down and grinned. "You last ones. Agent gone now, but I show you place myself. I live bottom unit, other side. You need something, I always here. My name Phi."

Laurie loved the place so much it made me jealous. She certainly hadn't oohed and aahed and carried on so ecstatically when she'd first laid eyes on me. The original house—probably a second home for some nineteenth-century San Francisco Gold Rush millionaire—had been converted into a duplex, and the upper unit was nothing short of glorious: two spacious bedrooms with high coved ceilings, big picture windows with leaded-glass panes, tasteful new carpeting, a large fireplace in a grand living room, built-in bookcases and china cabinets, a deck off the dining room, a remodeled kitchen with a Jenn-Air range—it was insanely great. And it was okay for us to have a cat. Our recently rescued Burmese would be moving from the streets to a dream home.

"Everything top-notch," the landlady kept repeating. "You make sure keep good condition." In the main bedroom, she gestured at windows on the east and west sides. "Best thing! Sun rise this room, all day never go way. Sun circle house this way, evening sunset living room. Light very beautiful, like Renaissance painting."

We were ready to sign a lifetime lease even before she opened the narrow door off the central hallway. "Come up. Show you what I do in attic." She led us up a slender switchback stairway almost too small for me. We emerged into an entirely separate apartment, which included a brand-new, unused bathroom. Skylights made the cloistered space feel airy, even expansive. Laurie dug her fingers into my arm. "Oh my God," she whispered, more emphatically than when we had sex. "This is unbelievable. This is perfect. I can run my business here. I don't need an office—*look at all this room.*"

As we took a final look around—we didn't want to leave— we spewed our life stories to Phi, lying that we were married and otherwise convincing her that we were model citizens with abundant bank accounts, rock-solid credit, guaranteed lifetime employment, and no vices beyond having recently rescued a small black cat. She finally raised a hand, stanching our flow of self-aggrandizement.

"You handy?" she asked, measuring me with a level gaze.

"How so, exactly?"

"Handy! You good fixing?"

"Oh . . . *handy.* Oh, yeah, sure. She calls me Mr. Fix-It."

Laurie was tall enough that Phi couldn't see the comically incredulous expression on her face. Truth was, I couldn't hammer a nail straight and I had a talent for stripping every screw I'd ever tried to tighten. But to score this place, I'd damn well *become* handy.

"Happy, happy," Phi said. "Glad you handy." When she smiled, she looked twenty years younger. She'd been an attractive woman once. She patted my chest. "You nice couple. I like you. You live here. I call company, tell them apartment rented."

Before I met her, Laurie had been a high school teacher, but that didn't work out, I figured, because every male student had crushed on her. She was a prize—smart, funny, empathetic, and beautiful in the most disarming, unself-conscious way. She had everything—but didn't like to be reminded of it. A public job, she'd decided, was not her style. She didn't like to be the center of attention.

By the time I'd fallen madly in love—and convinced her

we needed to live together—Laurie had been seized by the entrepreneurial zeal that energized lots of young people in the early nineties. Bush was out, Clinton was in, and suddenly for us lefties making money was a capitalist continuation of the counterculture we'd missed out on. Fight the Man by making dough your own way. Find a live-work space. Build your own business. Make a few million and *then* sell out to a big corporation. Retire young and do fuck-all for the rest of your charmed life. That seemed to be the strategy, based on the few examples I'd seen. Follow your bliss, business-wise.

For Laurie, this meant founding a greeting card company. She dreamed of doing it all, bottom to top: designer, illustrator, manufacturer, marketing manager, distributor, CEO. All this responsibility, of course, would be just until she established her brand. Then there'd be expansion and outsourcing, maybe fewer eighteen-hour workdays. It'd take maybe a year or more to reach that stage—but in the meantime she'd found the perfect place to build the ship, rig it just right, and set it sailing.

That's no casually chosen metaphor, by the way. I'd gotten a job in the traffic department of a big shipping outfit based in downtown Oakland. My department sold space on trans-Pacific ocean carriage. All those cranes you see lining the waterfront as you drive the bend of 880—they're all picking containers from gigantic ships off-loading the endless tide of shit that keeps the American economy humming. Not much goes the other way. My job was to figure how to reposition empty boxes—dead-heading, it's called—without the company taking too big a loss in the westbound lanes. Fascinating stuff, maybe even *important*—but not as gratifying as creating and selling a greeting card.

I didn't have much involvement in Laurie's business—beyond bringing in the steady, relatively substantial paycheck and the company medical plan, which allowed her to invest so completely in the development of her dream. I was left with plenty of time to learn new things on my own—like how to be handy.

After four months of blissful residency in the Garden of Eden, our cat disappeared. This would lead directly to my initial display of handiness. But first, for two days, the loss of our beloved Cricket threatened to capsize Laurie's unbridled determination. Did I mention empathy was one of her overwhelming traits? She could not function with Cricket gone. Thoughts of the cat injured, crying for help, killed by a predator—all too much to bear.

We were walking back from our third round of posting *Missing Cat* notices when Laurie heard a tiny meow overhead, from the deck of our apartment. Cricket, I surmised upon closer inspection, had strolled between the posts of the guardrail, slid down the shingled eaves, dropped into a rain gutter, and instead of clawing her way back up the shingles, had gone *under* them, into a tiny crawlspace beneath the deck. The hundreds of long nails that attach the shingles had been hammered right through—the poor cat couldn't crawl out without getting impaled.

I rang our landlady's doorbell. She came to the door wearing a silk robe and a frightened expression. It was already dark, but we couldn't stand the thought of Cricket alone for one more night.

"It's our cat," I explained. "We found her but can't get to her. She's stuck right up there, under the deck."

"Why you not get her?"

"I have to cut away part of the roof. The nails, there's hundreds of 'em, all in at an angle. She can't get past them."

She considered this for a moment, then said, "No back up. Tire damage."

I laughed. "Exactly."

"You can do? You cut hole, you put back—good as new?"

"Of course. Good as new. Better."

She knew I was a bullshitter, but didn't seem to care. All she said was, "You do now. Must do tonight. Tomorrow, no noise."

"Thank you so much, thank you, Phi." It was the first time I'd called her by name. Trotting down her porch steps, I tried to figure out how I'd pull off this rescue mission.

"Hey!" she called after me. "Mr. Fix-It. You need tall ladder. One in back. I show you."

That old saw about necessity being the mother of invention—I proved the fuck out of it. Before midnight Laurie was cradling Cricket in her arms, and Phi was shining a flashlight on the shingles I'd replaced after cutting out an escape hatch for the cat. There were seams—I wasn't a professional *yet*—but Phi had to squat down and stare intently through her wire-rims to see the cuts. I'd even vacuumed the sawdust from the rain gutter.

"Everyone happy," she said, standing up and patting my chest a few times. "You handy." She scratched Cricket's head and smiled up at Laurie: "He *very* handy."

The following day was a Saturday and Laurie came down from the upstairs office about two p.m. I'd fixed some leftovers for lunch and we both doted goofily on Cricket, taking ridiculous pleasure in watching her sleeping in a patch of sunlight, her furry belly rising and falling peacefully. Her ears suddenly perked at a clanking noise outside, and I went to the window to check it out. A white van was out front, its side doors open and a lift-gate extended. A guy in a wheelchair was being rolled onto the platform by a uniformed orderly. Phi scurried up the driveway to meet them. I couldn't see much of the handicapped guy; he was wrapped in a blanket, wore a lopsided baseball cap, and seemed comatose.

"What's this about?" Laurie asked, coming up beside me.

"No idea."

Phi clasped the orderly's hand and slipped something into it before waving goodbye. She pushed the wheelchair and its unmoving occupant up to her house.

"Huh—so that wooden ramp is *practical*," Laurie said. "I thought it was just another cool part of the landscaping."

When the van's doors closed, we saw the writing on the side: *Veterans Administration Hospital*.

Two nights later, just after two a.m., the screaming started.

Laurie and I bolted upright in bed. "Holy fuck," she gasped. "What the hell is *that*?" Cricket was at the foot of the bed, her back up, wide eyes staring at us.

The sound was coming up from the floor directly below. A tortured wail, worse than anything in a horror movie. This was anguish—real, primal, and terrifying. Laurie clutched Cricket, trying to keep her calm. I paced around, muttering, "What the fuck?" under my breath each time the howling started.

"Maybe you should go down and see what's happening," Laurie whispered.

"No, listen," I said, "it's not an accident or something. It doesn't change. He's just . . . screaming."

"It's so painful." Laurie began to cry.

Those forty minutes were an eternity.

It didn't happen every night. But from then on our sleep was fitful at best. The expectation of the screaming was almost as excruciating as actually hearing it. We took to having sex in places other than the bedroom, fearful that the sudden howling might contaminate our lovemaking forever. After enduring a dozens or so fits, Laurie began working later and later in the attic office, sometimes until three a.m. I'd come up and find her crashed out, head on the desk, and she'd be irritable all the next day. Over dinner one night, peering out into the darkness, she said morosely, "It was all so perfect before."

I can't explain it, but I felt her disappointment was somehow my fault.

Coming home from work one day I found Phi hunkered in the garden beside the koi pond. She was rigging a cage on the rocks bordering the small pool.

"What's that for?"

"Raccoon got fish, goddamnit!" I almost laughed at her cursing like a redneck. "Now I get raccoon."

"Why not just put a wire cover over it?"

"Not look *nice*. And raccoon too smart, too strong. Lift cover."

"But he'll just waltz into a cage? That wouldn't be smart."

"I use bait. Fig Newton and fish sauce. He not able resist."

"Really? Where'd you learn that?"

"I know many things," she said, flashing that younger woman's smile. "Not born yesterday."

That got us talking, which, of course, no one *ever* does with a landlord. I was just looking for some clues about the screaming, and whether there was any hope it would end. But after a few minutes, I'd forgotten about the nocturnal horror shows and was listening intently—parsing through her pidgin English—as she gave me her life story, telling me things that Laurie and I would never have thought to ask.

Her father worked for the Vichy government in Vietnam during World War II. Her mother was Japanese, part of the occupation of French Indochina. They had to keep their love a secret. Her father pulled strings to get her into the best schools. She eventually trained at a university to be an architect. She loved art history, made it her minor, with a special focus on painting. Her father was killed by communist insurgents who wanted to run the French off the Indo-Chinese peninsula. Then America decided to wage war against the Democratic Republic of Vietnam, the centerpiece of its global campaign against communism. Her mother was killed in the early sixties; collateral damage. War, she feared, was all she'd ever know. There had to be beauty in the world, she figured, because she'd seen it in art, in paintings. She grew up in hell, but survived. It was a skill, she explained, like sailing or carpentry. As the war was ending she volunteered at a military hospital, where she met a shell-shocked GI, Corporal Paul Gennaro. He'd lost an arm, part of a leg, and maybe more. He had no family, no home to be shipped back to. As Saigon fell, she proposed to him, promising she'd always take care of him. It got them both shipped stateside.

For more than eighteen years she'd been married to the screaming.

To be honest, the history lesson was hard to follow, since Americans don't know jack-shit about the world, or the wars we get into. I pieced most of this together later, from library books. At the moment, all I could say was, "Wow, you've sure had an amazing life."

"America save me," she replied. "But you know what I do now? Only one thing. Woman like me, here I only able do one thing."

"What's that?"

"Own property. America not see me, people here never see

me. They see money. See my money *good*. Eight property in Alameda. Vietnam, I design building. Here, I just own them."

My only response was, "Huh."

Then she said: "You hear him, my husband. You hear him in night."

"Sometimes, yeah."

"I sorry. Very bad. They keep him hospital but now only for short time, each time. Drugs they give make worse, not better. I so sorry. Not want to bother you. No, no, no. You and your wife work hard. I see—she hard worker. Like me once."

There was a big commotion out front a few days later. Cricket was freaking out, bouncing all over the living room. I realized what was happening and ran outside.

The raccoon was huge, practically filling the cage. It shook the trap viciously, its eyes burning red. Phi was standing casually nearby, staring at it. She had a baseball bat in her hands.

"Fig Newtons and fish sauce," I said. "I'll never doubt you."

She handed me the bat. "Here. You do it."

"Do what?"

"Kill it."

"*Kill it?* I'm not going to kill it." I was stunned. "There are people you can call, they'll take it into the hills and turn it loose. Let's just do that."

"That cost money," she scoffed. "You want to pay? It eat fish, eat my plants." She shoved the bat into my hands. I took it, just to keep her from doing anything drastic. "I open cage," she said, gesturing. "You smash quick."

By now Laurie had appeared, rushing out in a robe and bare feet. She took one look, made an awful crying sound, and rushed back inside.

"I'll pay to have it taken away," I said. "I won't kill it."

She studied me. It felt like I was being examined under a microscope. "Maybe you not so handy."

Later, when Raccoon Removal Service came to take the poor thing away—alive—Phi came out and stood next to me, watching them load it into the back of a van, where several other traps were already stacked, a half-dozen caged raccoons glowering warily. A guy in coveralls and heavy gloves did all the work. His partner sat in the passenger seat, wearing mirrored sunglasses. He only watched, a small grin never leaving his face.

Phi read my mind: "That one do killing."

"Don't say that," I moaned.

"Your cat get hit by car, cannot walk. What you do?"

"Take care of it the best we can, of course."

"It in pain, all the time. You think you help. But it in pain *all* the time. All it know—pain." She stared up at me, her usually squinted eyes sharp as glass. "All it feel, ever—*pain*. Maybe then you do it. Maybe then you do what need be done."

The screaming went on. And despite the misery—which had us seeking refuge at night in the living room, on separate couches, wearing earplugs—Laurie persevered. She started selling to stores in the area and steadily grew the account list and her territory. At all hours the fax machine in her office chugged away—a welcome sound in the night—spitting out orders from new buyers.

We'd succeeded. We'd achieved what all bright, young, hardworking American couples were supposed to achieve—but frustration was always there. We weren't happy here anymore. Our heaven-sent sanctuary had been snatched away. We were living above a psych ward, its night terrors erupting just when we thought they might be over. The VA, I found out, had cut off any further in-hospital care for Corporal Paul Gennaro.

* * *

Laurie met her twin at a local craft show, a jewelry maker named Remy. She was soon spending more and more time at Remy's studio loft in Jack London Square. They talked about teaming up to create a more expansive and profitable product line. Whenever they were together I was the outsider—even though I was the financial backbone of the operation. And though the business was growing, it was a long way from being in the black.

Then a terse e-mail notice arrived in my inbox at work: the company was moving to North Carolina. It was a shock, completely out of the blue. This was a gigantic firm, a cornerstone of Oakland's economy. The idea that it could just abandon the city, dumping thousands of employees, was unthinkable, at least to a human being. But then, human beings don't think like CEOs. Or their masters, the shareholders.

There was no way Laurie would move—she couldn't uproot a business she'd worked so hard to build. If I relocated, regularly sending back paychecks until her business was self-sufficient . . . well, that wouldn't work, either. I didn't trust she'd need me when I came back. I convinced myself that losing my salary, losing my benefits, losing the monthly rent—it meant losing her. I had to find another job fast, or somehow replace the income I was about to lose.

Actually, that's probably all bullshit. Just a way to rationalize what happened next. Something else entirely was at work, some gnawing part of me I didn't understand and didn't want to understand. Something I'm only now starting to comprehend, all these years later.

Laurie was at a trade show in Los Angeles—with Remy, of course—when the screaming, incredibly, got even worse. Instead of jamming in the earplugs, or finding an after-hours bar, or getting a hotel room for the night, I stretched out on the bedroom floor, closer to it than ever, and absorbed the brunt of its horror.

If she could stand it, down there in hell's black belly, so could I.

In the morning, before dawn, I rang Phi's doorbell. She answered, looking drawn, haggard, and devoid of hope.

"Okay, I'll do it," I said. "But it has to be tonight or tomorrow. Laurie will be back Monday morning."

She stepped onto the porch and pulled the door closed behind her. I laid out my conditions and she nodded sadly.

It happened that night, just as I figured. She'd been waiting a long time and wasn't about to let the chance go by. She let me in a little after ten p.m. No one was on the streets and the televisions would still be on in nearby houses. The place was dark but what I could see, just as I expected, was tidy and immaculate. The floor plan was almost identical to ours, so it wasn't difficult to navigate the shadows. She led me down the central corridor to the rear of the house. The place smelled strange, like incense mixed with disinfectant. We stopped at a closed door, directly beneath the bedroom Laurie and I shared.

She clutched the front of the black nylon jacket I was wearing and pressed her head against my chest. She made no sound, but I felt her sobbing. "No one even notice," she said softly. "I promise. No one notice."

She quietly opened the door, not looking inside. She didn't go in with me.

A small desk lamp cast a meager light. I didn't see him at first, just a shape in the corner, then I made out the wheelchair beside a small, unmade cot. His back was to me. That would make it easier, I figured. I approached, careful not to make any sound. But he moved his head, as if he knew. I saw that his left arm was gone. Then he jerked suddenly, like an animal sensing a predator, and in the half-light I glimpsed his wet eyes staring out madly from the scarred and discolored flesh that had been his face.

I took the cord from my pocket and clenched it in both hands. He looked right at me, right into me, the entire time I killed him.

In the years since, I've spent a lot of time in libraries—when they don't chase me out—reading everything I can about what happened to soldiers in Vietnam, trying to understand what I saw in his eyes. Trying to find some kind of explanation. There isn't one. He's still looking at me. Right now.

Days later, Laurie answered the downstairs bell to find Phi on our doorstep.

"Let me show you," she said, taking hold of Laurie's hand. "Get your husband. Want show him too."

She walked us around the bright, sunny grounds, proudly showing off the yard work she'd had done after the recent rains. The place had never looked better. Everything all cleaned up. She pointed to several big black bags of yard waste piled in the driveway.

"You take to dump?" she asked. "*Please.*" She stuck a couple of twenties in my hand.

As I got my coat, Laurie asked, "Why would she ask *you* to do it?"

"I'm guess I'm handy."

Three months later, Laurie went looking for a bigger office and never came back. Well, only to get her stuff. And the cat. I don't blame her. I was now the one screaming my head off in the middle of the night.

My company moved, but I stayed—even though there was nothing holding me here. I had no job, but Phi let me stay on upstairs—that was the deal, of course. No more rent, ever. The screaming stopped—my magical solution to saving our happy home.

With Laurie gone, I hated the place. Phi told me I could live out back above the carport, in the garret she used for storage. I'd need to fix it up—no problem for a handyman. A few weeks later I was watching a new young couple giddily take over the home in which Laurie and I had wanted to spend the rest of our lives.

Phi's properties always needed maintenance of some kind or another. She dutifully gave me fix-it jobs, even though I was pretty shitty at it. But I figured things out and got better at manual tasks. Odd jobs got me through a few rough years. At least until the morning an ambulance came and took Phi away on a gurney. She died in Alameda Hospital the next day. I kept a vigil in the waiting room until they made me leave. I wasn't next of kin. "There is no next of kin," I told them. Her next of kin was long gone, somewhere six feet deep in Indochina.

The state, of course, took her house.

Learning to be handy has served me well the past few years. It's helped me survive on the streets. I know how to jury-rig shit like I never imagined. I spend a lot of time at public libraries, reading mostly, and eventually I stopped typing Laurie's name into the computers. But I don't get jobs anymore. The roadside Mexicans have the day-labor market locked up. At least I've learned to sleep so lightly I never wake up screaming. I'm like a soldier in his tent, always on alert, living by his wits, hunkered down in the middle of a fucking war zone. Who knew it would ever get this bad—whole villages of us camped under freeway overpasses living hand-to-mouth. And wouldn't you know:

from where I am tonight, out of the rain but freezing my ass off, I can see the top floors of the empty office building on Harrison Street, where once I had a view of the lake.

ABOUT THE CONTRIBUTORS

KIM ADDONIZIO, an acclaimed writer of poetry and prose, is a Pushcart Prize winner, a National Book Award finalist for *Tell Me*, and a recipient of two fellowships from the National Endowment for the Arts and a Guggenheim Fellowship. Her works include *Jimmy & Rita, What Is This Thing Called Love, Lucifer at the Starlite, Little Beauties, My Dreams Out in the Street,* and *The Palace of Illusions.* Her new books are a collection of poems, *Mortal Trash,* and a memoir, *Bukowski in a Sundress.*

Lin Tan

CAROLYN ALEXANDER is a writer, storyteller, English teacher, and librarian. She revels in the use of the English language, and has written original material for single and tag-team storytelling performances as well as for the San Francisco Mime Troupe. She has a BA in English from Cornell University and a master's in library science from Columbia University.

Lena Alexander

PHIL CANALIN is a twenty-five-year public health finance manager in Oakland, most recently for the noted Health Care for the Homeless program. He loves writing fiction, poetry, and children's stories, and currently resides in Alameda with Sue, his wife of thirty-six years. His latest publication is *Invisible Society Fables,* short stories based on his experience with homeless people and their caregivers. For more information visit www.philcanalin.com.

Melissa Erikson

JAMIE DEWOLF is a performer, film director, and showman from Oakland. He is a National Slam Poetry Champion, NPR's "Performer of the Year," and has toured everywhere from Moscow to San Quentin State Prison. DeWolf is the writer and codirector of the feature film *Smoked,* and the host and creator of Tourettes without Regrets, the longest-running monthly underground variety show in Oakland. Watch his films and performances at www.jamiedewolf.com.

Mike Lloyd

KATIE GILMARTIN'S checkered past includes stints as a union organizer, bona fide sex researcher, and college professor. She now teaches printmaking classes and runs the Queer Ancestors Project, devoted to forging relationships between queer artists and their ancestors. Her illustrated noir, *Blackmail, My Love,* is set in San Francisco in the dark ages of queerdom: 1951. Winner of Lambda and Indiefab Gold awards, the narrative is a revelatory history of San Francisco's sexually complex underground.

Renee Mayer

JUDY JUANITA'S debut novel, *Virgin Soul,* follows a black teen who becomes a member of the Black Panther Party in the 1960s. Her short stories and poems have appeared widely and her plays have been produced in Oakland, San Francisco, Berkeley, Los Angeles, and New York City. *De Facto Feminism: Essays Straight Outta Oakland* traces her development as a writer, activist, and independent woman.

DOROTHY LAZARD manages the Oakland History Room, a special reference collection in the Oakland Public Library. She holds a master's degree in library and information studies from the University of California, Berkeley, and an MFA in creative nonfiction from Goucher College in Baltimore. Her writing has appeared in *The Public Library: A Photographic Essay* by Robert Dawson, *Essence* magazine, and the librarian blog *The Desk Set.*

JOE LOYA is the author of *The Man Who Outgrew His Prison Cell: Confessions of a Bank Robber,* and is the host of *The Allure of Crime* podcast. He homeschools his daughter, but has not initiated her in the art of banditry. Yet.

THOMAS MCELRAVEY was born in Tahoe City, California, in 1991. He moved to the Bay Area in 2009 to pursue writing and music. He has contributed to several local zines, all of which have disappeared into the region's remarkable creative commons. His contribution to this collection, "Black and Borax," is his first published short story. He currently lives in Oakland with his two cats, Serenity and Ichibad.

EDDIE MULLER, a.k.a. the "Czar of Noir," is a writer, cinema historian, and film preservationist. He has been nominated for several Edgar and Anthony awards, and his novel *The Distance* won a Shamus Award for Best First P.I. Novel; Muller is also the coauthor of the *New York Times* best-selling autobiography *Tab Hunter Confidential: The Making of a Movie Star.* He produces San Francisco's Noir City, the largest annual film noir retrospective in the world, and is a regular host on Turner Classic Movies.

NAYOMI MUNAWEERA'S debut novel, *Island of a Thousand Mirrors*, was long-listed for the Man Asian Literary Prize and the International Dublin IMPAC Award. It won the Commonwealth Prize for Asia and was short-listed for the Northern California Book Award. The *New York Times* called the novel "incandescent." Her second novel, *What Lies Between Us*, was picked as one of Buzzfeed's twenty-seven most exciting new books of 2016. She lives in the Temescal area of Oakland.

Nathanael F. Trimboli

KEENAN NORRIS'S novel *Brother and the Dancer* won the James D. Houston Award in 2012. His work has appeared in *Popmatters*, the *Los Angeles Review of Books*, *Inlandia: A Literary Journal*, and the anthology *Post-Soul Satire*. Keenan edited *Street Lit: Representing the Urban Landscape* and is a guest editor for the Oxford African American Studies Center. He teaches at Evergreen Valley College and Goddard College's West Coast campus and serves on the editorial board for the Los Angeles literary collective Literature for Life.

Akabunda Amazu-Lott

NICK PETRULAKIS has been a bookseller in the Bay Area for almost twenty years. His writing has appeared in various publications, including the *San Francisco Chronicle* and *Oakland* magazine. His cocktail creations, marrying fiction and spirits, can be found at drinkswithnick.com.

Al Wright

MAHMUD RAHMAN'S walk around Lake Merritt during a vacation compelled a move across the continent. Besides Oakland, his long-term hometowns have included Detroit and Dhaka. He currently works in Oakland and received an MFA in creative writing from Mills College. He is the author of the short story collection *Killing the Water* and the translator of Bangladeshi writer Mahmudul Haque's novel *Black Ice*.

Abeer Hoque

KERI MIKI-LANI SCHROEDER is a visual artist and writer based in Oakland. A fan of all things odd, experimental, or transgressive, Schroeder creates artist books and dark short fiction. After earning an MFA in book art and creative writing from Mills College in 2015, Schroeder now works for Flying Fish Press, an independent publisher of limited-edition artists' books, and teaches book art workshops and classes.

Micheal Wagner

Jerry Thompson

JERRY THOMPSON is an accomplished violinist, playwright, and poet. His works have appeared in *Zyzzyva, James White Review*, and *Freedom in this Village: Twenty-Five Years of Black Gay Men's Writing*. He is the coauthor of *Black Artists in Oakland*. Thompson owned Black Spring Books, an independent bookstore, and is the creator and organizer of the original Sister Circle Reading Series. He is currently working on a play about the prison system, a memoir, and a poetry collection.

Jane Tyska

HARRY LOUIS WILLIAMS II was born in New York City and raised in Asbury Park, New Jersey. He is an ordained Baptist minister who is known for writing gangster fiction such as the award-winning best seller *Straight Outta East Oakland*. In 2015, the Oakland city council recognized Williams for his work reclaiming the lives of young people lost to the streets. Dr. Cornel West calls his book *Street Cred: A Hood Minister's Guide to Urban Ministry* a "must read."